The Crimson Shaw

Lawrence and Keane, Volume 2

Elyse Lortz

Published by Elyse Lortz, 2021.

This is a work of fiction. Similarities to real people, places, or events are entirely coincidental.

THE CRIMSON SHAW

First edition. July 26, 2021.

Copyright © 2021 Elyse Lortz.

ISBN: 979-8201794842

Written by Elyse Lortz.

Table of Contents

To all those who make us smile. | And to the men and women whose profession makes it so. | And to those who went before us, | But walk constantly by our side..................... 1

PART ONE | Happy is the man who can make a living by his hobby. | -George Bernard Shaw 3

DEVON, ENGLAND | -to- | CALIFORNIA, UNITED STATES 5

—Late July 1948— 7
CHAPTER ONE........................ 9
CHAPTER TWO 17
CHAPTER THREE | Spring 1916—H.M.S. Greylag.....23
CHAPTER FOUR................................27
CHAPTER FIVE 35
CHAPTER SIX | Summer 1916—H.M.S. Greylag..........43
CHAPTER SEVEN..................................47
CHAPTER EIGHT | Summer 1916—Palermo, Italy......57
CHAPTER NINE 63
CHAPTER TEN | Summer 1916—Palermo, Italy 75
CHAPTER ELEVEN 79

PART TWO | Life is but an inspired series of events, | That just happen to end and one's own inconvenience. | -Brendan Keane.................................87

CHAPTER TWELVE......................................89
CHAPTER THIRTEEN | Summer 1916—Palermo, Italy 105
CHAPTER FOURTEEN.................................. 113
CHAPTER FIFTEEN | Autumn 1916—H.M.S. Greylag................................. 123
CHAPTER SIXTEEN 127

CHAPTER SEVENTEEN 141

PART THREE | Those who aim at great deeds | Must also suffer greatly. | -Marcus Licinius Crassus 151

CHAPTER EIGHTEEN.. 153

CHAPTER NINETEEN.. 167

CHAPTER TWENTY 179

CHAPTER TWENTY-ONE 191

CHAPTER TWENTY-TWO 201

PART FOUR | Death is the most terrible of all things, | for it is the end, | and nothing is thought to be either good or bad for the dead. | -Aristotle.. 219

CHAPTER TWENTY-THREE 221

CHAPTER TWENTY-FOUR... 233

CHAPTER TWENTY-FIVE... 241

CHAPTER TWENTY-SIX 253

CHAPTER TWENTY-SEVEN 265

CHAPTER TWENTY-EIGHT.. 277

PART FIVE | People do not lack strength; | They lack will. | -Victor Hugo 285

CHAPTER TWENTY-NINE 287

CHAPTER THIRTY 299

CHAPTER THIRTY-ONE 309

CHAPTER THIRTY-TWO 317

PART SIX | The rest of the story need not be shown in action … | if our imaginations were not so enfeebled by their lazy dependence … | -George Bernard Shaw..................................... 331

CHAPTER THIRTY-THREE | September, 1948 333

AUTHOR'S NOTICE | Meyer Harris Cohen................ 339

To all those who make us smile.

And to the men and women whose profession makes it so.

And to those who went before us,

But walk constantly by our side.

PART ONE

Happy is the man who can make a living by his hobby.

-George Bernard Shaw

DEVON, ENGLAND

-to-

CALIFORNIA, UNITED STATES

—Late July 1948—

CHAPTER ONE

"America?" I nearly choked on my tea. "Keane, you can't be serious. In all the wonderful and exotic places in the world, why would you choose America?" My companion glanced up from his enormous oak writing desk and lowered his pen atop a tidy stack of manuscripts. Ever since we had returned from visiting his sister, those papers had absorbed much of his valuable time. Hours were spent huddled over ink-splattered words; minutes moving past lazily as long pen scratches were etched into the unsuspecting page. But now...

"And why not, Lawrence? You yourself are an American and should be delighted at the prospect of returning to your homeland." Unlike what his English clipped voice so perfectly assumed, I was not *delighted*. I was not even pleased.

England and America, two countries separated by the same language...

"First of all, I was born in the state of aviation and lightbulbs, *not* California. Second, you know as well as I do, being born in a place does not necessarily mean you wish to spend your entire summer there."

"Really, Lawrence, aren't you being a touch over dramatic? Yes, I am well aware of your, shall we say, distaste for your fellow countrymen."

"Distaste?" I crossed my arms tightly over my throbbing rib cage. "Distaste is hardly the word for it. It's as if the whole country speaks without their mouth ever shutting completely."

"I agree Americans have always held an intimate affair with the exclamation point, but it would only be two months—three at most." Wonderful. Approximately sixty to ninety days with an average of 1800 hours and God only knows how many minutes. "Besides, it is an invitation from an—"

"—old friend. Yes, Keane, I remember. I also recall the last time you received a letter from an 'old friend'. He turned out to be your elder brother and we were almost murdered in a blizzard." My companion had the grace enough to look at least marginally pained by my heated response, but still he held fast.

"I assure you this is not another mysterious sibling. The man is not so much as a relation. You have, I think, heard of the name James Harrison?"

"Isn't that the director friend of yours?" Keane tugged on his ear.

"Indeed. I worked with him—briefly, mind you—back in the war, and now he claims he needs some sort of help." There was, I thought, at least a grain of truth in the statement, for no human being who had ever taken upon themself the mantle of theatrical director was ever really sane. But all the same, the assistance the letter was requesting seemed hardly one of an overpowering madness as it was a soft cry of a child in danger. I rocked on my heels, mind and thoughts tossing about as waves leaping over a ship's rail.

"Why the devil does a thespian need a professor of psychology? Not that it isn't a noble profession, but—"

"—I asked James the very question, but he insists any information must wait until we step foot on the great state of gold and flickering lights." I set my teacup against the saucer with a firm grunt of china.

"Keane, I heard a *we* in that statement. Would you care to elaborate?"

"You don't think I would go alone without your splendid company, do you? Of course not. Besides," He stood from behind his desk and grabbed a cigarette from one of the many bowls spotting the study, his back suddenly to me. "It would be good for you to see the United States again, even if it is a different portion than what you were used to." The rope was beginning to slip from my fingers. I felt the threads weaken and tear in my palms. All that had been tightly woven as one was unravelling into a thousand bits of life; therefore, I allowed myself to succumb into one of the most animalistic instincts.

I dug in with my nails.

"Really, I *can't* go. I have hundreds of appointments with my editor, not to mention the publisher breathing down my neck for another manuscript. I couldn't possibly—"

"—Cancel them? No need, I already did. Your schedule is entirely free." The feigned innocence on his face, the boyish grin which so often appeared when he knew he had won, often made me forget his fifty-something years. After all, it is often well past the borders of acceptable society to strike an older man.

But if he were younger . . .

"Keane, you really are quite impossible. Every time I wish to do something, you throw my life in another direction completely. It simply isn't—isn't gentlemanly of you." A silver eyebrow leapt high on his forehead.

"Me? Not a gentleman? Lawrence, have I ever said you were *required* to come? No, I haven't. I have merely made it possible to join me if you wish to do so. The choice is entirely your own. Of course, if your love of the theatre is not enough to tear yourself away from your work—"

THE PLANE TOUCHED DOWN late in the evening a few days later, and I had still not fully forgiven Keane for the black-mail infested offer of a trip to my home country. Even so late in the day, a wall of festering heat nearly bowled me over as I climbed down the ladder. The dim outline of palm trees caught fire in the evening sun, the tips burning feverishly above the shadow of buildings a few miles away. Not since our trip to Mexico had I felt such stifling temperatures, and at least then there was some sense of mystery, a subconscious drive keeping our adrenaline at soaring heights and the sleep far from our eyes. Here, we were welcomed by a long stretch of boiling pavement, a polished brown car, and a short, fat, middle aged man with a few wisps of white hair, a gold molar, and a thick cigar dripping from his mouth. His voice was gruff, near raspy, and the hand suddenly pumping mine was no better.

"Hello, Miss. Mister. You're the professor, right? I was sent to fetch you. Do you need a hand with those?" *Those* happened to be two rather depressed looking leather suit cases piled at Keane's feet. The brass corners were well past tarnished, and the handles had been fixed more than what was perhaps acceptable, but the lettering was still faintly discernible beneath a layer of international dust and grime. Before my companion could answer, the little man had shoved the cases into the car's trunk and opened the side door. Keane waited for me to clamber in before allowing his tall, slim frame to fold into the leather seats. Admittedly, American cars had always seemed far more forgiving to a man of his stature, rather than the cramped European automobiles; however, even with the extra space, I was made well aware of the almost sickening heat matted together with the incessant odour of cigars. Keane himself was a heavy smoker, but where his favoured cigarette tobacco was crisp with almost a pipe-like vanilla, this was a strong, blinding stench with no other purpose than to claw its way into our hair and clothing.

America had always been said to be a civilised nation, but, as the roads jerked the car unceasingly, I began to have my doubts. Twice I was bashed against the metal door, and, had it not been for the providence of Keane's presence on the other side, I could have sustained injuries far worse than a few darkening bruises. As it was, I suspected by the hand clasped behind his neck, Keane had already begun to suffer the inconveniences of his height.

Between the jolting, thrashing road and billowing stench of cigar smoke, my stomach wrenched itself into a tight knot and made me extraordinarily thankful for a lack of dinner. I folded my arms securely across my ribs and pulled my elbows violently toward my ribcage. I was not prone to weak bouts of inconvenient femininity, I thought reassuringly. I would not be sick.

However...

"Lawrence, are you alright?" I laughed, a dry, grating noise that did little to improve the ringing in my ears or the throbbing knots in my stomach.

"I swear, Keane, if you trade in your cigarettes for cigars, I will personally see to it you are abandoned at the home of some extremist puritans who drink milk and eat stale bread." My companion's rich chuckle was cut short by the painful slamming of teeth as we were thrown over yet another hole in the road. From somewhere in his jacket, Keane produced a small hip flask and offered it to me. I quickly unscrewed the top and took a long swig.

Brandy.

Once the tightness in my abdomen subsided ever so slightly, Keane himself took a hefty draw of the liquor before carefully returning the flask to his pocket. He had his faults, but, in the end, his character far surpassed those shortcomings. His stubbornness was both a sword and shield; defeat was never an option unless it led to total victory. In my innocence, I had foolishly thought he would never lose a fight, no matter the odds piled high against him. It was only when I was older—those drawn out moments spent wallowing in silence—that the truth occured to me.

He *couldn't* lose.

The darkened night enclosed the windows, and I felt increasingly aware of that sense of dread that presses upon your eardrums until a shrill ringing erupts through your head and shatters all memories of comfort. Where the lights of a rampant society ought to have been swelling and growing, they had fallen to little more than misplaced stars upon the horizon. The emptiness; however, merely worked to entrap us further.

"Keane, we're going the wrong way." My companion did not flinch at my words. Of course he didn't.

He had already noticed.

His long fingers slipped silently to the door handle and gave it a violent tug.

Locked.

Wonderful.

Had we been in most any other country in the world, his position would have been perfect; however, Americans had always seemed bound and determined to make life more difficult. Keane, ever the gentleman, motioned me aside, but it would have been a foolish move—a complete waste of precious time—to switch seats. There was no time for masculine chivalry. There was never time for chivalry. There was only time; time to choose between right and wrong. Death or life. Minutes or seconds. Today or never. There was only time.

I leapt forward and swung my arm around the driver's neck while Keane desperately tried to steady the wheel while staying well out of the way from the driver's thrashing hands. I could feel ever so clearly the pulsating of the man's throat in my forearm, the surging heat of life gradually challenged and drained in desperate measure. In a matter of sheer moments the car was no longer driving at a respectable pace, but careening dangerously along the edge of the road at speeds no sane man would ever tempt. A meaty fist met my face and sent me hurling back against the seats. I was instantly pinned to the leather, stunned and dazed as the world whizzed by. A deafening scream grabbed desperately at my ears as a hard left turn threw me into Keane's side at the same instant a near inaudible click peppered the chaos.

Then there was a great rush of air compressing my limbs as something strong grabbed me by the collar and gave me the unexpected sensation of God's hand bodily dragging me through the air and dropping as a mangled mass in the hard dirt. There was an enormous flash of light. The roar of a thousand cannons as singing fingers brushed over my twisted legs.

Silence.

I lay there motionless for a long while, taking a mental survey over my various pieces and limbs. Everything was present. Nothing seemed broken. Bruised and battered, definitely. Sprained, perhaps. But not, thank God, broken.

When at last I felt sufficiently at peace with my sorry state, I rolled onto my back and sat up to discover Keane in much the same position. His immaculate trousers had succumbed to a death of scorched threads dangling just above his socks. The knees were brown with glimpses of pale, bleeding flesh in between. I had thought him entranced by these, the long forgotten pains of a school boy who had skinned his legs and muddied his clothes. And then I too saw Lucifer as Keane's dirt-streaked face was set grimly upon a campfire down at the bottom of the steep hill. Rather than a sense of joviality at the prospect of a cheery flicker of flames, I found myself repulsed by the scene at our feet. The brown car had been so horribly mutilated one might have believed it a relic from the war so recent in our minds. Hot, burning shards of metal groped upward from the hellish ground in long, sharp fingers. The horrid smoke of burning rubber and petrol far outweighed the stench of cigar tobacco still present in my nostrils. It was as though Hell had reached its claws into our world to swallow us away, fires eating the earth greedily until the teeth were barred against us

And, somewhere lurking within the fire and ash, there was a skeleton.

CHAPTER TWO

I had hoped it all to be a dream; prayed for it to be nothing more than a horrible, twisted trick of the imagination to awaken me in a pool of pungent sweat. There were also several bruises, cuts, and a rather unappealing discoloration along my left cheekbone. The latter of these must have been perfectly dreadful the night before, which earned me more than a few raised eyebrows from the few people mulling about the hotel lobby when Keane and I came stumbling in close on one. We were revered as two buffoons. We had no baggage, nothing beyond the tattered clothing on our backs and the odds and ends hidden within our pockets. Fortunately, that included our passports and money.

I groaned and gingerly threw an arm over my sore eyes. What had begun as a child's drum tittering near the base of my skull had expanded into a full military band pounding and blaring until any bit of sanity was completely out of the question. At the climax of this mighty roar came one roaring bang that rang like gunfire through my ears.

"For heaven's sake, Keane," I moaned groggily. "Don't slam the doors." The thunder of even footsteps approached the bed and springs screeched of a new pressure as the mattress dipped slightly. A grunt above me proved my companion was not above the mortal scrapes and woes of such adventures to which we were constantly subjected. His voice was more of an elongated groan than individual words.

"I do apologise. Now, move your—language, Lawrence—move your arm away." I reluctantly did so and found myself overshadowed by a complete stranger who lacked all the dignity and grace I recognised. His iconic tweed suit had been replaced by a ratty, white dressing gown, and his combed, wavy hair shot out in damp, unruly curls. His right hand pressed a hot water bottle to his forehead, while the other sported a small collection of sticking plasters, winding together until they covered his little finger. Where the scents of crisp cigarette tobacco often lingered was now nonexistent. Instead he smelled only of soap. Boring, lavender soap.

I moaned and turned away from him and buried my face into the pillow, the motion shooting a burst of pain through my neck and into my battered skull.

"My head hurts like I was trampled by a herd of elephants on parade." Keane chuckled dryly, a sound that both amused and hurt me as it reverberated through my deteriorating brain. Something pleasantly hot and rubbery was gently laid on the side of my head as he stood from the bed. I was vaguely aware of his clear, blue eyes still lingering on my prostrate form, but it mattered little in comparison to the three ring circus between my ears.

"James will be here soon, Lawrence, and it would be prudent if you washed that filth from last night out of your hair. Don't bother with trying to salvage those clothes. Take everything out of the pockets and put them in your jacket. I must say it puzzles me why you brought that heavy garment with you. It isn't as though we travelled to the North Pole."

"It's my trademark." I muttered, suddenly aware of a dry grating in my throat. "Besides, it's durable and practical; two things of which you have always approved."

"Indeed." Keane peeled the leather RAF jacket from the floor and promptly held it away at arm's length. "It may take some effort to get the stench of petrol out of it, but effort does not mean impossibility. I already started the hot water. Ten minutes, Lawrence."

WHILE THE RING MASTER did not cancel the performance on the account of a flooding of senses, the hot water and steam worked miracles on my aching muscles. Much of the dirt and grime fell easily from my battered flesh, and what did not dissipate immediately was quickly persuaded by the bar of lavender soap lying idle on the porcelain edge. As the water gradually cooled, I slowly became reacquainted with myself. Long, jagged scrapes wrenched their way up my arms, and my legs were no better. What skin was not torn or cut was infinitely sore. Even my hair was slicked with bits of oil and dust. There was not an inch left untouched.

Not even my mind.

It was well past ten minutes when I emerged from the now tepid water and began drying my cleansed flesh, the dripping ends of my hair dropping long rivers of water along my shoulders. A fresh shirt and trousers had been hung on the back of the door. They were not an ideal fit—I had to roll the trouser legs up a bit and the shirtsleeves were an infinite battle—but it was far better than that with which I was naturally born. Swaddled in my new, ridiculous wardrobe, I reentered the main portion of the hotel room to find Keane in a rather amusing conversation with another man. He was about the same height and build as my companion, though perhaps a tad bit smaller in both areas of consideration. Where Keane's hair was a greying blonde, this man's was entirely white without so much as a speck of any former colour. His features were rounded and centred with an upturned nose that had been broken at some point in its existence. The lines on his face were partially masked by a dark tan that approached his shirt collar with no signs of stopping. But, beneath the sun's marks, he appeared pale and nervous; twitching erratically at times or touching the tail end of a scar that ran along his cheekbone. Had the man's fingers not held such a fascination with the deformity, I might not have noticed the thin etching at all.

He stood as I entered the room, prompting a bewildered Keane to do likewise. It was always startling to remember the one eternal difference between the revered professor and myself.

I was a woman and he was a man.

I shook James Harrison's hand, nodded to Keane, and sat down on a rather extravagant settee. Apparently money did more than merely talk. It breathed. The red, almost gaudy, upholstery was heavenly to a weary traveller and I understood why Keane had decided to spend the night there, rather than the bed as I suggested. There was no doubt in his gentlemanly nature, just as there was no questioning his stubbornness, or the fiery streak within him that flamed a temperament which could topple the strongest of men and the most prominent government officials.

He also looked uncomfortable.

"Keane, isn't that suit jacket a bit—er—snug?" My companion self-consciously tugged at the sleeves of the offending article. Perhaps *snug* wasn't the right word. *Short* was more accurate. The suit—well-tailored and reasonably expensive—appeared something Keane might have owned at some point in his life. Just, not now.

"As soon as you called saying something about lost bags, I bought it from one of the finest taylors I know." Harrison explained. "I went off of measurements from last I saw you. When was that?" Keane chuckled.

"Almost thirty years ago. *Orthello*, I believe it was."

"Was it really that long? We were young then." The director grinned roguishly. "And you, Brendan, were the ladies man, as I remember."

"Yes, well . . . " Keane tugged fiercely at his left ear, his blue eyes sparkling in nostalgic wonder. I had always thought these two reflections of embarrassment far more endearing than the reddening of one's face, and, as with everything, my companion retained the utmost dignity.

Dignity. Always dignity.

"You weren't completely faultless yourself. Started drinking at eight in the morning and carried on the entire day." The director smiled ruefully and pressed a hand firmly into his abdomen.

"I'm afraid those days are behind me. Have you ever had an ulcer, Brendan? Well, hope to sweet Jesus you never do. Hurts like shit."

What a pleasant American saying.

Keane grimaced and turned to me, face completely bereft of anything more than an anatomically correct facade.

"Lawrence, I'm positively famished. Could you go down and order something? It doesn't matter what it is so long as it is hot and edible. Don't bother with the tea, though." My companion glanced at Harrison. "Tea always seems to be a weak point in this country."

CHAPTER THREE
Spring 1916—H.M.S. Greylag

"WHAT THE DEVIL IS THIS swill?" The young seaman cursed, gulping down the tepid liquid before glaring into the glass as though bearer of the most fatal of poisons. A morning's stubble grew red over his long jaw, a stark contrast to the blonde, wavy hair and sharp, blue eyes. His uniform fit nicely over his masculine frame that began at a pair of strong shoulders and slimmed into a form well-toned by years at sea. The man standing over him was much the same, save a head of dark sticks for hair and a face that was more round than oblong.

"It's tea." The brown-haired man stated firmly, as if to convince himself of the cup's supposed contents. A dark pool of liquid still swirled about in its metal confines, but it was nothing like tea. Water and twice-used tea leaves did not make a proper cup of tea. It couldn't even pass as the watered-down coffee they were forced to drink every now and again.

"What's your name, man?"

"Seaman Second Class, James Harrison. You?"

"Brendan Keane. Seaman First Class." The younger man swung his arm into a salute and nearly knocked him upside the head. "What the devil do you think you're doing, Harrison? If we spent all our time bickering over ranks and nationalities we might as well let the blasted Germans have a parade through Piccadilly. Now—sit down, man—let me make one thing infernally clear. I am *not* an Englishman."

"You damn well sound like it, 'cept for that funny singing sound." Brendan's brow furrowed slightly, creating lines otherwise nonexistent on his face.

"That 'singing sound' is the last remnant of my brogue—my *Irish* brogue—and if you have something to say about it, you had best say it now while there's no one to watch you embarrass yourself."

"Ireland? But isn't that a part of England? Oh, right, that whole Easter thing." Harrison pushed himself back ever so slightly from the other seaman. "You aren't one of those rebels, are you?"

"No."

Not yet.

The Irishman took a long draw from the watery tea and allowed his brows to furrow together. One war was enough—more than enough—for any man. No mortal could live long beneath the shroud of death without fully considering its benefits.

Suddenly the ship gave a mighty heave and forced his body to sway in unison, an occurrence that happened constantly and, while not unpleasant, could cause untold havok if a man bore not the sea legs necessary. Brendan sighed.

In death there was no rain of led, no fires from above, no final screams as one sunk into a darkened abyss. There was nothing but silence—a cool, blissful quiet—to lay one's soul at rest and allowed them to sleep soundly in eternal arms.

Sleep. The young man scratched the red starts of a beard. Yes, that was something he needed—they *all* needed. How long had they been at it now? It seemed a string of several years, yet it had hardly been a day; one, dreadfully draining twenty-four hours.

Harrison took out a package of cigarettes—American by brand—and offered one to Keane. The Irishman smoked every now and then back home, but now it had become a constant; something to do with his hands while his mind wandered to safer waters. The bitter taste of tobacco had become pleasant to his palate as a pretty girl who smiles at you when she saunters past. That was another problem.

There was no female companionship. A man could not delve into the depths of his soul, for, to do show on a warship was a weakness. To do so to someone who listened and did their best to comfort, that was divine.

That was Natasha.

Harrison finished his cigarette first and debated whether or not to have another before deciding the better of it and instead shoved his hands into his coat pockets.

"Tell me, Brendan, when did you last have a good, hearty meal?"

CHAPTER FOUR

When Keane had said he was famished, I had taken it as nothing more than a polite excuse for me to leave the two men for whatever memories may take them. It had not crossed my mind that my companion—professor and war hero—was actually hungry.

Keane ate with gusto, downing entire cups of coffee between sentences and large helpings of eggs in the brief bits of respite between nostalgic tales. What dent Mr. Harrison and I made into the various dishes, Keane doubled easily. When had we last eaten? Dinner? No, we were in the plane and then... was it really lunch yesterday? I supposed that did explain the gnawing storms in my stomach, not to mention Keane's ravenous appetite. In battle the bacon was no match, nor the toast quickly slathered in butter. As the dishes ran down the conversation began to turn. Where there were the brighter, more amusing stories of war (Remember old Johnny Crackers? That boy was a walking lunatic. No danger in him though.), there were also old wounds which began to open and fester. Names of lost comrades fell heavily to the floor like stale vomit. Days best left buried overturned and wrenched their spindly hands toward the surface. All that ought to have remained unsaid was said, and yet there was so much still hidden behind their stolid expressions. The wheel again rocked the ship into dangerous harbours as

Keane proceeded to fill Harrison in with all the details of our night's escapade, ending abruptly with the ear-shattering screech of a fork on an empty plate. The American thespian leaned back in his chair and wagged his head incredulously.

"You're joking. That's the whole reason I called you down here. We just lost our leading man to an accident too. Hm? Oh, no, he'll be alright, but he is laid up with a broken leg. Some damn stagehand wasn't watching what he was doing and opened a trap door beneath Earl Bennet just as he made his entrance. Have you heard of Earl Bennet? No? It's just as well. The only thing he's ever on time for is a bottle of booze."

"That doesn't explain why we're here." I started flatly. The band in my head had gradually progressed from a waltz to something far more rampant that buzzed through my ears like lightning.

Harrison leaned forward on the table with his forearms entrapping his half-finished plate in a triangle.

"Brendan, how would you feel about going into the theatre again?" Keane's coffee cup hit the table with a mind wincing clatter.

"You can't be serious. I haven't been near the stage for years. More than a decade."

"And?"

"And I must say I am far too old to be playing Hamlet and leaping about in a pair of damn tights." I clasped a hand over my mouth as the tickles of laughter tempted my lips. Keane? In tights? Never had I considered such things to be uttered in the same conversation, let alone the same sentence. The image of such a thing—the sheer lunacy of it all—was far too much for any person to comprehend. Keane? In tights? Never.

And yet...

"Oh, you don't need to worry about that." The director quickly assured my companion. "We aren't doing Shakespeare. This season's production is Shaw's *Pygmalion*. You liked that, if I remember right."

"It is a well-written play centred around a rather intriguing idea. To think, a man crafting a common flower girl into the image of grace and beauty. If such acts were to become commonplace, the whole of society's natural class system would come crashing down more effectively than those daft ideas of Socialism." Keane smiled and shook his head. "An intriguing idea."

Part of me wished to remind my companion that it was not necessarily the infamous Professor Henry Higgins who instilled the seeds of ideal femininity and fierceness into Eliza Doolittle. Rather they had been there all along, had he opened his eyes to accept it when first she walked into his study. George Bernard Shaw was one of the first ties discovered between Keane and myself, and, as time passed, the reasons became all the more obvious.

James Harrison leaned back in his chair.

"What about it, Brendan? Think you're up to it?"

"You still have not explained what exactly it is I would be agreeing to. I may be able to pull a few strings—call in some old favours—to find you another leading man. There are a few amature theatrical groups I know that may have a few young men up for the job."

"What about you?" Keane's eyebrows arched high on his lined forehead.

"Me? I think I'm a few years too late for such a role."

"Hogwash. You'd be perfect for the part. After all, Leslie Howard wasn't a spring chicken when he did it in the films." My companion chuckled and tugged gently at his left ear.

"James, I think there is a few year's difference between forty-five and fifty-four." Harrison pushed himself back from the table and grabbed his hat.

"Don't give me an answer right now. Think about it for a while. Talk with Jo here. If you want to go back to England, fine, but the part's yours if you'll take it. You both can even stay in my beach house just a few miles from the theatre. I like to live in the city for convenience, so you'd have it all to yourselves. There's plenty of space—two bedrooms and such—and a beach if you want to swim. Even if you don't take the part, you could still stay a while. Who knows, you might find us Americans aren't so 'positively dreadful' as you'd like to think." Harrison scraped himself from the chair and moved toward the door. "Give me a call when you make up your mind."

I WAS AWOKEN LATE INTO the night—or perhaps early in the morning—by the light scents of cigarette smoke sifting through the crack beneath the door. Having known Keane for so near to a decade, I had long since learned to read the various forms of the white and spindly whispers of tobacco. Often it would merely be a simple trail pulled and released in gentle puffs, the sake of smoking for the sheer habit of the thing, but there were those instances when cigarette after cigarette would be fiercely burnt down to the butt before being stabbed mightily into an unsuspecting ashtray.

This, I could tell, was neither.

The smoke came white and mistlike with quiet traces of vanilla carried along with the tobacco. The fog-like fibres wove together into a blanket of familiarity that wrapped its arms silently around my shoulders. There was warmth in it—a beckoning—I could not ignore for fear it would disappear all together. It was an invitation engraved at his own hand and finished with a seal of burning wax.

I slipped out from beneath the covers, dressed silently, and gently pushed open the door into the main portion of the hotel room. Keane sat on one end of the sofa, the ill-sized suit coat folded neatly beside him and the collar of his shirt left open with the necktie hanging loose and limp around his neck. If he heard my approach, he made no announcement of it, but instead taped the burning end of his cigarette against the ashtray at his elbow. I pushed the jacket away and sat beside him.

"May I?" Keane handed me the packet of cigarettes, already half gone. When he had lit mine, he started another for himself and leaned back into the cushioned backing with a long puff of white haze.

"I haven't been on stage in years, Lawrence. Nearly twenty years." There was no nervousness or regret about him, no fear that his age might somehow hinder his performance. It was simply a fact. A cold, hard, selfless fact that he felt necessary to bring to light. He shifted subtly on the settee. "I think I shall do it. I have no other pressing matters to date. It would only be two or three months. Besides, it would be rather nice to do something theatrical again." Suddenly Keane's attention fell entirely upon me. "Of course, you must go back to England. It would be selfish of me to ask you to stay when you have work of your own. I will arrange transportation as soon as possible. That aeroplane—" I laughed.

"Really, Keane, you've forgotten something. You cancelled all my appointments with my editor, not to mention the publisher. I am liberated from work and worry for the next several months." My companion chuckled lightly, his brow creasing ever so slightly through the grey haze.

"Yes, I suppose that was rather poor foresight on my part. Even so, you can travel anywhere you wish. Spend a few months in France, perhaps?"

"And see a world racked with the fever of a passing war?" I shook my head. "I think I would rather stay here. If there is one thing to be said about this country, it is that you never hear of a wise old American, only a young and foolish one. This is the country of progress, forgetfulness, and absolute idiocracy." Keane nodded.

"It reminds me of Shaw's picture of Hell, a place of eternal pleasure. What could be more tedious?"

"A good many things, I suppose; the repetitiveness of day to day life until all time merges together and you are looking back wondering why you didn't accomplish something else when you could."

"You're much too young for that yet."

"Not true. Take our last little adventure, for instance. If I had known Michael would become so . . . infatuated with me, I might have been able to stop him before he had us both wandering about in a blizzard."

"But had that been avoided, we wouldn't have found Bridget. See, Lawrence, there are a great many things we could find in our pasts and wish that it had happened differently—that we could have changed it somehow—but doing so would alter the present result. Regret is one of the most useless of emotions. Guilt, when truly honourable and honest, is far better." I nodded slowly, Keane's sage words creeping gradually into my consciousness.

Regret may be useless, but it had a bite more cold and deadly than an onslaught of bullets.

CHAPTER FIVE

"*The carriage is waiting, Eliza. Are you ready?*"

"*Quite. Is the Professor coming?*" An older woman looked at the younger, though not very attractive, woman with an air of indignation only those withered with age can rightfully supply.

"*Certainly not. He can't behave himself in church. He makes remarks out loud all the time on the clergyman's pronunciation.*" The young woman turned to the man still seated in the elegant parlour.

"*Then I shall not see you again, Professor. Good-bye.*" The old woman swept over to the man who, though much younger than herself, still held the grace of age etched into his face.

"*Good-bye, dear.*"

"*Good-bye, mother. Oh, by the way, Eliza, order a ham and a Stilton cheese, will you? And buy me a pair of reindeer gloves, number eights, and a tie to match that new suit of mine, at Eale & Binman's. You can choose the colour.*" There was a cheerfulness to his voice, a carelessness that seemed willfully oblivious to the young lady's furrowed brow.

"*Buy them yourself.*"

"*I'm afraid you've spoiled that girl, Henry. But never mind, dear; I'll buy you the tie and gloves.*"

"*Oh, don't bother. She'll buy them all right enough. Good-bye.*"

I felt struck, entirely dumbfounded by the unusual affair. How many times had I seen the same thing—read those very words—and yet the soft English drawl that brushed my ears was far more real than any ink slathered over a page.

"Wonderful, Brendan." Harrison praised as he marched forward to the edge of the stage. "Wonderful. Now, if we could just run that last scene once more we can all go home and get some rest."

"You want us to do it *again*?" The young woman whined, her voice now completely bereft of all grace and beauty provided by the English language. "Well, *I* am going home. You all can stay and do it without me." She clambered down from the stage and stormed past Harrison without so much as a glance in his direction. To his credit, he seemed to hardly blink at her spoilt behaviour. Instead, he turned back to those still remaining on the stage.

"I suppose rehearsal is over then. Tomorrow is Sunday, so I will see everyone bright and early Monday morning." I grabbed my jacket from the theatre seat beside me and stood just as Keane came striding down the carpeted aisle with his hat under his arm. Before I could speak, his hand was at my elbow, edging me onward at a thrilling pace toward the door and out into the streets of evening. Window lights poured into the street in long yellow streaks upon blackened pavement. When we had rounded the block or so between us and the car, Keane laughed triumphantly and grasped my arm with an exhilarating amount of force.

"By God, Lawrence," He breathed. "I haven't felt that thrill for years; the words, the articulation, the wonder of it all. It's marvellous. Simply marvellous." I glanced at my companion's face as we strode rapidly onward. His blue eyes sparkled like a thousand lights laid out low over a glassy sea. There was a pleasantness to them, a long past longing hence fulfilled in a matter of instances wound together into a moment far too precious to be rightfully described.

"Mr. Harrison was right." I said. "You were incredible."

"Pshaw. I was adequate. Nothing more." How easily he said those words, how quick he was to brush them aside without so much as a nod to their meaning. Yet oh what pride there was in his face, and what dignity there was as the foundation for such a marvellous man as this. I would be the first to attribute him to ill temperament and, at times, utter neglect for the world at his fingertips, but he was a man different from all others. When he stood I stood. Where he walked, I walked. And, paying no heed to age or stereotypical roles, I could not help hoping that even the slightest bit of him might rub off onto me, that I might be such a fine human being as he.

Even if he should deny it.

Keane's steps slowed as we neared the car. We had refused a chauffeur, for reasons I believed to be more than obvious. A third constant variable meant another set of ears to hear even the most private of conversations and a mouth to carry them to the general public. Fortunately, Keane—man of many talents that he was—was able to skillfully drive in America, just as he was in Europe. I slipped into the passenger seat beside him.

"I still think you were magnificent." Keane grunted, though he could not hide the slight tug to the tip of his ear.

Old habits are difficult to break.

As we rounded the bend separating the seaside from the city itself, my companion began to hum merrily and drum his long, slender fingers against the steering wheel. Though I had often considered myself knowledgeable in the realms of classical music, his deep, melodic song drifted in and out between Vivaldi and Beethoven as natural as the summer breeze. Notes leapt from pitch to pitch with nary a falter. Key changes were bested by a quick adjective of the voice. It might have been considered childish, the constant singing that broke between each song with a gentle ease, but there was nothing false or foolish about him, just as his intelligence could not be measured in one area alone.

True intelligence never can.

MR. HARRISON'S HOUSE by the sea was stationed above the whispering waters with a presence so modern and overbearing, one could not fully escape from it's grasp. The plain, almost dull, white of the exterior meant nothing in comparison to the bright colours decorating each and every room. There were, of course, the less mind-shattering greens, beiges, and blues one could always expect, but the pinks, yellows, and other eccentric fabrics created something far different from which I had ever laid my eyes. And yet, sleep came without a qualm.

The next morning when I drifted slowly from the depth and warmth of the night to the cool of the morning, I found my mind whirling with thoughts and ideas so abominable that all I could do was hope a swift walk along the shore would banish them to the fire from whence they came. I got up immediately and began shuffling through the new suitcase filled with clothes that stank of starch and were as stiff as some ancient woman. There was a bathing suit (which I sincerely prayed I would never wear), a few pairs of rather eccentric pants, a few shirts, and—

And then I saw it, the lethal weapon that would doom me to a hell I wished not to walk.

The thing far more despicable than the devil himself.

The thing I hated more than sin.

A dress.

Damn.

The colour was not the problem, for I had always been rather fond of such a light blue (though perhaps not the exact shade). It was the idea of the thing—the principle—that burned my soul. The skirt was long and folded into vertical creases, while the upper portion was specifically made to emphasise those imphamous curves and caves of a woman's figure. Illogical though the perfectionist's illusion may be, it still existed to expect nothing less from the garment. It was the epitome of a grounded womanhood, built upon a femininity completely incapable of defending itself against anything more threatening than a slight fashion fopa or—heaven forbid—a farce while out to coffee. Complete femininity damned even the most capable of women to complete helplessness. The opening of a door was left to a male escort. The men drove the cars. The men worked in office buildings or shops. The men played politicians, pushing and prodding forein nations with little more effort than chess pieces on a wooden board. The men ruled the world.

Or so we women had been taught at the dusk of childhood innocence.

But then there had been the wars, both the first and second, to prove to the world the strengths of a woman; that the world would not revolve on its axis without our constant assistance. While the men slaughtered themselves on the battlefield, we had changed their bandages, clothed their aching flesh, and fed that pit in their stomach until they curtly thanked us and slogged back into the hail of bullets.

And yet, there was a dress.

Clearly it had not been I who had chosen such a truso, and Keane would most certainly never dare do such a thing. It had been left entirely to another.

Much to my eternal regret.

I at last emerged into the morning sun with what I believed to be a reasonable compromise of colour between a pair of brightly plaid trousers and white shirt. So armed, I trudged gradually down toward the ocean and began walking along the seashore. The sand glittered gold as waves of silver lapped upon their grainy treasure. Even in America I could not withhold that sense of glory in the presence of such sheer majesty. There was always such power in the waves as they whispered their forbidden tales of ships lost at sea, or the approach of those still yet to come. It was as if they had captured the whole of time within their watery hands and allowed only the briefest moments to drip through their fingers before they carried all the pains of one's past out to the sea. There was darkness in it too, an anger not even the purest of hearts could fully quell. It was there in the deafening roar as it threw itself desperately against the rocks. She flew with a hopeless cry as one who wished for the end without consideration for how it occurred. She held the lost spirits of a thousand sailors whose ship had not fulfilled the promise of safe passage, or those despite widows and lost loves who flung themselves onto her surface with pockets of rocks and other heavy objects. Final glory was all she wanted as she grabbed at my ankles with her wickedly cool fingers.

The end. The end. The end.

And yet, as I caught a glimpse of a wooden arm cutting along the heart of her, I knew but one thing.

It was just the beginning.

CHAPTER SIX
Summer 1916—H.M.S. Greylag

THE SHIP ROCKED VIOLENTLY, thrashing its crew about like the entirety of the world might soon collapse about their shoulders. Men became monsters, armed in their coats against the rolling of the sea. Their unruly hair was plastered to their dripping faces. The first shadows of a beard became wiry stripes of paint. To the world they were blind, though their hearts be open with a longing no one need say. Those who wanted a hot fire wanted a meal. Those who wanted a meal wanted a girl. Those who wanted a girl wanted all three. But there were none of these here. There was nothing but a bleary-eyed darkness that had settled upon them and clawed at their throats. There was no sound save the horrid screeches of death challenged by a captain's call. There was nothing to them but what was, even if that was very little. It had been said—by some strange old salt—that what would not break their spirits would most surely kill them.

Though Seaman Brendan Keane suspected half were already dead.

He knew not the time, nor the day, nor anything that could save them from a fate far worse than even the fires of Hell.

"Keep her steady, men!" The captain shouted, a mere whisper against the storm. Steady indeed. There was not a finer ship in all of His Majesty's service. The HMS Greylag was as fit as they came, strong and sleek as she was nice on the eyes. To Brendan she was more beautiful than half the women he had known, and he had known plenty to be sure. The young seaman grinned at the thought.

He had spent some of the better moments of his young life with a lovely lass on his arm as he paraded up and down the streets in his old number one. Even in those brief moments they were in port he could always muster up a girl to take on the town, and more often or not she proved to be the fairer of the fair sex. Hair thick and long as it flowed down her back or was wound upward in wondrous braids and curls. Those dresses that had made it their purpose to accentuate every curve of her figure. Oh, he didn't give so much as a fig to fashion. So long as the styles were suitable for the wearer, he was satisfied.

A monstrous wave hurled itself over the rail and smashed violently over the crews before rapidly retreating back into the dark and dreaded waters. Brendan shifted his weight against the winds and continued to carry on toward the hatch. The storm followed his lead and allowed its growl to swell into the frantic screams of a thousand hysterical women.

Women.

Of course, Brendan had no complaint toward the facade of the fairer sex. He was not a cad, but a man with the same heart and soul as most other men. Even when he was a boy he could get girls alright, but he had never known what to do or say in her company. Women, he thought solemnly, were not like men. Men were straight out, say what you like, sort of chaps. It was simpler that way. Women; however, often listened to every uttered line with uncanny scrutiny. One slip of the tongue and—

A sharp shout cut through the air like fire as another watery hand slapped the deck and grabbed at his feet. Where their fingers pulled, he fought bravely forward until he was very near to the hatch. Below would be a lovely warmth, dry from the squall's damning hand. It was like a wife; safe and sure against the obstacles.

A wife.

Brendan Keane was many things, but a scoundrel was not one of them. He'd loved and been loved. Was he a heartbreaker? He didn't think so. Oh, he may have dented them a bit now and then, but that happened in life. There had been some women who had kicked his heart around a bit, but, in the end, he was the same man. Most men he knew were never too horribly changed by the fickle finger of fate. Sure, there were those unlucky few who dropped a woman and picked up the bottle, but he would never be one of those. He would never forgive himself to step toward such a slippery slope to destruction; to be tied down forever to ragged coats and empty pockets. Such was the end of a man, and the birth of a thousand devils. Brendan fancied himself a free spirit, though that was a bloody hard thing to be when tied to a ship at sea.

Another wave crashed down upon him. The icy hands of death brushed his neck and ran down the open collar of his shirt. Every unruly hair on his head snaked against his scalp, the blond fangs biting his flesh with sickening ice. A sudden scream slapped him hard across the face as a dark figure was swept backward towards the rail and toppled limply over the edge. Without a second thought, Brendan dashed along the deck, fighting the wind and led rain. His boots slipped mercilessly over the lurching ground until at last he was at the icy rail. The metal bit into the calloused flesh on his palms as his body was brutally thrown forward by another shock of the ship. In an instant he had climbed upon the only barrier between himself and intimate death.

And then promptly hurled himself off of it.

Down he fell, deeper, deeper, until his body was submerged in black. Great nets of poisoned foam fell upon him in sheets as his trained arms pulled him through the shifting waters. Great boisterous calls echoed somewhere above him, but Brendan could see nothing but the final glimpse of a man's fingertips sinking further into the murk.

Further. Further.

Lower. Lower.

CHAPTER SEVEN

When Keane again resurfaced from the water, he was dragging a sailing ship behind him. It was not an enormous vessel like one would imagine in some great pirate film, nor was it a rickety old thing that could do nothing more than a lonely cork from a wine bottle. It was ship shape from stem to stern and the port and starboard side respectively. A stripe of clean, white paint shot along the sides, just as the sails cut through the morning sky. Everything about her was magnificent and dignified to be sure, but, when I said as much to the tall figure approaching on the sand, I received only a hearty chuckle.

"She's not the *Saint Gobniat*, but she'll do nicely, I think." And indeed she would, though Keane was quite right. This ship was most certainly not the same one he had left behind in England. I glanced at the painted letters upon her hull. *Mae West*. Of course an American would name their ship after a film star. I had seen a few of her films myself and, though they were admittedly enjoyable, the vessel's title was not quite so poetic as Keane's selection. *The Saint Gobnait*; the female patron saint of County Cork, where he had been born and raised until the war.

The first war, I corrected silently.

There had been two now; two fatal cracks to shake the world until it trembled at the knees. If the millions of deaths and an insane dictator were not sufficient evidence to the demoralisation of this hell in which we lived, the Americans had developed an entirely new form of warfare that could kill hundreds of thousands of people within a handful of seconds. Those who survived the blast were then racked with diseases that weakened their bones and induced vomiting no human could quell. Blackened corpses lined foreign streets, limbs twisted and bent like the victims of Pompeii. In thought, there was only one difference.

One was made by men.

Keane strode up onto the shore and began drying his face with a towel I had not noticed lying limp on the beach. His sopping trousers clung to his legs, dripping little rivers of water onto his bare feet. His hair was slicked back against his skull with enough laxity to retain some semblance of style. He was not—nor, I thought, had he ever been—a man to whom his wealth meant much more than a lack of poverty. However, in the years I had known him he had most always been cat-like in the upkeep of his appearance. His tweed suits were just as common to him as my jacket was to me. They were not so much what we wore, but who we were. It was a reflection of our lives, our ambitions, our hopes, our dreams, our past, and our future. They were a story woven tightly by the threads of our beginnings, a knot tied firmly at every day to prevent the fabric of our being from unravelling at the slightest slip of change.

"What do you think, Lawrence?" I blinked.

"About what?" Keane laughed, the strong sound of a trained baritone shaking through him like thunder in a summer's storm.

"Breakfast. I learned how to fry up a decent pan of eggs and rashers in the navy, and I did see some fresh oranges inside.

After that we can go into the city and buy some proper clothes. How does that sound?" I nodded and was rewarded by another shower of sweet rain. The birds sang in glory, and all of life fell once more into the tellable joviality one must always believe to lay just around the next bend. For every pain, there is a drop of hope. For every pint of blood, a salvation. And, for every friend, a companion.

Keane swung the towel over his shoulder, put a hand on my elbow, and together we trudged back up toward the house.

"BY GOD, LAWRENCE," Keane chuckled as he came out of the tailor's. "You must be the one woman on earth who can finish her shopping before a man. Either you are truly a fine example of the female sex, or that tailor took far too long with his measurements."

"I think I rather like the first explanation." I grinned. "At last you are admitting women can be more efficient than men."

"I beg your pardon? I said no such thing."

"Hm, well, you should. It would look far better to admit it now than to be wrong later." Keane's shoulders shot back and his eyes hardened to silver.

"Me? Wrong? Really, I—"

"—Relax, Keane, I was only jesting. Your pride can be most insufferable at times."

"Says the most stubborn, prideful, and infuriating woman I have ever had the pleasure of knowing." I really did not know what to say then, and my companion damn well knew it. A self satisfied grin quickly swept across his face at the very instant his eyes twinkled with amusement. In a flash he had stolen the wrapped parcel from beneath my arm and held it suspiciously with a scrutinous eye. "Are you sure you bought everything you need? No truso? No trunks? No ridiculous amounts of hats and curlers bubbling up to your ears? Or are you hiding a ridiculous amount of baggage nearby?" I snatched back the wrapped bundle, shaking my head with an exasperated sigh.

"Really, Keane, you need to think more highly of yourself. After all, calling yourself baggage may be a sure sign of oncoming depression . . . or dementia." He had not the chance to respond as a shrill voice warbled his name in such a careless way I had not thought it was his name at all.

"Mr. Keane? Mr. Keeaaannneeeee?" She came at us like a mad woman, sashaying her hips with such exaggeration I could have swore she would topple over on those high heels of hers. I needn't have looked at Keane to know every muscle in his body had stiffened into a stance looking every bit as depressing as an old Victorian banker.

"Miss Smith," He greeted simply, straining his face into the most excruciating of smiles. "You are looking well today." In fact, the woman was most certainly *not* looking well. Rather she looked every bit as ugly as she did the day before when she had marched out of the theatre. Her dark hair was the colour of sodden ash, burned by fire and soaked with styling products. (I was quite relieved Keane was not smoking at the time, else she go up in flames.) What I suspected to be a ruddy complexion was hidden behind buckets of makeup, just as her too-large lips were accentuated all the more by gaudy red lipstick. In addition to this, her nose was large and ill-shaped, her figure was rather lumpy, and her fingernails were painted such vulgar shades of blue I wished only to turn myself from her completely. A sickening knot in my stomach formed when her screeching giggles prodded at my ears with rusted needles.

"Ohhhh, you *are* a charmer, aren't you Mr. Keane. Or can I call you Brendan? I think I will. It's a *real* nice name. Real British-like. You are British, aren't you? You sure sound like you are." The woman suddenly turned to me as though I had clawed my way up from the burning earth with a third eye glued to my forehead. "And who are you?" Keane cleared his throat and shoved his hands into his pockets.

"Miss Smith, may I introduce you to Miss Joanna Lawrence." I offered my hand but, rather than finishing the greeting, the woman pulled her painted fingers away and glared at me with something very near to hatred.

"Funny. She doesn't *look* like a secretary." I felt my fists clench at my sides. Surely America held some laxity toward pummeling women in the streets. It was, after all, for a good cause. My dignity. Keane was first to the tackle.

"I should say not. Miss Lawrence is an educated young woman who is her own person."

"*Educated* isn't the word I'd use." The woman chirped. I ground my teeth. Of course it wouldn't, the cow. She probably didn't know any words longer than two syllables able to be said with any air of decorum. Keane finished the conversation—if it could be called a conversation—with a few gentlemanly words and—God save us—a cold, formal kiss to the wretched woman's hand. I thought she would faint dead away onto the pavement.

And I would have left it to Keane to pick up the shattered pieces.

As it was, we walked another three blocks before either of us had the courage to speak up again. Keane sighed heavily, reached for his cigarette case, lit one, and blew a long puff of white haze. With one, fatal glance, he caught me.

"Out with it, Lawrence."

"Keane, have you ever considered—may we walk through the park?" My companion's dignified brow furrowed considerably. Rarely—if not never—had I ever suggested such a thing so utterly ridiculous and off handed. I abhorred the storybook romanticisms that even bordered leisure, and despised the likes of those who made a life within its pages. Keane; however, obliged my request and, clasping his hands nautically behind his back, chartered a new course toward Shaw's Hell of pleasure.

The park was like most any other park I had seen. Green grasses, screaming children with sticky fingers, decrepit men on benches, and a variety of trees spotting the worn paths. In the heat of the morning, men had shed their suit jackets and women wore their lightest blouses and skirts. To my pride and misfortune, I was still wearing my leather jacket as Keane half-heartedly paraded us up and down the dirt paths. His monologue began as some effortless forms of polite conversation before trickling into the dull dribble only the most desperate could supply. I listened to him ramble on about the improvements made to help the millions of soldiers suffering from shell-shock, the benefits of physical exercise, the hot weather, the ocean, the history of sailing ships, the Flying Dutchman, Irish folklore, male fashions, theological similarities in American culture, America in general, England, Ireland, France, the division of German, the threat of a possible third war in the future, the conspiracies that another such war would include nuclear bombs fired from space by green creatures with four eyes and—

"Damn it, Keane, that's absurd!"

"Thank God for that." My companion exclaimed, dropping dramatically onto a nearby bench. "Really, a man can only carry on a thread of conversation for so long before truly doing himself a mischief."

"Why do you feel it necessary to say anything at all? Haven't you heard the phrase, *If you haven't anything nice to say*—"

"—Lawrence, you demean yourself."

"*I?*"

"Yes, you. Do you realise we have been walking for the better part of an hour and you have said no more than two fragmented sentences that entire time?" I folded my arms and glared down at Keane.

"And what would you prefer my reaction to be? Green creatures indeed. If you find my company deplorable, I'll go."

"Oh, Lawrence." Keane chided, wagging his head slowly and motioning for me to sit beside him. Which I did.

But at a respectable distance.

"Blast it all, Keane. What is so all-fired important about what I haven't told you? I keep a lot of things to myself. For instance, I have a distance cousin in Dover who is married to some fifth cousin, twice removed from Eisenhower. There, do you feel better knowing that? Or would you rather me tell you about this neighbour boy when I was little who was so damn fat he once got stuck in his chair at school? Or perhaps I should provide the tale of Bobby Hensle Jack, who was such an ass I clobbered him over the head with a complete volume of Charles Dickens' works. Or—" I did not stop out of a lack of oddities speckled through my life, but something far more sinister. Keane was laughing.

The damn man was laughing.

"By God, Lawrence, you do know how to avoid a topic, don't you. And just when I thought you had the nerve to ask me something serious."

"Oh?" I sat a little straighter. "And what, pray tell, would that question be?"

"I expect you were going to suggest we marry."

I slapped him.

It was nothing fancy or the blind swing of an emotional female, but a good, open-handed crack against his jaw.

I slapped him once.

Only once.

Hard.

Just as quickly as I had struck, I leapt to my feet with my fists ready to pummel the sod into the wooden bench.

"How—How *dare* you!" I spat venomously. Keane had not so much as flinched at my strike, though I noticed the slightest dusting of red along his left cheek. His eyes remained that steady blue and—damn the man—even his voice still sounded reasonable.

"Am I wrong? Tell me I am, and I shall apologise immediately."

"I—"

"There, see, you can't because it's true. You think we should be married, though I can't imagine why the thought occurred to you. Lawrence, I have met enough women in my time to know they hold the realms of matrimony on some idealistic throne. While it may have its social and moral advantages, and although

I am by no means against such an arrangement—please sit down, Lawrence."

"No." I would not 'sit down'. I would not give him the satisfaction of winning so much as a pawn on the chess board. But when my refusal hit his ears, he rose to his feet. I had stood before him a thousand times, yet it never ceased to amaze me just how much he towered over me when he took my shoulders in his hands and forced my eyes to meet his.

It was never safe to look into those watery blue eyes.

When his voice came again, it had lost some of the sharp English clip I had known for so long. Or, perhaps it had not been lost, but overshadowed by the sing-song brogue of Cork. It was just a smattering upon certain vowels—a mere brush—but it was enough to just be noticable.

"Lawrence, listen to me. I am fifty-five years old. I have long been accustomed to the freedom and seclusion of bachelor life. You would be wasting your life for something that could last only a few decades. I would not—*could not*—force you to endure such a fate."

"And you believe that you have the power in the world to speak for both of us? I never said I wanted to marry you." I tried to tear myself away, to wrench my shoulders from his grasp, but he caught my arm and tugged me back. His fingers dug into my sleeve, but my flesh was unharmed. And my soul burned.

"Think of it. No matter what, there will come a day when I will be dead, and you will have to live. What if we had wedded ourselves? What if—by some unread twist of fate—you would be my wife? When I die, you will be a young widow." Keane's voice, filled with an energy I feared to properly place, immediately dropped low about my ears. "And Lord knows there are far too many of those already."

"But I never said, or even suggested—"

"God, Lawrence, do you think I care so little you must speak your mind at every given moment for me to know your heart? I may be a man. I may be—on exceptionally rare occasions—rather dim. But I am *not* a bumbling buffoon."

"Nor are your words logical. Why would I want to marry you? Why? To stop some old hag who attempts to dictate morals when she knows not the binds of ethics or the sorrows of forgotten dreams?" The grip on my arm lessened, strength giving way to a heavy warmth spreading along my flesh. A sign of hope and sorrow. I had crossed a barrier too wide for my young mind to comprehend. But an inability to understand does not mean that I could not recognise the abyss over which I balanced. I had taken a step too far. A leap too long. A hope that was hopeless.

Keane's fingers became feathers upon my sleeve; an angel's breath of a door that should never again be open.

"Do you really imagine I would succumb to the bond of matrimony to stop busibodies—like Miss Smith—from wagging their tongues anytime we are seen together in public? Do you?" I said nothing. Anyone who has ever been in such a position has been told to do so. I said nothing. Not even my name, rank, or serial number. I just ripped myself from his hands and strode quickly away.

He did not follow.

CHAPTER EIGHT
Summer 1916—Palermo, Italy

"*. . . And should the ship not take its place*
  Upon the silvering tree
  Let not what was or would have been
  Become what's yet to be.
  Oh, hark the angels that do sound
  Let trumpets they do play
  Announce that what I have found
  Upon this forein bay."

"Oh, Brendan, that was beautiful." The young woman hummed as she buried herself further against his chest. How could he help but smile and tug her even closer to him when they sat on the front steps of her stucco house. Brendan Keane, seaman of His Majesty's Royal Navy, never ceased to wonder at the city's enchantment. Vividly painted homes speckled the horizon until gradually fading into a churning ocean that sang as crisply as a music box for all who lived near its waves. There was nowhere quite like Palermo in his mind. Nowhere in the world. He would be content to grow old in the warmth of her arms, to sail the painted horizon and return to nights of wine and dancing. He could write his poetry, or perhaps take up some new hoby as its brother. Writing had always appealed to him as much, if not more, than returning to University in England after the war ended.

If it would ever end.

It had always been his dream—his passion—to pen words to pages in hopes that some foreign soul might read it and be reassured by its splendour. But when he returned to England, he would be just as content to study the mind as Dr. Sigmund Freud had written. Perhaps he could arrange to meet the Austrian. Of course, Freud was an unusual man at best, but wasn't that true about most any genius that had walked upon the earth? Yes, once the war was over, his world could again fall into place.

Just as the woman in his arms.

He could have drowned in beauty of her. Thick, auburn curls hung well past her shoulders. Her eyes were the delightful shade of melted chocolate that splashed and rippled with every smile. And her laugh. Oh, what a laugh she had. It was the sweet twittering of birds in the warmth of the morning. There was nothing to fault in her. There was no sin to be forgiven by God or man. She was entirely perfect.

And she was his.

In thinking so, he pulled her tightly to himself in a firm embrace before wincing ever so slightly with the effort. She pushed back from him and ran a hand over his lapels with the weight of butterflies.

"Is that shoulder still troubling you?" Oh how sweet her voice; how pure against the smog of life. She was the epitome of womanhood, the angel of femininity, and the goddess of

Palermo. The young man hummed as he brushed a few stray curls from her ear.

"How could anything trouble me when I'm with such charming company?"

"You are an exasperating man; frustrating, aggravating, incorrigible—"

"—And marvellous." The young woman laughed. God, how he loved her laugh.

"A marvellous fool. James told me how you dove off of the ship to save a man. In the middle of a storm, no less." Brendan chuckled and wrapped his arm around her petite waist.

"Natasha, have I told you lately how much I adore you?"

"No, but you should, or I might be liable to forget."

"Forget?" Brendan pulled her face up to his and lightly brushed a kiss atop her lips. "There. You can't very well forget that, now can you?" Natasha shook her head with a grin Brendan could not see as anything less than endearing.

"How could I when you seem adamant to grow that infernal beard?" The young seaman raised his hand absentmindedly to stroke the trimmed hair along his jaw and lip.

"I think it makes me look rather dignified." He defended.

"Well I think you look ridiculous. It's too red. It makes you look Irish."

"Then I shall keep it."

"But I hate it." Natasha argued. Brendan stood and offered her his hand.

"Then I shall shave it off. Really, me dear, you're far too much of a blasted female; telling me what and what not to do. Shouldn't a man be able to wear his own hair if he likes?" She laughed, lifting a hand to his face that her thumb ran gently over his lips.

"Do what you wish, Brendan Keane, but you won't get another kiss out of me with that infernal thing in the way. And you certainly won't receive any . . . other benefits?" The seaman nearly toppled off the steps.

"Natasha!"

"And I haven't heard you asking anything that could make our little affair official." Where the young woman appeared entirely unshaken by what she had just suggested, Brendan's face would have proven a vivid red had his facial hair not have been the same eccentric colour.

"I won't ask until I feel it's time." The woman rested her hands on the soft curves of her hips.

"Oh, really, and when is that going to be?"

"Natasha—"

"Brendan, I see you once a year—twice, if we're lucky—and each time we continue this proper courting as if we had all the time in the world."

"And have I not been a gentleman?" The beautiful woman sighed and ran her small hands from the buttons of his pea coat upwards until they were encircled around his neck.

"That's the problem. It's as though you haven't any feelings at all. Each time you return to Palermo, you come to my doorstep with sweets and flowers. A woman can only have so many of those without wanting something more. Something . . . memorable."

"Have I not written you letters? Have I not expressed my affections each and every day I have been absent from your life?"

"You have written me *words*, Brendan. You always give me words, but even a cad can do that. Don't you understand? I want you. *You*. Not some feeble representations of your feelings, but something more substantial that could tide me over until I see you again. Else . . ." Her voice drifted away into the evening dim, but the sun was only beginning to rise on Brendan's anger.

"'Else' what?" Natasha unclasped her hands from behind his neck and settled them on his lapels.

"There *are* other men in the world. And I should consider my options before I reach the dreaded spinsterhood."

"Natasha, be honest with me. Is there another—"

"—of course not, Brendan, but we're not getting any younger and I have half a dozen friends who are already married and are working on their third child. We aren't even engaged. So what is it? What do you want after the war? A life of passion with me here, or your life of study in England?"

CHAPTER NINE

I turned down one street and onto another, not bothering to learn the names or directions of either one. It was of no importance where I went, just so long as I kept increasing the distance between myself and Keane. The argument did not bother me in the slightest. With him, such squalls were a way of life. More often than not, they were rather entertaining when one reflected on the long moment spent bickering over both the superfluous and commanding. However, as I dodged out of the harrowing path of a fruit cart, I had no intention of looking behind me.

The audacity of the man. To think I would suggest *marriage* of all things. Never had I even considered such an outlandish thing. Or, on the few—*very few*—occasions when I had, they were nothing more than brief glimpses of 'what if'. Often they were gone by morning as a dream that never came or a nightmare that was not quite so frightening as one may first imagine. In either case, I most certainly never would say such a thing out loud. Thank God I hadn't, else that entire situation would have been made all the worse. Worse than that pitying look that made one feel entirely useless against the world. Worse than the warmth of his hands on my shoulders. It was worse than most anything in the world, save his disappointment.

When we met again, the conversation would be nonexistent, as if it had never occurred and shaken our fragile world. Perhaps it had not. Perhaps the obstinate man had asked something innocent and kind; something that could not force our world into trembling shards. Yes, he was obstinate. And the most infuriating, aggravating, sarcastic, damnable, and temperamental man I had the ill-fortune of meeting.

And yet I could not help but adore him.

However, in the shadow of doubt and as I wound up and down the obnoxious, pulsating streets of morning, I could do nothing but hate myself for this weakness.

ABOUT AN HOUR OR SO later I had cooled enough not to bash the face of any person who said 'hello'.

Hello.

Not 'good morning' or even 'good afternoon'. They said 'hello'. How entirely American.

I turned down an alley, popped up at another road, and came face to face with a colourful diner with bright, spindly lights that, in a twist of glass and metal, spelled out a single word. Dilly's. A loud string of music escaped through the walls and poured out into the street. Trumpets blared while drums pounded out some intelligible rhythm that wreaked of life and energy. I shoved Keane far out of my mind.

Damn the man, I was going to enjoy myself.

A small bell above the door announced my presence to the dozen of other young people who peppered the booths and stools. A few high-pitched girls gathered around a jukebox in the corner, stuffing coins into the overworked machine until it blared out the newest songs. The tin, lifeless noise was hardly a consolation to my battered brain. Voices became only scratches of steel, and horns a shriek for sanity. As I sat down at the long, metal counter, I found myself examining the linoleum at my feet. Large white and black squares chequered the floor before vanishing at the painted walls. They were so different. Complete opposites, in fact. But they were also the same; the same size, same shape, same design. To a buffoon, they were to be separated, but to a wise man, they were meant to band together to create a much broader picture.

Life.

"What would ya like?" I glanced up to face a scrawny, ruddy-faced boy grinning from behind the multiple levers of the soda fountain. Sharp, brown sticks pricked outward around his white cap, and the black bow tie of his uniform did nothing if not accentuate an all too prominent Adam's apple. What truly struck me as odd was his eyes. They were not an exceptionally unusual colour, but different colours themselves. The right one was a rather dull green, while the left a gentle brown that only made his standard Californian tan more noticeable. I smiled wearily.

"What would you suggest?" The boy didn't even blink.

"Our burgers are good."

"I'll have one of those then, and coffee too."

"Sure thing." The boy disappeared and I was again submerged into my surroundings. It was so entirely American, and yet I found nothing displeasing about the affair. Every so often I even recognised a voice crackling through the room. It was not my own environment, but I could accept it as much, should the need arise.

Perhaps there was good reason to say America was made for the young.

The food came when I was into my second cup of coffee and I was soon entrapped in the almost film-like innocence. I was the young child who had run away. I had run away to the little diner where you could buy a feast for a pocket full of coins and listen to music that would either make you smile or deafen you into stupidity. The only sign of true existence—*my* existence—was a set of eyes resting on my shoulder as I slowly mopped a chip (or were they fries here?) through a receding pond of ketchup.

"You aren't from here, are you?" I glanced up at the boy, uncomfortably aware of his optical abnormalities as he spoke. His voice was not of poor quality or annoying by any means, but it held some undertones—an odd lilt—I couldn't quite place. I swept another fried potato through the red paint splattered across my plate.

"Not here, no."

"I didn't think so. Your voice is different. More—what's the word—refined. Are you from England?" Idaho? No. Missouri? No, that wasn't it either. Further east perhaps?

"I have spent some time there, yes." The boy nodded toward my jacket.

"Did you fight for 'em?" I fingered the worn bits of leather toward the edge of the sleeves.

"No. It was a relation's."

"Oh." The young man's multi-colored eyes darted immediately to the floor. "Sorry. I didn't mean to—that is, er—I lost my brother in the Air Force."

"The world lost a lot of good men." I stated simply. Then, as if we had said all we could on the matter, I thrust out my hand with a nod.

"My name's Jo Lawrence, by the way." The boy completed the handshake.

"I'm Frank. Like the singer. 'Cept my last name's Collins. Have you ever heard him sing?" I mentally scrubbed through my exhausted brain until I fell upon the only reliable conclusion: the vocal shooting star.

"All the time. I take it you do too?" Frank grinned from ear to ear and stabbed his thumb backwards into his ribcage.

"Sure I do. I came from the same town as him: Hoboken, New Jersey." New Jersey. So that was it. It certainly explained his tendency to pronounce his 'er's as 'oi's. "There's a heck of a lot of things in New Jersey, but California has something that li'l state'll never have."

"And that is?"

"Sun. Lot's and lots of sun. Not to mention . . ." Frank leaned over the counter with a grin and nodded toward the high-strung group surrounding the thumping jukebox. " . . . Girls." I laughed, a short biting sound that made the little man hunched over in a booth writhe in surprise. If most any other person had said such a thing, I would easily have reached over the counter and grabbed his lapels until his face turned blue, but this young man held that uncanny ability to communicate the unspeakable.

That too, I thought, was strictly American.

As if summoned, a woman, perhaps a few years younger than I, climbed onto the stool to my left and waved her hand to order. It was my cue. I downed the final dregs of my coffee, dropped a fistful of change onto the metal counter, and left the bright little diner.

I wandered about for some time after that, not wishing to return to the beach house while still overwhelmed by the sheer size of my surroundings. 'Large' did not so much as scrape the surface, and 'enormous' came only marginally closer. I was not more than an insect placed beneath the heat of a microscope and society's scrutinous eye. A few people glanced casually in my direction. Others stared. Some did both. I was well acquainted with these discomforts that were often magnified when striding beside Keane. It was not quite so despicable here, for indeed to not know a person is to remain oblivious to their opinion. And yet, there were those—damn that Miss Smith—whose tongues God had made too large and their brains too small. (In select cases I suspected the good lord had forgotten the latter entirely.)

I passed a druggist's, a tobacconist's, a hotel, several shops, a grocer's, a barber's, and several cinemas before turning right along a street crammed with bodies bashing into each other with heated words and snide remarks.

Wonderful.

I edged through these with as much dignity as any human being may accomplish after charging headlong into a scruffy sailor, brushing the arm of a prissy man in clothes bereft of all signs of work, and apologising profusely to an old lady who, even in her flickering years, still had quite the mouth on her. It was a hideous, wrinkled, filthy, and toothless mouth, but a mouth all the same. Her dry lips were not but a stiff line carved into dark, rotting wood. Her bark-like skin seemed eager to fall away and leave nothing but a described skeleton well past burial. I have always had the same amount of luck with understanding old women as I have young men: none. Perhaps that is why I was satisfied with my nonexistent marriage status and avoided social events as one would a plague. The old women always want the young ones to marry quickly, while the young men want the same for their own advantage. Both ideas were entirely useless unless one was trying to dramatically increase the surplus population, or decrease it exponentially by those who sought a desperate end. In either case, the result was appalling.

I dug my heels in near the end of the street and turned away from the thrashing crowds with their high-pitched exclamations and violent frames. From that point I turned West toward the sea, walked leisurely for a mile or so, before deflecting sharply from the waves. I did; however, stride quickly toward a book shop.

In all the world, books are very much the same; pages bound together with the glue of knowledge and the mustiness of time and tragedy. An author myself, I knew all too well the exhausting effort that occurred between the first, brief spark of an idea to the finality of that hard-covered book, or, to Keane, the intellectual manuscript read by scholars throughout the world. We were well-met, he and I; two minds wallowing in the intellectual deprivation of modern society while still clinging to some form of sanity.

It was never much of a decision about which section to begin with when it came to books. I bounded from thrillers to poetry, and murders to tragedies. Between the four, there was little they did not share. What poetry does not speak of thrilling moments? What murder does not mean a tragidy harolded by man's fist? Many of the names were familiar to me, be it by a fondness for their work or a recommendation through Keane. I also recalled a select few from some rather unfortunate moments plotted in the dull beginnings of a child's education.

Plucking a volume from the dusty shelves, I leaned my shoulder against the wood and began flipping idly through the first few pages. There were those tepid few that lacked steam and drive (. . . *oh but flowers, how they weep, and how the winds do blow, and if I pull them one by one, there shall not be a row* . . .) or (. . . *and with the waving, whipping winds I trudged upon the dew, and though I saw it many times it was still fresh and new* . . .). These ripped at my soul as a dull blade would my flesh; the stupidity of it all was excruciating. I had nothing against flowers, though I was not particularly fond of the symbolism of such things, nor did I scorn the summer winds that rolled lazily across the sea. They were forces of nature enjoyable when one had the proper time and company. But, ah—

I stared down at the page open in my hands with an impish grin smeared across my features. God, it would infuriate him. It would send him into a whirlwind of words best left on a merchant's vessel. By George, he could drop of a heart attack within seconds.

Marvellous.

I soon left the little shop with the book pinned under my arm, only to bow beneath a sheeting of soaking rain. I rushed along the megre shelter of shop awnings, my shoulders and head soon claimed by the downpour. What had begun as a clear day had suddenly demoralised itself into the dreary English climate. I sped along with my spine hunched low as my clothing clung to my flesh. Where the morning had been hot, the droplets of water smacked my neck with a biting cold I had met in Ireland. My blood turned to ash at the memory and I immediately waved down a taxi. Though my muscles jerked with the incident upon our arrival, I was overjoyed to note the man behind the wheel was not smoking those hideous cigars. He was; however, well equipped with a heavy raincoat and the collar pulled up around his neck. His hat was pulled low over his brow, but that was not unusual. Few things were in this country. My mouth was half open, ready to give the address of the beach house, but a quick glance at my billfold sent that hope far out of my head. Damn. Why hadn't I brought a bit more, rather than stashing it in a dresser drawer like a child?

"Caldwell Theatre." I instructed the figure behind the wheel. A compromise. It was not so far I would pay a small fortune, and it most certainly had a telephone I could use. If I didn't feel up to calling Keane—God, what a joke he'd make of it all—I could wait until the squall passed then walk back. It wasn't unreasonably far and, as Keane had so eloquently pointed out, I was still considerably young in my own life. I sat back against the jaunting seats, allowing myself to be lulled by the rain pattering against the windows. Peeling my jacket from my shoulders, I laid it over my legs and pressed my forehead to the glass. What a world it was out there; constantly changing and shifting with every human whim or fancy. Where there had been horses there were cars. Candles became electric lights. Dirt became pavement. And life? Life was nothing more than a facade made real by millions believing it so. What fools we were to think it would last; that this chaotic tranquillity would continue as we wished. Perhaps it was the war which had stolen logic from our minds, or perhaps it was only an excuse for us to do what we had in the beginning. We were not but people. We were not gods, nor lords, nor any other sense of divine royalty. And yet we thought we were. So often we believed the world was ours; that we were the nucleus to all that had been in existence since time itself began.

What fools we were.

I was not aware the vehicle had sputtered to a halt until the figure in the driver's seat caused the springs to creak. Shoving a few bills into his wrinkled hand, I bounded up the steps leading to the theatre doors. Locked.

Damn.

I ran back to the taxi just as it began to pull away and threw myself into its odorous clutches. My soaked clothes weighing me down, I fell back against the seats with a heavy sigh. Like clockwork, the motor growled to life and began skittering along the roads.

"Where to, Miss? I know a good place to get warm and catch a bite, if you want?" I smiled.

"That would be wonderful." And indeed it would. Warmth is most always a thing of bliss, but when it comes with the promise of food, that is truly heaven. I once more settled back into the seats, more at ease with myself then I had been for some time. My mind relaxed into oblivion until the car sputtered to a stop just between two claustrophobic walls darkened by shadow and fear.

"Where is this?"

"Right where ya wanted. There's a place just down the road there." I squinted out through the sheets of rain.

"Road? That isn't a road, it's a blasted alley. What the hell is this?" The heavy, sandpaper voice dropped half an octave lower.

"Hasn't anyone told you it's dangerous for a good girl to go around with strangers?" The concealed man shifted around until his overshadowed face leered at me and I noticed something sticking out from his clenched fingers. Something cold, silver, and undeniably lethal.

Before so much as a single strand of hair stuck up on my neck, I found myself in that odd situation held between hurling myself bodily toward my attacker, or laughing hysterically.

I chose the latter.

"Good God, Keane," I gasped, grabbing my heaving sides. "What on earth are you doing here? You gave me a start." A soft chuckle floated to my ears as my companion folded down the collar of his coat until I could see those familiar blue eyes flickering merrily in amusement. Something, even through my own hilarity, I did not fully appreciate until several hours later.

"I assure you that was not my intention." He opened the silver cigarette case poised in his hand and casually pressed one of the paper-wrapped cylinders between his lips as his long fingers searched diligently for a match. When one could not be found, I pulled a lighter from my pocket and tossed it in his lap.

"You still haven't answered my question. What are you doing here?"

"Driving. You have no idea what I endured as I waited for you. For the majority I had no problems, save the ordinary, international imbecile; however, there was one couple that would have been arrested if their little dance of repopulation on a street corner." Keane flinched visibly. "Has America no morals?"

"*'Morality is only moral when it is voluntary'* Besides, you're one to talk, how did you get the taxi?"

"I assure you I was entirely within the law. I borrowed it from a friend—yes, I do have friends—who just asked that I return it before four this afternoon. Had you continued your plight for another hour and a half, you would have made a liar out of me."

"You? A liar?" I chuckled. "Now there's a hell of a confession."

"Really, Lawrence, you're language."

"Sorry. So, are you having fun?" I could easily hear Keane's quiet and—heaven forbid—undignified groan.

"Less than a week in the country and you have already adapted to the American slaughtering of the English language."

"I was born here, remember. Fine. Are you enjoying yourself?"

"Quite, but I would do so even more if we got out of this cramped piece of abused machinery." I peered out the dripping window once more. There was still nothing but faded murk played by a smattering of watery bricks and clutter melting into the bleary outer walls. Every natural colour had faded and darkened into the final smears of an artist's paint as thick globs of the world refracted through the window and ran slowly along the glass. It was as if the entire world was melting into the palm of my hand, leaving nothing but drab streaks of grey and the dull tedium of little pellets berating the taxi's metal frame.

"Where would we go?" I said. "There isn't a restaurant or pub out there. Is there?" Keane chuckled, a deep, rich sound that echoed effortlessly through his chest. It was a sound I had come to love just as much as I had learned to despise. I was aware of the final wisps of a cigarette and a brief tap to my arm before I was once more hurled outward into the finality of a soggy world.

CHAPTER TEN
Summer 1916—Palermo, Italy

"BRENDAN, YOU ARE A man among men." Young Seaman Fingal O'Malley roared as his hand slammed down on the Irishman's back, nearly throwing him from the chair.

"It's true." James Harrison nodded, downing half his drink. "You are a braver man than I to let a girl as good as that get away. If I could get a dame half that pretty to beg me to love her, I could march back on that damn boat one hell of a happy man." The celebrated seaman pinned between the two men could hardly agree.

"It was the principle of the thing." Brendan Keane stated, rubbing his hand over the red scruff on his jaw, though it had darkened toward more of a chestnut brown, rather than a heated fire. Harrison again slammed his hand onto the red and white chequered tablecloth.

"Principle, shminciple. I've never seen you happier than when you had a girl on your arm."

"Or when ya were kissing her in the back of a cab. Brendan, me boyo, you are a master in the art of women." The young man cradled his drink between his hands.

"Master or not, I still let her go."

"Didn't take long for her to find another though. She must have seen half a dozen men this past week." James Harrison finished his liquor and patted the front of his uniform. "C'mon, fellas. Let's get something to settle in our stomachs." The seaman was just about to order when a well-dressed couple entered the restaurant. The man was, without a doubt, Italian. His coal black hair and moustache were immaculately groomed and, though he was not nearly so tall as the present threesome, he was not short either.

But it was the woman on his arm that had young Keane's full attention as she sauntered past. The floral dress she wore clung excessively to every curve and dip in her figure. He wished he could disappear. He wanted nothing more than to turn to ash and flit away on the billowing winds. But there was no such luck. She passed, making a special effort to sway so close to Keane he could easily have been intoxicated on her perfume, had the liquor in his hands not already finished the task.

"Why, Brendan, isn't this a surprise. Are you and your little friends on a search for ladies." She turned to O'Malley and Harrison, raising her voice enough to call the attention of some unfortunate customers at the nearby tables. "You might as well leave this one behind, boys. He hasn't got the nerve to go out of the starting gate." Keane's face burned and his blue eyes turned to the grey of flint. The spark was struck and the flame raged.

"How dare you." He growled. "I'm as much a man as all the men in this room, and perhaps more so. You asked something immoral; something I dare not supply out of respect and—God help me—love for you. I see now what you are, Natasha Barra, and I am quite relieved I was able to scrape together the dignity you so obviously lack." Before the woman could find some feminine retort, Keane was pinned backwards over the table with the Italian soldier's hand strangling his collar while the other was pulled back in a solid fist. Down the mass of fingers came, slamming into his face with a heavy crack.

And then there was darkness.

CHAPTER ELEVEN

In January of 1920, three years before I was born, the government of the United States passed an amendment that prohibited the consumption, trade, or sale of alcoholic goods. If I lived to be a hundred, I would do so without ever having understood why a democracy would dare tempt fate. The 18th Amendment was passed.

And all hell broke loose.

In those thirteen years, the first decade of my life, legends were made. Unlike those great heroes like Lawrence of Arabia or the Red Baron, these were the shadows with automatic weapons slung over their shoulders and a fat cigar dripping from fowl mouths. As Keane led me down the alley and through a door pressed far into the wall, I recognised the establishment to be one of those created by the men in the pin-stripped suits. Time (and the 21st Amendment) had caused the place to be one of fresh *legal* liquor and calm jazz wafting about our heads as thick as the tobacco smoke. It reeked of colour, and yet was not completely unappealing to the eye. A woman, dressed in a costume I felt better tailored to fit Shirly Temple, took Keane's coat and hat before leading us to a small table near the stage. The place was no bigger than a large living room. Each table was within arm's distance from another without enough of one certain type of chair to fill the room. Instead there were three floral—and damnably eccentric—garden chairs, several wooden ones that folded at the seat, and even a handful of armchairs that had seen most anything from air raids to moth brigades. The tablecloths were patched together from fabrics not related by blood, nor nationality. Had someone welcomed me to Wonderland, rather than dropping to a fit of hysterics, I might have asked whether the Mad Hatter would be available for tea.

"Keane, you never told me we were going to a speakeasy." I hissed over the slurred roar of music. My companion chuckled as he began to light one of his infamous cigarettes.

"As they say, *noise is a language used all over the world*." I shook my head in mock shock.

"You wound me. I rather like this song, even if the drummer is half a beat off."

"You noticed that as well, eh? '*As practice makes perfect, I cannot but make progress*.'"

"Van Gogh, wasn't it?" Keane nodded, taking a long, calm draw of his cigarette. The quotation, while practical, also bore the bitter taste of irony as the poor drummer fell further and further away from the rest of the band. Within another few minutes, I feared the set's throbbing would rapidly slip from generally amusing to unbearable, and I most certainly did not want to spend the night in jail for pummeling him over the head with those blasted drumsticks. A glance at Keane; however, and I was not convinced it would be I who did the violent deed. His brow had furrowed deeply toward his Roman nose as he took a tentative sip of the strong liquor. I did the same and my throat was immediately in flames.

"Good God," I gasped, slamming the mismatched glass onto the table with enough violence a bit of the clear liquid leapt over the rim. "What is that stuff? Petrol?"

"I believe it was called 'bathtub gin.'" Keane muttered, staring down at the offending drink. "Though why they would serve the damn stuff is beyond me. Nostalgia perhaps?"

"Who would even want to drink it? And don't even think about giving me that *desperate times mean desperate measures* talk. I thought all this had gone out in the thirties." As if he found an answer, my companion took a gulp of the dreaded gin, held it in his mouth, and swallowed. The creases in his forehead immediately disappeared.

"Come now, Lawrence, it isn't so bad as all that. It just takes a bit of patience." My laugh entered into the world as a half-hearted wheeze, lungs still burning from the legendary alcohol.

"Just mind you don't get too comfortable with the stuff. You're driving."

"Indeed." Keane grumbled and shoved the glass further towards the centre of the table. In a matter of seconds, a fresh cigarette was between his fingers. I watched as he dragged his eyes lazily over the collections of individuals spread across the small room. There were perhaps two or three characters tossing back the gin like it was water and glancing over their shoulders constantly, but, for the majority, they were those intolerable young things on the endless search for frivolity without thought of cost.

I could have been—could *be*—one of them if I wished. I could go about without a worry in the world, but what sort of world would that be? Would I be living, or merely wallowing in the pit of existence? Would I be me, or merely some vague idea of myself? And what would Keane think? Not that I really gave a damn of his opinion, of course, but there was always some satisfaction in his approval, just as there was great pain in his disappointment.

WHEN THE MUSIC BECAME discombobulated enough that no amount of hard liquor could ease the pain throbbing through our ears, Keane found his coat and led me out into the remainder of the world. The rain had stopped, having its signature in the long puddles strewn about the streets. What had once been hot had cooled into the blissful chill of a passing spring, bringing too those recent memories of Ireland; the lush, green landscape, rolling hills, rigid stones, and a rose garden just outside a little cottage. I might have been born an American, but I was by no means an ethnocentric.

Keane and I reached the taxi with a half hour left to return it to his friend. I clambered into the passenger seat while he settled himself behind the wheel, his tall frame accommodated by the vehicle's bulky size. Nothing was said as he drove along the busy streets, and it was not until we were climbing into his rented car that I recalled my brief excursion to the book shop.

"Here." I thrust the paper-wrapped parcel to his chest and waited with baited breath as the twine gradually gave way with his gentle tuggs. An eyebrow immediately climbed high on his forehead.

"Poetry?" I grinned.

"Come now, Keane, don't look so dubious. It's not as though you have a hatred for the art of the verse. I dog-eared the page I thought you might enjoy."

"Dog eared!" He roared in mock fury. "I would have thought, of all the literary people in the world, you would show more respect for an author's work." I watched impatiently as his sharp, blue eyes flickered over the page. As if suddenly possessed, a dark anger erupted shamelessly over his features before falling away as deep barks of laughter shot to the surface.

What stubborn things a man can be;
A dog, a mule, an ass need be.
What priggish things on rainy days,
When sun shan't show it's ragged rays.
And seamen be the worse of these,
For they no not a woman still
Who's made not of wood
And flesh, not sail.
What ill-gotten goats those men so be
When days arise without the sea.
But none are quite so hellish
As the bright ones with a mind
And though they bluster
And temper still
They're a hell of a find.
So patience still, oh lass and lady
And throw them not to sea
For without men we'd have no problems
And oh what a world it would be.
And oh what a world it would be.

"WHERE THE HELL IS SHE!" James Harrison shouted, waving his script viciously through the air like a sabre while pressing his other hand into his stomach. Keane stared down at the raving director from the stage.

"Belay that, James. No doubt she will be here momentarily."

"No doubt? Brendan, we've been waiting thirty minutes! What does that woman think she is? A princess?" From what I had seen of Miss Daniel Smith, Harrison wasn't far from the truth. The older woman standing near Keane—a Mrs. Bernice Klein—edged forward.

"Calm down, James. Remember your ulcer." I expected Harrison to roar something entirely masculine, damning his ulcer or some other such nonsense, when the doors at the theatre entrance screamed open before slamming with a heavy thud. The director whirled around.

"And where the hell were you?" Miss Smith sashayed forward, tilting her head slightly.

"What do you mean?"

"Rehearsal began at seven sharp. It is now—" Harrison glanced at his wristwatch. "—seven thirty-one." The young woman's face puckered as she planted her hands on her hips.

"*Well*, if you're gonna treat me that way, I might as well leave."

"Daniel, dear, don't be ridiculous. Of course we want you here." Mrs. Klein cooed from her perch on the stage's edge. (Come to think of it, with those spectacles on, she really did look rather like an old owl.) Miss Smith smirked and sauntered down the aisle.

"That's better. Now, what part are we doing?" Harrison, who had at least gained some composure in this time, stood stiffly in front of Keane.

"Act two." The young woman's face immediately returned to its unappealing scowl.

"But I don't like act two. It's boring, and that old man can't act." When it at last registered that the 'old man' was Keane, I was infuriated. Surely he had ten times the talent of this poor excuse of a woman. Again Mrs. Klein took up her halo and smiled.

"Don't worry, dear, we'll get it done quick and you can leave."

'Quick' was not the word for it. Excruciatingly long, yes. Each line that passed through Daniel Smith's lips was so dreadfully wrong for the part of Eliza Doolittle. Where there ought to have been inflections, there was none. Nor was there any emotion aside from a boredom completely uncharacteristic to the young flower girl. Harrison was constantly having to stop the rehearsal, debate some inconsequential nonsense with the delusional actress, before sending the three back to their places, each time Miss Smith looking paler than before. When at last Mrs. Klein—who had stepped in as Colonel Pickering, as the other gentleman actor was unable to attend that morning—at last said her starting line for the millionth time, I was teetering on the brink of insanity, and Keane looked no better as they reached what was what I thought to be the true epitome of Henry Higgins. His already deep and rich baritone dropped to the most thrillingly beautiful low tones that wavered just above a whisper and yet still carried the power and dignity of an entire civilised nation.

"By George, Eliza, the streets will be strewn with the bodies of men shooting themselves for your sake before I've done with you."

"What the hell do you think you're doing?" The young woman shrieked, swinging her arm back with her fist levelled directly at Keane's head while the other hand allowed her pristine script to tumble to the wooden boards. "You old fool, you messed up the line again!" My companion pulled his shoulders back as his eyes froze grey.

"I assure you I followed Shaw word for word." Miss Smith's pale features whitened still as her body began to shake.

"You did NOT! You made a mistake! You—you—" Keane appeared fortified against any slanderous insult, his chin raised high as no doubt he had done in the navy when entering into the thick of a storm. The sharp crease of his lapels shone gold with vallour and no salt of earth's stale minds dared embed itself into his polished shoes.

He was a man.

He was a sailor.

He was a captain.

Keane was not; however, prepared for the woman to collapse into his arms.

PART TWO

Life is but an inspired series of events,

That just happen to end and one's own inconvenience.

-Brendan Keane

CHAPTER TWELVE

KEANE WAS KNEELING by her in seconds, his fingers gingerly lifting her eyelids before pressing deeply into the middle of her wrists. Her pale face had faded to near transparency, and even beneath the smears of villainous lipstick, splotches of icy blue appeared. Keane turned to Harrison, who was clutching his abdominon.

"For God's sake, James. Get an ambulance out here." As the man staggered off toward the miniscule office behind the stage, my companion rapidly clasped his hands, one over the other, and began pushing into the woman's chest hard and fast.

(*One. Two. Three. Four. Five. Six...*)

Keane threw his lean body forward with every count.

(*...Thirteen. Fourteen. Fifteen. Sixteen...*)

The woman's neck jerked forward, but still there was no sign of impending life.

(*...Twenty-six. Twenty-seven. Twenty-eight...*)

I moved myself nearer to the woman's head. Good God, did I really have to do this.

(*...THIRTY.*)

My fingers pinched deftly over her cold, horrid nose and, eyes clenched shut, I began to lean forward and commit myself to the creation of artificial respiratory functions to bring life back into this poor excuse of a human. A slight gurgling taunted my ears just as my face dove rapidly downwards.

"Lawrence!" I never knew if it was the sharp exclamation of words or the sudden hand on my arm that snatched me back from the woman's limp figure. In either case, I quickly found myself sprawled out on my back with my head laying against the stage and Keane bending over me with his handkerchief pressed to my mouth. Rarely demonstrative man that he was, the tips of my ears burned.

"Damn it, Keane, what—"

"—Did you get any on you? Lawrence, for God's sake, open your mouth." I did so, if only to protest, and found his hands splitting open my jaw and twisting my head painfully toward the glaring theatre lights. I made some vain, guttural noise as a glob of saliva settled in my throat. Before I could gag or—heaven forbid—begin revealing the remains of a scarce breakfast, Keane let go of my face and allowed me to clamber to my feet. Damn the man. What was he trying to do? Show the whole of society the state of my teeth? Admittedly they were quite good, but that was no viable excuse for such an action. Keane rested his hands on my shoulders, not so much out of some unnecessary form of comfort, but as a barrier between myself and whatever lay behind him. I stepped forward. His grip strengthened.

"Keane, if you don't let me go, I'll—" My voice caught as my fists clenched at my sides, but my companion's vice did not lessen.

"I have no doubt that you are a capable and, God save us, an independent woman, but I really must insist you go into the hall."

"Because of my femininity?" Keane said nothing. "That's it, isn't it? Well, I don't need your chivalry. I will be fine. Now, step aside." I expected many things. I was prepared for many things. In my own lifetime, I had witnessed events that had thrown grown men into madness and several sound minds over a bridge's rail. But I was nothing if not curious when my companion stared down upon me, released a long, low sigh, and let go.

The weight of his eyes was still heavy upon me as I edged around his shoulder and toward the corpse motionless against the shimmering floor. She was indeed dead and just as attractive and unpleasant as I had known her to be in life. Her almost anaemic body jaunted upward along the cracks of the stage, the bones in her ring-infected fingers clawed a path to Hell.

To think such things were, at best, sinful, but sin is rather like the whole of life; everything is relative. I did not think myself damned for believing such ideas, nor did I regret the venom with which they stewed in my mind as I peered down at the final form of the woman. Her pale skin was drenched in sweat, her eyes not but glass, and her fingertips blue against the pale white. I saw too why Keane had pulled me back. I saw and was glad of his swift actions.

A thick, almost yellow pillow of foam had risen out of her still mouth and trickled down one side in curdled globs. Had someone spilled spoiled milk over her, the result would have been identical. In fact, it might have been somewhat of an improvement. I stared at the corpse for as long as I dared before swiftly retreating into Harrison's office; far away from death. Far from the buzz of those left to live. Far from my own sins and failings. Yes, sin may be relative, but one's belief can make sin into the scale between eternal life and eternal damnation.

And I knew not which path I walked.

I WAS NOT SHAKEN IN the slightest by death. Death becomes rather like an old friend after you live through a war. I had seen worse—far worse—on our first trip to Ireland a little less than a year before. A fizzion of dark energy shot up my spine at the mere thought of it. A child had been mutilated, carved so deeply one could see the dark organs climbing out from the pale abdominon. His arms and legs ended abruptly where his hands and feet ought to have been. But they were not there, and neither Keane, nor I, ever discovered them. My body jerked again, forcing my throat to clench. No, I was most certainly *not* disturbed by the woman's death. She was gone.

So be it.

The fist came as efficient as a battering ram, but I denied it enty, though, under what right, I remained unsure.

"Lawrence, are you indisposed?" His voice was low—hesitating ever so slightly with each vowel—but there was a hopefulness too, as though he said something for the sake of conversation itself, rather than a true answer. I folded my arms together, while keeping my back toward the door.

"Of course not."

"May I enter?"

"No. Go away."

"Lawrence." There it was, that seaman's growl hanging heavily over the thrashing waves. It was sharp enough to cut through wood unaided, and yet it caused no more harm to my flesh than a blade of grass beneath my shoes. "Lawrence, open the door."

"Why? I believe I have answered all your questions sufficiently. I am not ill, nor am I depressed. Nor, I think, am I in the need of a psychiatrist. There. Go away." Keane did not, in fact, 'go away'. His shoulder proved quite capable as the gasp of hinges heralded his arrival. I leapt up from the corner of the large oak desk and faced him square-shouldered without fear of reproach.

"It wasn't locked, but I suppose you're just too well-educated to consider such matters." I snapped as Keane gingerly fingered the abused door behind him. My words either did not affect him, or missed the man entirely. With quick, deliberate steps, he had swept up my leather jacket from a nearby chair and shoved it into my arms.

"Put that on; we're going back to the house." I wish he had said home. If he had I would at least hope that he meant England, or Ireland, or some such land that was far from the heat of sunny California. "*Now*, Lawrence."

Later, as I considered the events of that moment, I wasn't entirely certain what prompted me to do it. I am still not quite sure. But oh how satisfying it was to see Keane's face when I hurled the leather bomber right back at him. It was a pitch worthy of any respectable baseball team out of New York, but they were on the other side of the country, while I was here with a red-faced Keane towering over me. By some show of physical strength and verbal eccentricities, he got me into my jacket and herded, prodded, shoved, and pulled me out onto the pavement and into the car.

It is a miracle we survived that ride, for nothing short of an angel's touch kept Keane from veering off of the road as he forced the machine along at speeds no automobile ought ever go. Unlike the country roads of Ireland, these were straight and well paved; therefore, I was not afraid of the path itself, nor the motorcar's capabilities, nor most anything else. I was not afraid.

But I did not like that look in Keane's eyes.

I did not like those flecks of grey pulsating through the blue of his irises, nor the ruddy colour invading his square-jawed cheekbones. The hands gripping the steering wheel had been crudely carved from blocks of wood, tapering into fingers when necessary, but only so much as the general shape with a slight bleaching where the knuckles ought to have been. His posture was painfully stiff as his right leg pressed violently against the accelerator. Only once did his foot flinch toward the brake, and even then I was thrown into his shoulder by the centrifugal force. The other turns were equally heart-stopping. Those scarce few that were not were hardly bends at all. Rather, they were merely interruptions to my companion's unshakable purpose. I could only hope he had not planned to end our lives by sending the automobile over a cliff's rigid edge.

At last Keane came to an abrupt halt in front of the beach house, nearly tore off the car door as he got out, and stormed over to my side. The vice-like grip on my arm was not at all worse than his bite. More so it was that uncomfortable reminder of his temperamental masculinity as he pulled me into the house, allowing the door to shut with a resounding crack. Keane thrust me toward the nearest seat of the sitting room before plucking the cigarette case from his pocket and smoking each one violently; thrusting their final stubs of life into a rather audaciously bright ashtray. As he picked at the gaudy green and blue fabric of the chair, I noticed a second pack of cigarettes peeking tentatively from Keane's breast pocket. I glanced at my wristwatch. Seven thirty-five.

God, it was going to be a long night.

My companion suddenly shoved himself up from the chair to lean against the mantle of a large, and most certainly obnoxious, fireplace. The redness had drained from his features, only to be replaced by long shadows hanging from him like cloaks. One, long hand scrubbed tiredly at his face as his voice came only a fraction louder than an ocean's midnight hum.

"Out with it, Lawrence?"

"Out with what?" A slight flash of grey splashed over his eyes.

"You know very well 'what'. You wish to say something, now say it and let us move on with our lives."

"Really, Keane, I don't—"

"Damn it, Lawrence. We're in private. There are no other eyes to prod at our minds; no outsiders to judge our thoughts." No, there was no one. We had no witness. We had no third party. We had no fence; no net; no safety. There was only Keane and myself, and that was more than enough to convince me to say nothing. Another cigarette passed through this life. Then another. Keane was soon reaching for the second package and began to tug one of the little, white cylinders from its snug rest. I had rarely seen him falter from most anything the world placed before him, and certainly he had never held any trepidation about a hearty smoke. And yet, the match paused—if briefly—before meeting the paper end and burning the first wisps of dried tobacco. The faint orange circles branded themselves into the cigarette, accentuated with each slow draw. Keane's attention had turned slowly to the ashtray's yellowing rim. I inhaled deeply, allowing the tobacco and brisk smells of the ocean to fill my lungs. When I released them, I too allowed the question—that horrid breach of conscious thought—to slip carelessly from my mouth.

"Will I go to Hell?" Keane's long, thin fingers toppled from the smooth edge of the ashtray, spilling a small pile of dark powder atop the white mantle. His eyes sought mine in an instant.

"I beg your pardon?"

"I know it sounds dreadfully childish, and you needn't answer if you feel it below the line intellectuals must draw, but . . . " My voice fell away as if I expected his answer to come at that very moment; to have a pool of infinite wisdom pourn at my feet from which a conclusion may be properly drawn. However; he was silent. So horribly silent. As the tobacco smoke drew on, I began to fear he thought less of me for asking such a thing. It was infantile, I admit, but it had fallen to the floor with a harrolding of destruction and could therefore not be repaired. Fear was not an emotion I made use of often, yet I felt it deeply as my fingers knotted themselves further into the chair's faded and fraying fabric. A heavy cloud entered the air.

"Lawrence, you do realise I am not privy to such information." I nodded and opened my mouth in some pitiful defence, but Keane raised his hand. "I am not God. I am not something above human weaknesses and morality. There are times when I am not even certain I am a good man. In fact, I know I am not. But I will tell you that, in the years I have known you, I cannot think of anything that would doom you to such a fate." Again I nodded, but this time, rather than preparing some string of ill chosen words, I remained dutifully silent as my companion reached for the box of matches. The brisk scent of sulphur sighed as it took light. "May I ask what prompted you to ask such a question?"

"Am I not allowed to make certain philosophical statements from time to time?" Keane chuckled lightly, causing the flame to dance in rhythm to his deep, rich baritone.

"Statements? Lawrence, that was hardly a statement."

"True, but it brought up an important discussion."

"About death?"

"Yes, death. Do you not consider that important?" Again the match danced, the yellow flame scarcely above Keane's fingertips.

"At my age, death is a topic discussed easily and with about the same amount of enthusiasm as an ulcer."

"But you are only—"

"Fifty-five? Yes. And you are twenty-four. I ought to be testing your mental state for considering such dark and dreary paths, but, as your youth has been infested by a global disturbance, I shall say nothing more unless you give me a reason to do so. Now, I am awaiting your excuses, Lawrence, and if you say you have none, I shall be testing you for dementia, as well as depression." I sighed, which slowly slipped into a nervous laugh that was quickly matched by Keane. The jovolity lasted only an instant, but even the briefest of moments is enough to give necessary strength. My companion edged away from the mantle and disappeared into the kitchen. When he returned, he was escorted by two mismatched glasses and a bottle of something too good for American whiskey and not quite so adored as his beloved Madeira. He poured a generous amount of the pale liquid between the two cups and, having handed the first to me, returned to his place at the mantle. I stared dubiously at the liquor in my hands.

"I do hope this is not the same stuff we drank yesterday." I joked, swirling the pale substance until a perfect representation of a hurricane was visible in the glass. They say that there is nowhere so calm as the eye of the hurricane. And yet, to enter into that world of tranquillity, one must endure a hell lethal to human life. I stood there now, teetering on the edge between storm and bliss as Keane took a long, slow sip of the wine.

"Lawrence, do you recall the name Dionysus?"

"You mean the Greek god of theatre, ritual madness, wine, and—" My face burned a vivid red, but Keane, ever the gentleman, remained unshaken.

"Fertility? Yes. It was believed he was raised in a cave and fed on honey. In many depictions he can be seen holding ivy-wrapped wands from which bountiful streams of the gold nectar flows." Keane raised his glass, allowing the pale wine to sparkle in the last lights of evening. "Behold the sweat of his prosperity: mead. The nectar of the gods and the love of all things sacred among men." I tentatively sipped the sweet liquor, allowing the gentle fragrance to mingle politely with the tobacco still lingering in the air. It was a light wine, delicate to the extent one might hardly believe the masculinity of the thing. I suppose there is, in some men, that poetic nature I so often saw in Keane, but there too was his voracious temper quelled only by the knowledge and wisdom time often provides. There was also, to my eternal consternation, that gift for reading people as effortlessly as books, and not being satisfied until the end has been completed and analysed.

"Lawrence, you still have not answered my question." I tipped the glass away from my mouth with only a small pool of wine left within its crystal walls.

"How did that woman—Miss Smith—die? I know you haven't an autopsy report, but, by your own judgement, what do *you* think the cause was?" Keane chuckled; harsh, dry, and—what was that? Regret? Guilt? Or a past to which I knew little?

"That phrase alone suggests you have already plotted some of your own theories."

"I had thought it was drug use gone awry, but . . . " My words fluttered away with a defeated shrug just as Keane relinquished his perch at the mantle and settled his tall frame in a rather depressed armchair. His cigarettes were again at hand, but, as the first began to burn, he did not smoke it. Rather, he gazed despondent at the dreary tail of smoke that gracefully curled and danced through the air. With one great, heaving sigh, the waltz became a ballet then dissipated completely into something held tightly in memories.

"I saw it first in the war." Keane muttered deeply. "I fear it is something inescapable no matter what time has passed. I have seen fathers, mothers, even children affected by its horrid hands, and yet—" He took a stiff draw from the cigarette dangling between his fingers. "You are quite right, Lawrence. Could you name what drug might have caused a reaction? It was opium, or some derivative thereof. Did you note the slight jaundice in her eyes?" Of course I hadn't. He had pulled me away. "That, along with the profuse sweating and foaming of the mouth, create the clear signs of an overdose. A thoroughly damning sight, but not, I thought, one that would affect you so."

"It wasn't that."

"Oh?" Keane's eyebrows arched high on his head, as if he had suddenly recalled I am not so feminine as to shirk from sights ignored and overlooked by society. "Would your reaction then have something to do with that little theological conference we just had?" Damn the man, it did. He knew it did. But how smuggly he looked as he awaited my confirmation that it was so. I would not give him that. My self dignity would not withstand such a blow. Instead, I turned to him with an Englishman's stiff upper lip and hurled my words at him with a strength entirely deceptive to my own self.

"Do you think Miss Smith went to Hell? I do. God help me, I do. I know I shouldn't think such things—that it's disrespectful and a mortal sin—but I honestly believe I'm right. I *want* to be right. I want her to burn for the things she said. I'm just so sick and tired of not caring what society thinks that I want to be accepted, leather jacket and all. It is acceptable for soldiers to return without arms or legs or even a living soul, but here I am, shaped and affected by war and still invisible to the world's good graces. I am tired of being thought of as a harlot. Lord knows I've never thought about being such a thing. But they don't see that. They only see a woman with a man slightly older than herself and—God, Keane, what is wrong with me?" He was silent, which was just as well as I could not face him. How could I have thought to tell Keane such things? He was a Victorian born Catholic. He had been raised amidst the starched collars and enforced folkways. He had been brought up in the Irish traditions of strength and dignity.

Dignity. Always dignity.

I was dead. I could feel his sharp, blue eyes drilling into the side of my face. After an eternity, the thin smoke disappeared completely, leaving only silence to strangle my lungs. A part of me wished to be struck by lightning, drop of a heart attack, be swallowed by a sinkhole, *anything* other than facing Keane. He cleared his throat.

"You think this?"

"Yes."

"And did you wish the same fate upon Michael?" The gun fired. A bullet slammed into my side and dislodged a desperate rush of words.

"No. I could never think of such a thing. Or at least I didn't after a while."

"But you did consider it." I sighed, my shoulders heaving forward as a shield over my head.

"Not when he died. I was always sorry about that. But, when he held that revolver on you while you offered to write—and commit—suicide, I—"

"—you were more angry at me than you were at him." The gun fired again, this time lodging the bullet between my eyes.

He was right.

Damn the man, he was right.

Perhaps he didn't even know how right. I hated him at that moment. I had hated him with everything in me as he asked for the pen. How could he—a man far better than any in the world—be ready to die when he had so much to live for?

"Lawrence, I—" I cut him off with a swift string of words.

"I know it was—*is*—a horrible thing to think, and I shall endeavour not to do so any longer. If that isn't enough, if you wish that I would leave, I can always go back to England for a time, or however long you need. Perhaps I could go to Italy. I have always wanted to go there, and you yourself have suggested it now and again. If that's what you want, I can leave tomorrow morning."

"Why would you do a blasted thing like that? Jo, I don't consider those thoughts to be unusual, or even entirely immoral. You are having a natural reaction to traumatic circumstances. I am not at odds with your words, only that they did not appear sooner. Those 'sinful' thoughts of yours are to be expected—and, dare I say, commended—as a show of your own strength and morality." I could not believe what I was hearing. It was an explanation so reasonable compared to mine, so damnably reasonable. I lifted my head toward the other side of the room to see Keane's face, a mirror to all the confusion swirling around in my brain. Though, in his case, the chaos had been quelled through the accumulation of wisdom bestowed upon him by the bettering of years. He had lived through two wars, and I only one. He had served in the heat of battle, while I had passed the last years wallowing in his company. He had been my rock—my cornerstone—for so long I could not imagine my life differently. Everything had been set in its rightful place. Who was I to change that now?

With an elongated huff, Keane ended the final puffs of his cigarette, smearing the darkened ash into the tray. He rose from his chair, stretched, and took a few methodical steps along the carpeted floor. And then, as by a magician's sleight of hand, Keane's dry chuckle floated as easily as his tobacco smoke.

"My dear Lawrence, morality—or, at least, the definition of the word—stretches so far as to distinguish the extent to which an action is right or wrong. Right actions—*honourable* actions—dictate one's character, while the actions of those such as Miss Smith and Michael give only one purpose to life. You come to live for the evils of mortal natures. It swallows you whole without thought or glance to your true nature. If I am thankful for anything in my old age, by God, it is that the world has not ceased creating those great shows of youth, finished with wisdom beyond their years." He picked up his cigarette case and slipped it effortlessly into his pocket with a nostalgic twist playing at the edge of his thin lips. "*That*, Jo, is the greatest purpose any man can have in life, and, as long as there is another person with such love and kindness toward humanity, I may live fully and be glad of it."

CHAPTER THIRTEEN
Summer 1916—Palermo, Italy

HE'D RATHER HAVE BEEN drunk.

He could survive being drunk. He understood the pain of excessive alcohol lingering in his veins. He had experienced hangovers more pleasant than the constant churning in his stomach as he struggled out of the creaky old bed. His long legs remained oblivious he was on land, rather than the pitching and tossing deck of a ship. After a long, painful, but successful mission, the young Brendan Keane leaned over the cracked mirror looming above a battered washbasin.

By Jezus, he looked a fright.

The rust colored scruff on his face had thickened into an unruly mass of hair. It wasn't too long, but it wasn't holding the same dignified effect the young man had hoped for. There was no doubt he would have it shaved off that very day. That very moment, if he had mind to do so. He ran a hand through his blonde hair, noting it too was in desperate need of a trim before he looked like Jesus himself staggering up to Calvary. By George, he already did. Wincing with the effort, he fingered the darkened skin encircling his left eye. The spreading purple infested with yellow blotches was an unfortunate comparison to his natural pallor.

Immediately the events of the evening before roared into his memory with the force of a thousand tanks, tearing down the better, more beautiful trees with its filth. Fury, hot and deep, burned his soul as surely as the devil's own trident. He rifled desperately through the decrepit wooden stand for a package of cigarettes he had stashed there upon his arrival in Palermo, but there was nothing but empty packaging. Nothing. God, it would be better if he had been drunk and hung over. It was more acceptable to be drunk than bruised. He wished he was drunk. He wanted to be drunk. There was more dignity to it in a country drowning in wine.

'Dignity. Always dignity.'

Yes, that's what his late father always said. Old John Keane, dead at the age of forty and leaving a young boy a man. That had always been a point of bitterness best left overgrown and unattended. Thomas was the eldest. It was his responsibility to care for their mother, himself, and—

Brendan shuffled further through the drawer, shoving aside shirts and socks until at last he found them lying carefully against darkened wood. The little folded papers bound together by an old necktie which had shrivelled into little more than a collection of poorly intertwined threads. It was difficult—near impossible—to find a serviceman without such a collection, hard to find a man who didn't have someone waiting behind the curtains of home. Someone dreading the telegram. Yes, there was always someone. Some had a mother, but she was dead too. Many had their pretty darling, but he'd been in most every capital in the world and still hadn't found her. No, he had a sister;

a dear, sweet, innocent girl wronged by anyone who dared not understand her enough to love her. She had been born when he was seven, and by God he was going to protect her no matter what happened in the world. He was all she had. Heaven knows Thomas and their mother hadn't given her the light of day. And their father had died when she was still just a wee infant tossing in her wooden cradle. Their father, a man sitting by the fire with a pipe clenched between his teeth and a ring of bluish haze encircling his head. A man who had little enough time for him, unless it was overrun by a string of holy beads. Conversations of life—a child's life—was undignified, and that was not to be endured.

Dignity. Always dignity.

God, Brendan thought, he needed a smoke.

It took some effort, but he managed to dress efficiently despite the constant thumping between his ears. As he reached for his necktie; however, his stomach gave a nauseating lurch and he quickly abandoned it on the bed before tentatively tugging the suspenders over his shoulders. His shoes were a bit more of a struggle, but he was soon ready to enter into the world with as much enthusiasm as a man near death might.

The late morning sun graced the clear sky as a dancer would a stage. Everything had its place. The gondoliers whistled their gentle tunes while embarking on the constant voyages up and down the river. There were fewer of them than Brendan recalled from his first visit to Palermo, and some cynical part of him could not resist wondering how many of those boat men now laid face down on enemy soil. No doubt the numbers were excruciatingly high, but such was war.

War.

How he despised that word.

What did war mean but millions of young men slogging through shallow trenches with the knowledge they may not live to see the light of day again. War was nothing. Nothing save a fulfilment of humanity's need for violent killing until the other side surrendered to their wishes. It made him sick, and yet, if it was his hand upon the trigger, would he hesitate? Would he dare? Or would he become the dignified epitome of a war hero?

Dignity. Always dignity.

Stiff and tired though they were, his legs carried him dutifully to the tobacconist's on the corner, then on toward Romanici's. It was a small establishment that overshadowed the churning river with such grace and life as man ought to know a thousand times over. Like the villas stationed on either side, it was brightly painted with vibrant decor scattering the exterior.

It was also the only restaurant Brendan knew that was run by a gentleman under fourteen stone and without a moustache spotting his upper lip. A pair of wiry spectacles had settled on his long, defined nose and made his eyes twice as large as anatomically possible, engulfing half his face in chocolate pools darting back and forth across the various tablecloths. At the instant the scrawny man caught sight of Keane, the seaman knew he was doomed and quickly found himself in the small man's vice-like embrace.

"Eh, buongiorno amico mio."

"Buongiorno, Gaetano. Come va?"

"Sto bene. You're improving, my friend. Good. It is always good to go somewhere, rather than nowhere." Keane chuckled.

"Wise words from a wise man." Gaetano held the taller man out at arms length.

"Me? Wise? No, amico. I'm only a small, skinny man."

"With a large heart and a fine taste for wine and food. Speaking of which . . . " Keane nodded toward one of the wooden tables pushed furthest into the corner of the well-lit room. The owner smiled.

"Oh, sì. You wan'a eat somf'ing good to eat. I'll tell Angela. She'll make you a somf'ing that'a fill you up in no time. And wine too?"

"Isn't it a bit early?" Gaetano slapped Brendan on the back. Considering his rather unconventional size, it startled the seaman by just how strong the man's arm really was.

"It's never too early for some good wine among old friends, eh? Now you wait here while I go have mia moglie make a little somf'ing for you."

'A little something' indeed, Brendan thought as an enormous plate of sauce-laden pasta was soon set before him. Mozzarella cheese had been heavily grated utop the steaming mass; creating both a masterpiece and a feast.

"Eat, my friend." Gaetano urged him as he placed a large glass of wine on the table. "It's no good if it's cold."

"It's only one in the afternoon."

"Good. Lots of time for it to digest as you tell me about your life. Young man like you should have plenty of stories to tell old Gaetano. How you got that black eye is a nice beginning. Now, eat up. It's no good if it's cold."

"EH, SO IT'S WOMAN TROUBLES that's got you in so sad. Have more wine. Wine to a man is like prayer to the soul." Brendan Keane accepted the red liquor with a steady hand.

What was it? His third? His fourth? Funny, he just didn't seem to care anymore. It was as though all the troubles of the world no longer were large enough to bother him. Gaetano poured another glass for himself and leaned back comfortably in the wooden chair.

"Yes, you've got woman troubles, my friend. But don't let that hurt your spirit." The Italian swung his arm wildly back toward the half a dozen couples peppering the restaurant. "There are'a thousand girls out there. Thousands. And they'd all like you. They like Englishmen. 'Ow you talk'a gives them da goose pimples. Make 'em all go crazy." The young seaman shot up in his chair.

"Why the devil would I want all of them?"

"I know, I know. You want Natasha."

"And why wouldn't I? She's intelligent and—"

"—and you love her." Keane slammed back into the seat, the wooden hind legs teetering dangerously. His voice; however, was steady and lethal as a poised gun.

"I never said that. By God, Gaetano, I never said that." The little man laughed, encouraging the red wine in his glace to dance and swirl gently. There was a little more laxity to his chortle, just as an obvious flush had settled over his nose and an extra twinkle was added in his eyes.

"You didn't need to. You, me amico, are like me: are a man of amore. You love the woman's mind and heart like a drunkard loves the vino. You will find your amore someday, but not today. Tomorrow you might. Tomorrow you might fall for a girl so hard your head spins in circles. But that is not today. So drink up, and toast the woman you will love like the drunkard does the vino." Brendan chuckled and moved his glass toward his host.

"God, I will miss this, Gaetano. All of it. The warmth, the language, the wine. All of it." A splash of liquor missed the glass.

"You 'a leaving me so soon? When your ship leave? A few weeks? A month and you leave me? Tell old Gaetano when."

"Friday."

"Three days?" The Italian sighed, almost offended by the mere thought of leavins such a glorious land. Does one dare think of leaving Heaven? Of leaving Paradise? But he did not know time as Brendan did. He did not question death, for he believed it far away. Gaetano was a man of moments, and if those millions of moments somehow created a passing of years, so be it. He would not die, he thought. He would not leave his beloved country. He would live life as it ought to be lived, and that was enough for him. It ought to have been more than enough for any man. This was his land of moments, a world of colour and joy up until the day the moments—those valuable acceptances of a life lived to the fullest—stopped.

With great gusto, Gaetano Romanici raised the glass above his head, allowing the red wine to sparkle in the midday sun. "Three days is not long enough to live a lifetime, but I am an Italian, and a lover. Then let us drink. Let us drink and drink and drink until we are drunk in love of Palermo."

CHAPTER FOURTEEN

"CANCEL!" KEANE BELLOWED from his perch on the edge of the stage. "Why the devil would you want to do that?" Harrison hardly flinched from my companion's steel glare. Brave man.

Or an incredible fool.

"I don't *want* to do it but I don't have any other options. A girl has *died*, Brendan. Doesn't that make a difference?"

"Of course it does. I'm not debating that. But shouldn't that give us all the more reason to keep the show alive?"

"I agree with the professor." Mrs. Klein stated evenly. "I think we all knew what . . . troubles . . . Daniel had, poor girl, but that's no reason for us not to continue on as planned. Besides, James, think of all the money you have invested into this project."

"Money?" I leaned forward in my chair. "Just how much money are we discussing here? Three hundred? Four?" Mr. Harrison shifted between his feet, a hand pressed securely against the side of his stomach. The amount was more of a shock than the director's previous announcement to obliterate the show itself.

"*FIVE THOUSAND!*" I feared Keane might teeter off the edge of the stage. He was himself a well-established man and, though I never knew the exact extent of his financial standing, I suspected he could live a hundred years in the finest luxury without so much as a glance toward his account books.

But *five thousand dollars*?

A cold chill shot up my spine.

"James," Mrs. Klein said gently. "Couldn't you find another girl, someone else who could play Eliza." I quickly saw the conversation's dangerous direction, careening wildly toward the nearest cliff over which it might hurl its desperate want of steadfast loyalty. I glared back at the several sets of eyes, especially the pair glittering blue with amusement. A few quick strides sent me retreating toward the carpeted aisle.

"No. Absolutely not."

"But think of it, Lawrence—"

"—No, Keane, I won't. It would be a disaster. Find someone else; someone with more experience in the theatre. I simply will *not* have five thousand dollars balancing on my theatrical ability, or lack thereof." Keane huffed and, violently tugging on his left ear.

"Someone of your age should be more confident."

"Confident? Keane, confidence has nothing to do with it. And, for heaven's sake, don't look at me like that. I am *not* one of your blasted patients."

"No, you are not. I would never ask them to fulfil so dentranmental a task. Now, will you do it?" I could distinctly feel his thin, trained hands tugging the rug out from under me.

"If I don't?"

"Then we can both return to England without anything more adventurous than having seen the effects of an opiate overdose—something we have both seen before—and live out bogusly important lives in a world that is itself bogusly important. There is no summer finer than having spent it surrounded by musty old books and imbeciles haunting you at every bend. The Autumn chill shouldn't be quite so horrid as last year, and I'm certain your publisher would be able to reschedule your appointments in, oh, three months or so." The frayed threads of an impish grin played at the end of his thin lips and his eyes were entirely bereft of all smatterings of grey. They were as blue and bright as an endless ocean glittering beneath the evening sun.

A sun that burns for light.

"Fine. You've convinced me. When do we start?"

"Right now. This very moment." Keane laughed, rubbing his hands together with energy enough to conjure a storm worthy of God himself. "What say you, James?" The director looked upon me appraisingly.

"I think she'll do alright. Does she have a quick ear for these things?"

"The finest." My companion assured him with far more conviction than demonstrated in the cold sweat approaching the nape of my neck as Harrison considered the proposition. At last, my fate was sealed with a solid nod.

"Good. Alright then, we'll start from the beginning." A wave of his hand brought an immediate surge of cast members taking their place on stage. There a world was created and recreated as we drilled the first act repeatedly until my mind swam in a hollow murk. Syllables became severed letters. Seconds became painful accentuations of a needle. And every breath stung with an acute urgency one had best ignore, else they become enraptured with the ill-gotten glory.

I was not a complete novice to the theatre by any means. I knew how to stand that my face was open to the audience's ridicule. My voice reverberated crisply through the hollow emptiness of the establishment; bounding from one wall to another and capturing the ears of all who might bear witness to listen. It was not quite so nice as Keane's clipped English, for his not only echoed, but danced in tones I had heard a thousand times.

And yet it never ceased to amaze me.

William White—a balding gentleman who never ventured so much as a punctuation from the script—was far from how I had imagined Shaw's Colonel Pickering. Rather than the character's polite light-heartedness, the man reeked of aristocratic boredom. There was none of that considerate charm to counteract Higgins' bullish lines. He lacked any gentlemanly goodness that ought to have erupted from a monument of kind mannerisms. Rather than being drawn to the noble character, I was suddenly repulsed by a snide, bald, old man.

The young man chosen as Freddy Einsford-Hill—a Walter something or other—was, I thought, well suited for his role. Not out of some incredible talent for acting, but rather a general stupidity that flowed from his pores as thick and dense as mercury. I would not deny him his looks (a girl constantly dripping from his arm cemented that), but, were Behan a topic of conversation, I would not be the slightest bit shocked if he claimed the man to be his tailor. It was only by nothing less than divine intervention that I survived the first few hours, and if I were to carry myself into the evening without my sleeves tied together by leather belts, I knew I very well might require an appearance from God himself.

When at last Harrison announced the lunch hour, I was aware of Keane cajoling me toward the door with Walter following close behind. God, how irksome his voice was; piercing the air in an octave typical of a young girl and with all the tact of a three year old boy. My companion steered me along the blistering sidewalks with a heavy hand to my shoulder. His long legs effortlessly swallowed the strips of pavement, the soles of his polished black shoes chewing the pebbles crumbling from the cracks. Walter must have ventured down another street, for I immediately felt Keane's maddening pace slow enough for him to thread my arm through his. He bowed his head low to mine that I could feel the warmth of his breath even through the unforgivably torrid day.

"*'Against stupidity the very gods themselves contend in vain.'*"

"Friedrich Schiller." I dodged out of a cyclist's oncoming path. "You used one of his poems for an essay, didn't you?"

"Ah, *The Fortune-Favoured.*"

As the poem's mighty words began soundlessly trickling through my mind as calming waters, it was impossible not to recall Keane's sure and steady hand penning the final lines of that most acclaimed essay.

"*Men are not but overgrown children. There shall forever be those who trample the forests in lust of gold. There shall be those who dirty the rivers with all that is not coal. And then there shall be those—that mighty few—for which the world was made. They see the world, but are not of it. They taste the sweets of riches, but do not fall prey to its blessings. They love with all their might and soul, but have been hurt enough to know it is better to love in pain than to hate in death."*

Keane glanced down at me with something I had rarely seen furrow his noble brow or invigorate so sharp a tongue.

Pure shock.

"Lawrence, I would not have thought those words necessary to put to memory."

"Necessity comes from what is true. It is almost like you had written them from experience, rather than merely scratching out some theory." My feet faltered and stopped, pulling Keane to a screeching halt. "I am right, aren't I? You were that third type of man." He said nothing for so long a time I expected him to leave me wandering aimlessly through the wordless hush. It was a common practice of his, as habitual as the sun in day and moon at night. I had thought nothing would come of it, but, with a morose look down the bustling street, Keane again threaded my arm through his.

"We all lead our own lives, Lawrence. We all love and hate with the same fervour as any other. My life is no different. I have made my mistakes and paid for them dearly. In the end, you must be able to live with yourself knowing you have given of your very best."

"'*To love oneself is the beginning of a lifelong romance*'" My companion chuckled, his blue eyes shedding away those few flecks of silver daring to appear.

"Exactly, though I find myself rather different from that young Lord Goring." I laughed. Keane was not only different from Wilde's carefree character, but the exact opposite for as long as I had known him. Rarely did my companion enjoy the trivial for its own sake. Such things were, to him, ludicrous and deplorable.

And yet, his distinct joy and adoration for life had not once wavered.

Keane seemed to have a far better grasp of our destination than I, for the arm through which mine was securely threaded worked as a diligent rudder, steering a course along the pulsing streets. I have never again seen sights their like by any relation or relative acquaintance. Buildings jutted upwards along each side until one felt entirely surrounded by their presence. Lights danced below the sun. Pavement stunk with the heavy odour of hot rubber. Blinding colours vomited upon the world until the palm trees appeared to be sculpted from painted plastic and the buildings themselves whittled down to nothing more structurally sound than a wooden shell expertly positioned on a sound stage. For a place famous for glamour, it was no better than a facade of life. The great rushes of people all lead lives of their own, and yet they were threaded together by both lies and truths alike. The truths worked to create and strengthen a utopia idolised by all, and achieved by none, while the lies' only success fell upon a want of advantage in a world that, in theory, ought be advantageous. It was a web of iron, weakened with the rust of corruption.

KEANE LED ME INTO A little restaurant many blocks from the theatre. While it was of no major inconvenience, we had passed several other diners and cafes in favour of the light touch of music and the jovially Italian atmosphere. Each table was draped with identical cloths centred with freshly cut flowers.

Several paintings spotted the walls with their various representations of life. Many were landscapes of colourful villas smiling over a rippling sea, but one or two depicted people walking the length and breadth of the canvas without having a care to where they were going or when they got there. A violin played giddily in the corner. Not Keane's usual choice, but, knowing him as I did, the food was far more important than the exterior.

A middle-aged man with peppered grey hair slicked back against his head merrily herded us into a booth shoved close against the front window. I slid first along the elongated leather seat while Keane slipped into the other side. He needed nothing more than a brief glance at the menu before sending the waiter away in his own tongue. I gaped at him.

"Is there any language you can't speak?" Keane chuckled good-naturedly and tugged at his left ear, a habit that was almost as infamous as his smoking.

"I must admit oriental languages are rather less than my forte, but with romance languages, understanding one is nearly sufficient for them all. No doubt I could hold a conversation with any Spaniard and be the better for it."

"And the Italian?"

"Ah, yes . . . well," His slender fingers pulled almost violently at his ear. "That was taught to me by a rather good friend."

"When you say friend, do you mean a friend, or a *friend*?" Keane's posture had never been straighter.

"Really, Lawrence, you should learn to control that female curiosity of yours. Or ought I ask you about any male counterparts in your history?"

"Point taken. However, if you so much as insinuate curiosity is a disease only befitting my sex, I should warn you that I still have my pocketknife and I would not hesitate to practice the Italian art of close shaves."

"Then I should also warn you I too have some familiarity with the realms of sharp weapons and would not hesitate to protect myself if I felt it necessary."

"Why, Keane," I grinned unashamedly. "Are you saying that I may pose a threat to your mighty and masculine world? Or is it that bachelorhood you are so fond of that has made you fear the noble advancements in the lives of women?"

My companion had not the chance to answer, for hot plates of fish covered in oils and a red sauce suddenly appeared before us, and our knives were mercifully occupied by the baked sea life, rather than each other's throats. The fish—salmon, I thought—was incredibly light considering the thick tomato sauce. The pasta was divine, an exquisite partnership between flavour and craftsmanship, and I made it a point to tell such to my companion. Again, he chuckled and his fork paused, if briefly, between the plate and his mouth.

"*La vie est trop courte pour boire du mauvais vin.*"

Life is too short to drink bad wine.

Mercifully, lacking though my Italian may be, my French had been planted and moulded at Keane's hand from the moment I made his acquaintance. More than not, it was through the works of Victor Hugo, but there were others (Voltaire, for instance) who too watered that seed of knowledge interred within my mind.

Now it flowed as easily as . . . well . . . good wine.

CHAPTER FIFTEEN
Autumn 1916—H.M.S. Greylag

HORRID SCREAMS OF IMPENDING doom forced the boat to tremble as thousands of lead devils whizzed through the air. The turrets on the enemy vessel swung back and forth, spraying the deck with an onslaught of bullets. They needed to leave—to escape from the massacre—but where could they go? There was not but ocean past the ship's rail. Boundaries had been painted in red blood as man by man dropped dead. Their flesh, once warm and full of life, soon laid cold against the stirring sea. And if it ever occurred to them, in the dawn of their youth, such a horrid fate might befall them, they showed no fear. The glassy eyes—unseeing as they were—would never again know the world as they had walked only moments before. A tangled mass of punctured limbs grew heavy as the end washed down upon them. Their fallen arms groped at the ankles of those left to carry on. The storm grew stronger as the devil's rain ceaselessly dove down upon the screaming decks, but what could they do? Men fell like birds being picked off a wire, dropping away from the guns. As each weapon was freed, another man stepped forward only to be shot down into the sea. Brendan Keane heaved those breathing few onto his shoulders and carried them down below. Their bloody burdens grew lighter as he went. The sight of death—the stench of flesh—became customary to his senses. There were a few occasions when he would bend and pull a gasping friend onto his back only to lay him down again as he felt their grasp give way to an everlasting sleep. Sleep. Sleep. Eternal sleep. Everlasting sleep.

Death.

Each time he threw one of the lads onto his back, he muttered a quick prayer of thanks that it was neither James nor Fingal. But it was John. And John's brother, Mark. And Ethan. And Brutus. And Edward. And Peter. And Jacob. And Mathew. And Lois. And Scott. And Reginald. And Maximous. And Charles. And—

The screech of tearing metal singed Brendan's right shoulder as a blast of feverish heat erupted in a mass of billowing smoke. It was as black as tar and just as thick in his lungs.

He bent down and slung the next man's arm over his shoulder and recognised him to be a Joe something or other. While the two men were approximately the same age, Joe's thick build was nothing like Brendan's slim and sturdy frame. God, he weighed a ton, but he was also at least semi-conscious and did his best to help. Together they made it to the hatch where several hospital apprentices stood by to take a gasping Joe Brown—yes, that was his name; Brown—down to the surgery. Brendan himself was panting, each quick indraw of breath burning his lungs with the black smoke of burning oil.

Through the groans and cries along the deck, Brendan caught sight of Fingal a little ways off, slinging two—admittedly scrawny—men over his shoulders and fighting his way through the sea of corpses. Good man, he thought to himself as he staggered forward just as another round of bullets hailed the demise of another row of men, including a brown-haired youth who had been bravely manning one of the larger guns off the starboard side. God, if they lost that turret—

Brendan could not finish that thought completely, his mind whirling as he began sprinting along the blood slick decks with his long legs propelling him over the battered limbs. His cap had long since disappeared into the throng of discarded bodies, leaving his sand-blonde hair matted to his scalp by the ocean's merciless arms. The front of his wool pea coat was soaked in the blood of several dozen men, but, by God, if he didn't get that gun working again, there would very well be another several dozen lying on the deck.

Not to mention himself.

He threw himself behind the metal machinery and began swinging it back and forth across the enemy ship. It brought him no pleasure to see those other lads—the enemy, as they had been forced to believe—dropping into the water, but he had no viable option. There was a war on—a damnably enormous war—and he was going to help it along to its inevitable end. The steel in his hands was ice cold and nearly froze his fingertips, but he kept on, pummeling the other ship harder and harder until his heart thumped in rhythm with an ache in his head. A horrid scream dulled his senses in one instant, and yet, he was entirely aware of the strange sensation that he was flying. Flying? Men—*human beings*—certainly can not fly on their own accord. It was improbable. Impossible. Ridiculous.

Get a hold on yourself, he thought wildly.

For God's sake, pull yourself together.

But he could not, for just as his mind whirred back into motion, he realised something was wrong—terribly and horribly wrong—with his left shoulder.

His flight ceased.

He was falling.

CHAPTER SIXTEEN

AS THE STORY GOES, Jesus was dead for three days.

But for three days I walked through the hell only those entirely dedicated to the stage would willingly endure. James Harrison—director, producer, and devil's advocate—mashed lines and blocking into my brain as a teacher tortures their students.

(*That's the wrong line!*)

I played my role with dignity.

(*Louder, Jo! Project!*)

I carried myself as a soldier.

(*Move downstage!*)

My tongue was my weapon.

(*Faster Jo! Pacing!*)

My history was my present.

(*Damn it! Show some emotion!*)

And, most of all, I became ill with what can only be properly described as theatrical shell-shock. It was a disease I had not thought existed until I awoke abruptly on that third night with my arms gesticulating wildly through the bedclothes and a cold sweat chilling the vulnerable flesh on my neck. I immediately slipped into a dressing gown a size or so too large and shuffled off toward the kitchen. God, I needed something good. Something strong. Something—ah ha!

I pulled the half-empty bottle from the rack and sought out a vessel through which my evil deed may be set. The cupboards were mostly bare of any practical china, but I did manage to find one of the chipped brandy glasses Keane had used a few nights before. There was a spider in it now, spinning a web along the cut patterns. The small thing looked at peace with its comfortable situation. Lucky bastard.

But I suppose not everyone is meant to be so fortunate. Here he was, weaving his own path within the glass, while my world seemed to spin and whirl whenever I made a foundation for my life. Each time the tremor sent a crack into the concrete and I was either forced to fix it, or do away with what I had and start anew. In any case, it was a pain in the ruddy—

"You should never drink alone." I hadn't heard him come in (damn carpeting) but I was more than aware of his presence by that sharp English tone that danced every so often with the last remnants of his Irish brogue. I began digging around in the cupboards again.

"I read something about that once. *Gone With the Wind*, I think. Anyway, I was awake and it was here. Oh, Would you care for some?" There was that rich chuckle as he strode across the room.

"Do you know what time it is?"

"Should I? I thought time was relative." Keane made a light humming sound as he gingerly picked up the bottle.

"It is, in fact, four in the morning. Much too soon for this fine drink. Though I must say, your taste is improving. How about tea?"

"An Irishman turning down liquor? And I thought I had seen it all. Wait, you said America doesn't have proper tea." Keane swished some water around in the tea kettle, that impish glow absolutely radiating from his face as he bent over the sink.

"My dear, Lawrence, you have forgotten one important fact."

"And that is?" He allowed the water to spew out the spout before filling it again. When that was set on the stove, he reached his hand into one of the vulgarly bright cookie jars, which was shaped—or rather misshapen—into the head of a disfigured elephant. From the animal's porcelain head, my companion pulled a metal box I had seen inhabiting the cupboards of his own home in Devon, as well as the family house in Ireland. Or at least, it had been the family house. Now it sat—bereft of human life—with only Keane's monetary support to continue the long traditions hidden in its walls. He dropped in on the counter with a comical clatter.

Damn the man, I couldn't help but laugh. He looked almost military, the collar of his cotton pyjamas pressed neatly beneath his dressing gown and his greying hair fingered into something that dutifully resembled control. By God, he was almost like a man who had just staggered from the straight jacket, and I would have informed him so had the telephone not rung at that exact moment.

"Blast the infernal machine." Keane growled, abandoning the first puffs of steam from the kettle as he stormed into the sitting room. I took the tea tin from the counter and began turning it over in my hands. Keane's tea was like his cigarettes, always there and always available. It stared down at the lid.

Barry's Tea.

Of course.

He seldom drank any other, unless it was put before him by a thoughtful—but nieve—host. The kettle began humming, then singing, then absolutely screeching for attention away from my thoughts. Instinctively I reached my hand out toward the angry pot, turned off the stove, and listened with an air of victory as the desperate cries settled to a soft whimper. I gingerly poured some of the loose tea leaves into a metal strainer before dropping it into a mug (of course an American would never have any available teacups) and pouring the steaming water into the pour excuse of ceramics. Once that was done, I reached for a second, equally hideous, cup which had no relation to any of the other objects in the cupboard.

"Keane, would you—"

I was interrupted by a startling coalition of heavy sounds that ended in my companion bellowing out a series of oaths that were not only imaginative, but increasingly heartfelt the longer he continued. As tempting as it was to enter into the hot winded squall, I was exceedingly pleased I had not when Keane stormed back into the kitchen dressed in his day clothes with his coat fully buttoned.

"Get dressed, Lawrence, we're going out." You could have blown me over with a stiff wind.

"Out? But you yourself said it was only four in the morning. Why the devil—"

"Either get dressed or, by God, I'll drag you out of here as you are. I'm certain it is nothing *too* scandalous to go around Los Angeles in one's night clothes."

THE CRIMSON SHAW

I WAS SUITABLY ATTIRED and out the door just as Keane started the car and together we were off at a feverish pace before the sun had so much as yawned over the flickering horizon. The darkness was only sparsely spotted with street lights or the brightly curved letters announcing the California nightlife. My finger's instinctively went to the leather seat as Keane nearly ploughed over a man teetering along the thin edge between the pavement and the road.

"Good God, Keane! Someone will think you're drunk!" He didn't even glance at me.

"Is that really anything unusual in this city? Besides, if a man is roaming the dark streets at four o'clock in the morning, he would probably be drunk too." There was a coldness to his voice—a stiffness—I had seldom heard in the years of our acquaintance.

And I might not have heard it again were it not for Keane's quick action to avoid a light pole that leapt into our path. It was another few moments, or a collective two seconds, when Keane slammed onto the brakes just before pinning our fragile limbs to the rear of a large truck parked just outside the theatre.

A very large, red truck.

Keane had scarcely stopped the car before he was out of it, running along the pavement like a madman. His was an act hard to follow, but I did my duty dodging in and out of the throng of people stationed arm to arm around the theatre. It was an army of drunkards, showgirls, robed men, and women with hair curlers chattering loudly above the last few shrieks of sirens. I at last arrived at the man standing at the door just in time to see Keane lift him easily by his coat lapels. It was quite a feat, not because I thought my companion incapable of such things, but because the young man was built more like a steam boat, rather than a human being.

"Hawkins, what the devil happened?" The stagehand shrugged out of my companion's grasp, but I noticed that glint of fear that so often loosened tongues and rattled rusted minds into action.

"Gosh, I don't really know. Thought I saw a light in the back and, sure enough, a fire had been started right in James' office." I understood the situation then, the faint odour of smoke and the overall bustle of human bodies jamming against each other for a better look at the sudden rush of news old bitties could pass around over cups of coffee as they waited for their life to drain away into a wooden box nailed shut at the ends. Someone ought to make a newsreal for them, something like the OBA.

Old Busibodies of America.

No doubt we would hear about this tomorrow in the black, inked titles or, more likely, a small article strategically placed just below the obituaries. The front page was reserved for something nationally important. Like the horse races.

Keane pushed his way further toward the group of uniformed men for a moment before quickly returning for another interrogation.

"Where is James? With the firemen?" The young stagehand shook his head violently.

"Couldn't get a hold of him, so I called you instead. Hope you don't mind getting up at this hour, but, gosh, when I saw those flames—"

"—I understand, Hawkings." He may have understood, but Keane's temper had not quelled. It was; however, controlled.

For the time being.

"Did the men get the fire out?" I asked before my companion could risk his slim composure.

"Oh, sure. It didn't take them long. They even said there wasn't any real damage to the building, just to some of the furniture. Oh, and the smoke might have ruined the wallpaper, not to mention those potted plants. But, gosh, when I saw—" Keane, who obviously didn't give a rat's ass of what the frightened man saw, cursely thanked him with a few well-valued bills and shoved me back toward the car.

The second trip was far calmer than the first, but still retained that edge teetering between mere moroseness and complete insanity. Buildings passed like ominous old men glaring down at those of us still left to amble the earth. Their glass eyes were as unseeing as those of death, and yet I could not shake the feeling that they were watching our every move—every breath—as though it ought to have been theirs and was not. The first glimpses of morning light had clawed upwards toward the horizon, just as sleep's skillful hands pulled me down into the murky depths. So low did I fall, I was not aware of the shoulder beneath my head until it disappeared, awakening me with a startling jolt as I fell across the leather seat. I did not receive so much as a muttered apology as the tall frame to which the shoulder was connected, again scrambled out of the automobile with an agility that might have been impressive for a man of fifty-five, had I not grown to expect it. I sluggishly followed after him toward the grey, dull building; more out of curiosity than a true desire to go. Keane quickly strode up to the third floor, his long legs swallowing every other stair. God, did every building have that many stairs? I stood behind him as he pounded on the door. I was exhausted, groggy, but I was there. I was there too to witness my companion—rarely demonstrative, look of an Irishman, and soul of a poet—ram his shoulder brutally against the door and send it flying open with a solid crack of wood.

The director's rooms were, for the most part, well kept. The colours were a bit more reserved from the house he had offered Keane and I, but they were still incredibly obnoxious.

"James?" Keane's bellow echoed through the papered walls and was answered by a groan from one of the connecting rooms. "James, you son of a sea serpent, get out here this instant!" And indeed a door did open and the director stepped out into the room.

And all my exhaustion was forgotten.

I did not sink to the female practice of hysteric screams or nervous giggles. I was too shocked to say anything really. I forced my eyes to remain on the man's face; to examine the constricted pupils, the light brush of sweat, and the slight pallor of his lips. It took Keane an excruciatingly long moment of tugging at his coat sleeves to pull a comprehensible string of words together, and even then it was only two accentuated nouns and an exceptionally firm verb.

"James! Clothes! *Now!*" It is one thing to see the completeness of a person's anatomy when it is spread out at a morgue or some other establishment to which such disclosure is necessary and hardly a pressing fact, but to find it staring back at you—living, breathing, and somehow entirely tan—that was a different matter entirely. Keane's cheekbones turned a fierce, violent purple as his blue eyes flecked grey. As a man born under Queen Victoria, no doubt he felt a young woman of nearly twenty-five ought not see such . . . things . . . until after they had been gagged and bound in the holy chains of matrimony. But I had lived through a war, and injured soldiers on the brink of death rarely followed the gentleman's dress code. Hospitals often were constructed of several rows of bloody men covered only by a single, white sheet, which in itself left very little to even the most sluggish of imaginations.

I was quickly aware of Keane's hand on my arm, shoving me none too gently toward a pitiful collection of chairs that could hardly call themselves a squadron, let alone a proper sitting room. His voice came like a bolt of lightning.

"Sit."

I sat.

I sat and watched silently as Keane began ransaking through every drawer and jar in the room. First he began with the smaller things, then he graduated to sticking his arm up the fireplace and wiping the soot away in his hair, creating dark streaks through the light morning. As his efforts persisted, I noticed the top button of his coat had come undone and exposed his pyjama shirt, rather than one of his nice white ones that went with those brown trousers of his. Just as Keane was growing desperate enough to shake the entire building upside down, Harrison reappeared in an unusual assortment of what I suspected to be the pants of a tuxedo and the brightest, most gaudy bathrobe I had ever seen in my life. Even so, it was a great improvement. Keane was still far from pleased.

"Where are they, James?" The director blinked a few times.

"Where are what?" But Keane had seen the mysterious item in the man's bedroom and showed no qualms as he returned with the little bottle half filled with white capsules. He waved them just a few millimetres from the American's nose.

"I thought you gave these up years ago. By God, man, don't you know what these can do to you? Didn't you see what happened to that Smith girl?" However dulled Harrison's brain might have been, his anger appeared quickly as a solid flush appeared on his tanned face. His voice was slurred, but somehow still retained that cold edge that can do nothing but harm its intended victim.

"We can't all be as perfect as the great Brendan Keane. Not everyone can be *that* perfect." The man, who seemed scarcely above a drunken stupor, swivelled his body toward me. "Ya know, your friend here has survived jumping off a boat in the middle of a storm, being punched in the eye by an goddamn Italian, and some shrapnel from a German deck gun?"

And being run down by an automobile, I added silently.

What happens in Ireland stays in Ireland.

With James Harrison; however, it seemed that what happened in the war was a no man's land; able to be used as a subject whenever he damn well pleased. I was all too thankful when he again turned his attention back to a painfully rigid Brendan Keane.

"Do you know what happened to me, Brendan? Do you? Shell-shock. You survive a hunk of shrapnel with nary a scratch to your shoulder, while I get shot down with damn shell-shock. Do you know what that's like, Brendan? Do you know what it's like to wake up in a cold sweat with your hands trying to strangle the fucking life out of your pillow? Or your wife? She married me right after the war. I was alright then, as you'll remember. Quite the ladies' man too. But then I snapped and she left like I was a fucking lunatic. A beautiful woman like that, and she ran off like I was a goddamn bastard. You shake those pills in front of my face, but they are the only thing keeping me from those hellish nightmares that have made up my life."

Ah.

Addiction.

By definition it was a physical and psychological dependence. However, to the human being not to be found in the rotting pages of a dictionary, it was pure hell. Dependence was often found the serviceman's curse; instilled upon them as the world thrust armies forward into battle, only to abandon them as stupefied sacks on street corners. I had never collected the nerve to ask, but I suspected that it was in the navy Keane had developed his taste for cigarettes. I watched curiously as he pulled a packet out of his pocket, lit one between his thin lips, and slumped into an obnoxiously patterned chair. A thin veil of smoke enshrouded his head, a brief reminder that made him again raise his eyes to Harrison, who was half sitting, half lying on a chaise lounge.

"I didn't come here to reprimand you, James. David Hawkins—yes, the one who mans the curtain ropes—rang me this morning to tell me there was a fire at the theatre and—" Of all the emotions I might have expected from Harrison (perhaps an uncontrolled, even violent anger that sent him barging toward the door), his reaction far surpassed them all. He leapt from his seat and began closing all the curtains over the windows until the only light in the room was the orange dot spotting the end of Keane's cigarette. I flicked on a nearby lamp, almost turning it off by the animal-like glare from its owner. But it wouldn't have made any difference. The man dropped back into his seat, threw his head forward into his hands, and wept like a child. Keane said nothing. Rather, he looked upon me as though my femininity might have somehow instilled the solution to such matters; as if I could wave my hand and make the uncomfortable situation disappear.

Not bloody likely.

I opened my mouth, closed it, and opened it again with just as much to say as I did on my first attempt. Damn Keane's irrational beliefs of my sex. I was nearly as inept as him when it came to ridiculous, emotional people. No, I was worse. Where Keane might carve them mercilessly with his sharp tongue, I would do so and finish without guilt or sorrow. At last, on the third attempt, a phrase did come out and, a pitiful excuse of a question though it was, it served its purpose with as much dignity as even Keane might have mustered.

"What the devil is the matter?" Harrison's weeping immediately ceased—thank God—and was replaced by short gasps that warned more of hyperventilation, rather than something weak and womanly that would soil his reputation as a man.

"God, they—they found me. I knew they would. I knew it."

"James, who the devil—"

"*They. They* found me." A long sob grew into a moan as Harrison clutched the side of his stomach and began rocking forward and back in his seat. "Oh, God. I thought I could have—but of course I couldn't have hidden from them. Not *them*. Oh, God. Oh, *God*. They will ruin me. Leave me to the streets. Burn my theatre. They already tried to kill you. God. God. *God*. They'll kill us all. Murder us in our beds. God. Oh, God. Oh, *God!*" Keane leapt from his chair at the very instant Harrison's thick, urgent tones turned sour with wrenching throws of cold vomit. Great globs of bodily slime filled an empty vase. I feared the worst, but painful moments with his head bowed down against his knees proved far more beneficial than a doctor's overzealous hand. Long, laborious breaths gave way to another bout of quiet sobs. Each weeping cry sent his shoulders to trembling; his body rocking as a madness set down upon him.

And then it stopped.

Everything stopped.

Keane, who had toyed indefinitely with the silver edging of his cigarette case, allowed the object to slip into its pocket with the air of a gentleman, and the compassion of a saint.

"James," My companion waited for the man's head to lift slightly from his hands. "James, I can not help you if I do not know of whom you speak."

"Cohen." Harrison groaned.

And all the world shook.

CHAPTER SEVENTEEN

I WAS ONCE MORE TUMBLING over into the abyss of sleep when Keane returned from helping the weeping man back to his bedroom; the mournful squeal of door hinges crying behind him. The angry flush had vanished from his face, but the consequences of an ill-used night had begun to make an appearance. Dark shadows suddenly lingered beneath his eyes with a thin scruff long since settled over his jaw. I sat up, expecting Keane to immediately dive into every nook and cranny of James Harrison's many vices, but instead he ambled off to the kitchen and returned with a bottle and two matching glasses.

"I believe now would be an ideal time for a stiff drink." He announced, handing me the first glass poured with a moderate hand. I had half the mind to point out it was now only a little past six in the morning, but, as he filled his glass to the brim, I thought the better of it. Wasn't there something Shaw said about not wrestling with angry sheep? Or was it pigs?

God, I needed sleep.

Keane threw his head back and dumped half the glass' contents down his throat. It seemed to have done some good, for the stiffness in his shoulders began to ease away.

"I think," He began carefully. "I think that I should stay here a while longer to make sure James comes out of it alright. These damn pills . . ." He pulled the little bottle out of his pocket and handed it to me. My tired eyes were none too eager to be put to proper use; however, after a few seconds, the brown smudge along the label became letters strung together into a single word.

Hydrocodone.

Keane tapped the bottle slowly with his forefinger.

"They used to prescribe these in the war. Then they became self-prescribed when the shell shock set in. In essence, it is a painkiller with a thousand other devilish purposes." I noticed when he uttered the last sentence, his hand came up to brush his left shoulder, as if he was dusting away a shadow.

"Does it hurt? Your shoulder, I mean. Does it still bother you?" There was a dry, rough chuckle in my ear.

"Lawrence, that was over thirty years ago. Are you still sore where you injured yourself as a child? No, I thought not." Of course it didn't hurt. Ridiculous thought. Perhaps it would become sore—even uncomfortable—if he went several nights without sleep or overworked that particular muscle, but beyond that? No. Poppycock. He downed the rest of the whiskey and poured himself another, more conservative glass. "If you want to go back to the house for a while, you can take the car. I'll get a cab later when James wakes up again." I tried to pull my exhausted features together in what I thought to be an offended expression.

"Me? Take the car back? I'd crash into a tree with the lack of sleep. No, Keane, you can't get rid of me that easily." He nodded before we allowed the room to slip back into silence. Surprisingly, I did not drift easily into the realm of dreams as the minutes ticked passed on a clock shaped eerily like a black cat.

Instead, I watched the curled tail swing back and forth. Back and forth. Back and forth. Back and—

"Keane?"

"Lawrence?"

"Do you really think all this trouble—the incident when we arrived, the Smith girl's death, the fire—is because of Harrison? Or rather, his ties to this Cohen man?" I felt my companion shift beside me, but his eyes stayed stolidly marked to the wall.

"Remember, Lawrence, Meyer Cohen is not the only leader of the Los Angeles underground. For all we know, it could be another dozen groups—or even a madman—who want to ruin James."

"But, if he owes Cohen money—"

"That does turn the scale a bit, yes." Keane ran his finger along the edge of his glass. "There was a part in the Bible—I cannot recall where—in which it was said those who provide temptation are related to the devil. Certainly the black market provided the drugs, but it is Miss Smith, James, and others like them who willingly enjoy their effects. They enjoy the chemicals, but financially?" He needn't have finished. I knew all too well of the stories of the late Capone's mafia out in Chicago and the hundreds of other groups who appeared across the country who made millions off of selling drugs to former soldiers; however, until that moment, I had only heard the stories. And that's what it felt like. A blasted story. Everything about the entire adventure seemed incredibly surreal, from the little fat man with his damn cigars to Harrison's stupefied entrance. It was no better than a blasted fairytale.

A damn story.

Keane stood from the seat and stretched leisurely with the heels of his palms planted firmly in the small of his back.

"I think it would be prudent if we watched ourselves for the next few days. Nothing paranoid, mind you, but the simple things. Staying away from excessively large windows, not eating or drinking anything you are not absolutely sure is safe, and—do you have your knife with you?" I pulled the folded silver object from my pocket and held it out palm up for Keane's inspection. "Good. Carry that at all times." It was a superfluous statement; suggesting a habit which had existed since he first bought me the piece. My curiosity, on the other hand, was not only justifiable, but necessary.

"And what will *you* be carrying? A sickle? A sabre?" I thought my companion had gone mad, or, at the very least, was on the brink of doing so. One by one he unbuttoned his coat, his fingers moving slowly but with an exquisite sense of purpose. It was not until he threw it over the back of a nearby chair that I saw the full extent of his pajamaed torso.

Including a holster and pistol.

I couldn't believe it. But then, as logic and reason washed upon me, I found I could. He had been in a war. Of course he owned a gun. I had seen a few scattering various drawers of his house in Devon. Yes, I had known about these, but to see him with the holster strapped over his shoulder, it shook me. Him, with his vivid, blue eyes and poetic expression, wearing a firearm over the warm cotton of his pyjama shirt. It might have been comical, had it not been a matter of life and the lack of such.

"Has no one told you never fight fire with fire?" It was a joke; a poor, weak, futile joke muttered with a voice scarcely audible above the pounding in my head. Keane grimaced—the first step toward a smile—and gingerly pulled the weapon from its spot against his chest. He handed it to me.

The little pistol was only marginally longer than my palm; coming several inches short of my fingertips. I had held a hundred revolvers such as this, and fired them just as often. I had no qualms to their use just as I had no doubt of their intense power. There was power to survive, and power to die. Power to live, and power to shorten the lives of others. Power to love, and power to hate.

Power.

I cleared my throat.

"FP-45. Small, but effective." I returned the weapon to Keane, who slipped it into the holster.

"It may not be the best in the world, but it will suffice until I find something more suitable. You have used them before, I believe."

"More often than I would care to admit." Keane nodded slowly.

"*'Doubtless there are times when controversy becomes a necessary evil. But let us remember that it is an evil.'*"

"Arthur Penrhyn Stanley; *Dictionary of Burning Words of Brilliant Writers*. Published in 1894, wasn't it?"

"1895, but the words still hold the same meaning." My companion finished buttoning his coat and sat down beside me with the air of a defeated man. His shoulders slouched low toward his knees; his hands falling uncomfortably in his lap. "I really ought to apologise—"

"—Don't you dare. You might injure your masculinity. And besides, *'Qué será, será.'*"

Whatever will be, will be.

"Even so, if I had not cancelled your meetings—"

"—Then I would be bored to death in England. Really, Keane, this is much more fun." He was silent then, as if I had just raised a flag of surrender for the sake of his pride. That was, of course, partially true, but not completely. Nothing is ever entirely truthful, no matter how hard one may believe it to be so. He knew as well as I that my publisher was a common goat of a man who was just as existing as an unsolvable algebraic equation. Lord knows I would have rather spent the summer months with one of my disgruntled relations than endure those tedious meetings. All Keane had done was to provide an excuse to save my sanity.

I began to sip at my long forgotten glass of whiskey.

IT WAS KEANE WHO AWOKE me. Not the scruffy, furious Keane who talked of weapons, but one who had recently shaved (*the brisk scent of his shaving lotion*), combed back his hair (*with that one little curl refusing to go behind his right ear*), and dressed fully in a three piece suit (*the lingering vinilla of cigarette smoke still clinging to the fabric*). The dark blotches were still quite apparent under his eyes, but they were not quite so heavy as before. In fact, if I hadn't been looking for them, I might not have noticed at all.

I was also equally aware of a steaming cup being shoved beneath my nose.

"Good morning, Lawrence. Or should I say afternoon? By God, if you had your way, you'd sleep the entire day into oblivion. Now drink this—no, it's not coffee; though are you certain your distaste for the beverage is not psychological—you're quite right. This is no time to discuss your many mysteries. Now get up."

I accepted the tea, allowing it to liquid to scald my throat and jerk me into reality. My mutterings of thanks scarcely passed my lips before I realised the suit he was wearing was too loose at the midsection and short at the ankles. The necktie too, I thought, was not his colour.

Yellow never was.

I took another long sip of the strong liquid.

"And how is the patient this morning?" Keane pulled at the ends of his suit cuffs (which weren't nearly long enough to conceal his wrists) and cocked his head to one side as a doctor might when preparing to give a diagnosis.

"His breathing and heart rate are normal. Pupils seem alright. All and all, I think he has come out of it right enough."

"And what are you going to do about the Hydrocodone?"

"Do?"

"Of course. I can't believe you would stand by and watch that man—your friend—slowly kill himself. It isn't in your nature." I would have said more, but I neither wanted to inflate his insufferable ego, nor puncture that great collection of hot air called masculinity. Instead, I sat with the mug of tea cradled in my hands and an expression wavering dangerously between curiosity and the expectancy my companion would suddenly announce some ingenious plot to forever rid Harrison's system of the little, white pills. But he said nothing. No great exclamation of marvellous insight came. There was only the thick murk of silence between us as he pulled out his cigarette case and began smoking the treasured things one by one. A thin shroud of smoke encircled us in a scent slightly more bitter than vanilla, but just as pleasing to the senses. I observed every twist of the flitting clouds that rose about Keane's head in a slow, mystic dance. The memory of those Irish pubs, heavy with the smells of smoke and stout, fell upon me in a wave of nostalgic impulses. I wanted to return again. I wanted to be free of this place. I wanted to be free of my past, just as Keane wished to be free of his. But I could not. A hundred stings, a thousand welts.

At last, as the final trails of smoke ceased to take breath from his cigarette, he slowly ground it into a nearby ashtray and glanced at me down the bridge of his nose.

"My dear Lawrence, I am hardly a role model for the 'straight and narrow path' as they say. I have my own problems—my own addictions." He waved a thin, clean hand over the ashtray. "And until I am willing to give them up—and Lord help me if I ever did—how am I to say I am in the right and poor James is in the wrong? After all, everything is relative."

"But there are some religions that even encourage smoking. The native tribes, for one."

"You mean the same tribes that use hallucinogenic mushrooms for their various rituals and other ceremonies? No, Lawrence, we are back where we started. I absolutely will not—*cannot* invoke upon my friend a hell I do not wish to walk myself. It goes against my code as a gentleman." Damn his blasted code.

"But Keane," I paused to collect the words rushing about my brain. "What if—What if it was *me*. Would you be so unable to do anything then as well."

It was a low blow. It was, dare I say, ungentlemanly. But I was not a gentleman. I was a woman, a skillful, conniving woman, who had dreams too great for realities, and realities too awful for nightmares.

It was also a risk. I was wagering the whole of the future on the thought that our relationship might have been so ingrained into him as it was to me that it would topple all fears he had at being an inadequate temperance worker. William Wilberforce, one of the great British politicians and author of *Real Christianity*, once said in a speech to the House of Commons in 1789;

'You may choose to look the other way, but you can never again say that you did not know,'

Keane stared at me with his jaw stolid against the rest of his features and his eyes stone against stormy seas.

"Confound it, woman!" He growled, circling around the back of his chair until I festered some vain hopes he might sit down.

"But, Keane—" I had scarcely uttered his name when he was upon me completely, my coat lapels twisted in his clenched fists as he pulled me to my feet and then some until our noses were but a breath from one another. I stared into those pools of blue flecked heavily in grey; those two oceans rippling in colour as the black centres darted back and forth between mine. His lips were pressed tightly into a stiff line. I knew that look well. I knew that look of intense thought, of measuring the consequences of a situation quickly with his mind reeling in a thousand directions at once. I knew most everything about that look; every line, every crease, every muscle, every movement of his eyes. I knew it. I knew it because I knew him. The years of our acquaintance, our companionship, our friendship, our—God, if our faces got any closer—

He suddenly released me and I fell back into my seat. We had been thrown back into our separate corners of the ring, but, by the soft, tentative nature of his voice, I did not doubt he remembered the bout in the middle.

"You are quite right, Lawrence. Quite right. It was . . . callus of me to say I could do nothing. Perhaps, with a little effort, I might be able to create some plan of action." He said it with such conviction I was hard pressed not to believe him.

I watched him awhile then, miserably aware of my own failings in life while perfectly oblivious to his supposed sins. He bent down for his coat (accentuating the insufficient length of his trousers) and hung it over his arm. "I am going out for a while. An hour—two, at most. Will you be alright here? Of course you will. No, I am *not* about to leap over a bridge, and I would appreciate a change in your humour. It has been rather dismal lately, and certainly not complimentary to your intelligence. Tell James when he awakens he had best cancel any rehearsals for the next two weeks. He and I have work to do."

And then Keane—Keane in a yellow tie and too-short trousers—was gone.

PART THREE

Those who aim at great deeds

Must also suffer greatly.

-Marcus Licinius Crassus

CHAPTER EIGHTEEN

THEY HAD DISAPPEARED like the final scenes of a dream. Their words rattled through my mind as clearly as the moment when Harrison emerged into his sitting room. The weight of the situation was well upon us, and our understanding reasonably questioned the sure path of the world. After all, it is difficult to take a man seriously in anything when you have seen him in nothing.

My mind wandered briefly to the strength of Keane's hands pulling my head above the petty thoughts deemed for the common man. Yet his grasp did not hurt me in the slightest.

They had gone and I had stayed. It was that simple.

And yet it was so horribly complicated.

I had watched Keane practically drag Harrison into the car with a final shout in my direction. They would be staying in the beach house and I, in turn, should stay in the director's apartment. I assured him I would.

And then caught the first available taxi and registered in a nearby hotel.

The clerk gaped down his sharp nose at me; a figure in a pair of plaid trousers, loose shirt, and shoes that bore a multitude of scuffs and filth. I had no doubt my short hair was also a reason for concern, but that was irrelevant. Anything was irreverent when it came to those such as he. Polished leather was not bright enough to create his boots, and no queen or king hath power enough to bow before him. I slipped a few extra, large bills across the counter, signed my name (or an alias thereof), and was rewarded with a key. The bellboy, having only recently entered out of the shadow of childish youth, attacked me with an arsenal of jokes that would have made the most vulgar bow their heads in shame. With each abhorrent line, his irrotic cackling nearly sent my single piece of luggage clattering down the stone staircase. The third time I caught it myself and instructed him (none too gently, I'll admit) to open the door when we got there. He did. I paid him. He was gone.

Thank God.

Ask most any Englishman, Keane especially, and they will tell you that American hotels have always been designed for the staff's convenience, not yours. He once compared them to Victor Hugo's Thenardier; picking money from your pocket with all those little wastes one has not requested, and could very well live without.

And yet, it was not as horrid as I might have feared. A single bed had been shoved into the corner across from a worn armchair. Below a row of windows set a writing desk, complete with a select amount of stationary and pencils that were short enough to fit into a reporter's hat band. The dresser had been topped off with a vase of flowers. Really, aside from the striped wallpaper, I had no complaints.

I dropped my luggage onto the bed and turned immediately toward the lavatory. The bathtub would have fit the former president Taft, and still had room to spare. I immediately twisted the taps and cajoled a steady stream of hot water from the pipes. Peeling off the woven ilk of my clothes, I stepped down into the porcelain bowl and allowed all my worries to sprout wings and take flight far from the realms of my mind.

I am convinced there is nothing so wonderful in the world as a good, hot bath; the tingling sensation of the water as it pulls the dust and grime from your skin, breathing the aroma of soap as it bubbles upwards towards the water's surface. All pains and frustrations were slowly tugged away from my person on the golden chariots of fire. The world no longer grabbed at me with frozen hands. It was a heady combination of absolute bliss. Not something I was permitted to experience very often. My mind drifted aimlessly from the whitewash ceiling to the cream tiled floor. Everything smelled of those meadows of Summer after a Springtime of rain, barring only the slightest brush of smoke wafting from somewhere below.

A shock shot up my spine. No matter how many times I came to that exact moment (*The screech of tires as the machine fell from the brink of control . . .*), it still felt like the last pangs of a nightmare (. . . *the burning cigar ash flinging into my face. . .*); the fingers of a fevered mind clawing its way to the layer of reality rarely punctured (. . . *and the vice grip on my collar jerking me out of the car just before—*)

I sat up in the porcelain tub just in time to watch a cloud of steam fly upwards with the sudden motion.

(*. . .and the blast of hot air as a pillar of black, oily smoke shot into the night sky.*)

I extracted myself from the bath soon after, fully aware the water was still warm but not caring in the slightest. What was comfort to the body when the mind is unwilling to succumb to rest?

I dried and dressed with the intention to do nothing more than write for the remainder of that day. Pulling out the wooden chair of the small desk, I took my battle position; pen in hand to fend off all enemies of the literary arts.

And then I waited.

And waited.

And waited.

At last, when nothing would peek its head upon the horizon of malleable ideas, I slammed the fountain pen onto the stack of stationary with the cold vomit of black ink spewing from the silver nib.

The first mark I had made in hours.

I shoved my hands together and stretched them high above my head with a painfully satisfying pop of my stiff shoulders. God, since when had I become a domestic? Extracting my leather jacket from its prostrate position upon the suitcase, I left the room and jogged down the stone steps into the lobby. The greasy-haired clerk stationed behind the desk grinned as I quickly approached.

"Leaving so soon." It was not so much a question as a hopeful proclamation.

"No, but I would like to know where the nearest library is."

"Oh." His cold smile faltered to the point of near extinction. I would have to remind myself to check for reptiles under my pillow before retiring that night. "Well, I think there's one if you walk down the street a bit, turn left, turn right again, and keep walking for a block or so." He might as well give me the directions to Siberia, for all the good it did me.

I thanked him curtly, my fingers flitting near my pockets as I turned abruptly and stalked out the door. It is a forbidden thing to look over one's shoulder; a sin to Lot's wife and degradation of all human sanity. Shadows lurk beneath one's heel, though they hide well. Even windows become eyes when the heart is not willing to stand alone in a world to which it does not belong. I wondered how long he would stand there with his hand outstretched in the most common form in the art of money making.

Begging.

I DID NOT ATTEMPT TO follow the man's directions, for the only thing one ought to do with such advice is to pass it off to someone who believes a broken match is the equivalent of a burning candle. The heat of the sun was doubled by the pavement that insisted on crumbling away at the most inconvenient places. The heavy stench of exhaust felt thick on my tongue, far thicker than one of Keane's cigarettes and infinitely less appealing. One can find the oddest people in such places; the endless stream of people aiming their cameras at most anything, the men with their tinted glasses, the women strutting about like disillusioned film stars. And then there was another person—the faintest glimpse of a shadow—that was constantly appearing among the crowds. I stopped and allowed the bobbing hat to catch up and stared into a face I knew, and which, in a moment, recognized me.

"Joanna?" She gasped. "Joanna, is that you?"

Ruth Woodsworth, one of my few ties to America that had found me. We had been schoolmates, she and I, though 'friendship' might be too broad of a word to truly emphasise our brief acquaintanceship those final months before I left for England. She was the iconic sort of female posted across billboards; slender, fair skinned, and that blonde mass of hair scorched by curlers.

Iconic, but with the obnoxious resemblance to a plastic doll. Cheap.

"Yes, Ruth. It's me." I said calmly as her eyes drilled holes into the scars accumulated over years of adventure.

"Gosh, you haven't changed a bit." She noted with something edging near distaste. Of course I had not changed. She was right about that. My hair was still a short, curly mass of a colour deceptively near to that of wet sand, and, unlike the makeup meticulously spotting her face, I had never made an effort to conceal my ruddy complexion. She wagged her head. "Still into leather jackets and men's clothes, huh, Joanna?"

"You might say that. And my name is still Jo." A quick feminine giggle bubbled into the air.

"Gosh, yes. I remember you giving Tommy Tanner a black eye for using your full name. You don't do that anymore, do you?"

"Only when necessary." Ten to one she thought I was joking.

"And what brings you back to the old country? Got tired of England? Or trying to get into show business?"

"None of the above. I came with a friend. And you? I thought you said you were never leaving Ohio; farm country turned industrial, or something like that." Her hand flew into the air, revealing a gold band.

Ah.

Marriage.

"Guess Mr. Right just didn't follow my plans. Now, is this friend of yours..." Ruth wiggled her eyebrows.

"God, no. Only friends." Her brow fell disappointedly. I had seen that look before, but more often from those relations shoved into my past, rather than an acquaintance from over a decade ago.

"I swear, Jo, you're going to turn into an old maid. Is that what you want? Oh, that's right, you always said you would never marry unless he had—What was it you said? Oh, it doesn't matter. You always did like the idea of being some old spinster."

"I prefer 'bachelor'. 'Spinster' sounds like a damn spider." Her eyes grew wide for an instant before that tedious giggle again surfaced.

"Well, if you ever do marry, he had better be a sailor. My Robert would never put up with language like that. He is such a wonderful man. We should all go out some time. I'm sure he'd get a kick out of you." Not if I kicked him first.

"That sounds grand, but, like I said, I'm here with a friend and it wouldn't be right if I just abandoned him." Not that I could anyway. He had already abandoned me to save his other friend.

At my insistence, of course.

Ruth smiled.

"Of course you can bring him along if you want. The more the merrier. And I want to meet this mystery man." Again an edge was laid to the words I did not appreciate. I could make no note of it; however, before Ruth had spun off again. "Say, how about you and I go get something to eat right now. Coffee alright? Or would you rather tea? I have a few hours before I need to finish my shopping, and Bobby wouldn't mind a speck if I took just a little longer. A girl needs her friends, don't you know?" In truth, I hadn't known. But, of course, that made no difference. Her fingernails dug into my jacket as she began hauling me down the pulsating streets, tittering on all the while. "I think it's wonderful you came back, Jo. Bobby would think so too. You'd like Bobby. He's smart—*real* smart—went to college and everything. Or do you call it university now? They didn't take him for the war though. Said his feet were all wrong. Something like that, anyway. I've seen his feet plenty of times. They look fine. But you'd never see me parading like a turkey in one of those uniforms. I mean *honestly*, do you really think they'd want Bobby for the war anyway? They can take all the dirty men off the street, so why should they want good, educated men?" I held my tongue. Keane had discussed the same topic frequently, but our shared opinions had never crossed this threshold so near the brink of immorality. Why should educated men be spared? The man in the firearm factory was just as valuable as a daft scholar. A great deal more so even.

Ruth hardly stopped for a breath before continuing. "I mean, gosh, if you want a lot of men, get the ones who aren't working. Lucky they didn't get Bobby. Do you know what he does for a living? Insurance. Makes a lot of money off of it too. Of course, I'm not like Penelope Hasselhemmer. Do you remember her? She was a dirty cow for some of the things she used to say. She was so stuck up about money and things, just because her parents were rich. Well *I* am not like that. Gosh, if she saw me now she'd take back all those things she said about my clothes in an instant. I bet she doesn't have a new car. And I *know* she doesn't live in California because I haven't seen her."

"This is only Los Angeles."

"*Only* Los Angeles? All sorts of big Hollywood stars live around here."

"Do they indeed?"

"Gosh, yes. Just last week I saw—Oh, look, we're here."

'Here' was the ground floor of, what I could only imagine to be, a women's club. Unfortunately, where the gentlemen were content with tobacco smoke, newspapers, liquor, and billiards, these women seemed prone to prattle endlessly over pots of tepid coffee. As Ruth led me through the well-lit room, I caught a few snippets of conversations that would no doubt be of great use to the political leaders of our separate countries.

"... and little Tim and teething still..."

"... hear about Madeline Shoemaker's party? Fell to pieces. I think she is having problems with her husband too..."

"... but if you smear butter on that..."

"... poor Tim was crying through the whole night..."

"... or if they devorce..."

"... the butter melts and..."

As it happened, I did not give a fig about a little Tim, nor a crumbling marriage, nor, thank God, what to do with butter. I was; however, infinitely disappointed that these women, the children of those brave suffragettes, would so willingly relinquish their progress and slowly crawl back to the impending stereotypes. It was their safe haven—their blanket—and ought to have been ripped away back when the 19th amendment took hold.

Ruth stopped and sat down at a table already occupied by a woman swaddled in the latest fashions and absolutely reeking of peppermints. How fitting it was then when Ruth introduced her to me as Mrs. Candace Caine. Better known to her friends as 'Candy'. As she shook my hand daintily, I noticed her eyes flickering toward my other five fingers.

"No ring, honey?" Her voice, unlike her name, was heavy and unwelcome upon one's ears.

"No. Nor am I married."

"Oh, too bad. Are you English? You sound English. You must know a lot of handsome boys over there." I assured her I did not.

"Jo is here with a *friend*." I did not appreciate Ruth's added inflection to the final word, but Mrs. Caine positively swallowed it.

"A *friend*? Well, that's different. I'm all for modern girls. Wish I'd had an affair or two before I married." I shuddered. What a laugh Keane would get out of all this.

At my expense, of course.

"He's only a business colleague. A professor, actually."

"How romantic! I read last week that professors can make the best lovers."

"I wouldn't know." Just as Keane would never know of this conversation. "And what is it you do, Mrs. Caine?"

"Do?" She laughed, a rough, dirty screech. "I'm married, honey. I don't have anything more than that. Why? Don't tell me you're a professor too." You would have thought intelligence a fatal disease from the over exaggeration of syllables flung distastefully from her mouth.

"No, a writer." A coffee glass shattered on the floor. Mrs. Caine appeared unaware of the fact, gradually floating upwards toward the conversation's surface, as though my chosen profession had dragged her under.

"Ah. A writer. Well, I suppose we need those. Don't we, Ruth?"

I DEPARTED FROM THE pair of vocational wives soon after, though it was not so much a departure as a retreat to the sanity of solitude. As evening had alighted upon the tips of buildings, the higher classes had dissipated with the sun and made room for those energetic night lives to make their appearance. It was rather like a ballet; when one group exits, another pulls the full attention of the audience until that first is hidden safe behind the curtains. They were comfortable there; hidden behind a shroud of duties and expectations.

And yet, I was not.

I stopped briefly at some obscure restaurant in the hopes of a cup of tea, but found none. Instead, they made a liquid with the same name, though the taste resembled a handful of lawn grass boiled in a pot of sewage. Liquid sewage perhaps, but even the form could not improve the horrid odour reeking from the glass. I took two sips, paid my bill, and was off again toward my room at the hotel, where I fell asleep moments after hitting the bed.

The following morning I was vaguely aware of an ache in my lower abdomen that only increased as I bathed and dressed myself for the day. It was a feeling I had felt several times throughout the course of my life and possibly more than the average person of twenty-four years.

Hunger.

I did up the laces of my shoes, grabbed my jacket, and was out the door in a matter of seconds. The morning air was heavy with fresh exhaust and the streets cluttered with the bodies of a few drunkards who had not made it to shelter during the night. Men in freshly pressed business suits pummelling the pavement with their well-polished shoes, while women shuffled about with armloads of shopping bags. Such was the life they chose to live.

Such was the life I was working so desperately to avoid.

My legs pulled me back to Dilly's Diner, which had few customers in spite of the breakfast hour. I slipped onto the same stool as last time and began glancing over the menu when an enormous clatter erupted somewhere off to my right and an object was suddenly hurling toward my head. In a burst of animalistic instinct, my hand immediately shot up into the air and grasped the glass between my fingers. The weight of it brought me back into reality just in time to realise I had an audience greater than just the boy apologising profusely as he began to sweep up the other glass shards spotting the floor like a minefield. This second person was leaning over the counter with his different colored eyes staring at me with a newfound respect.

"If it isn't Jo Lawrence. Hey, you didn't tell me you could catch like that." I pulled the menu up to my nose.

"Good morning, Frank. Now, I think I'll have—"

"—What a catch. Can you throw too?" I laid the paper on the counter, inadvertently brushing the glass I had left cautiously beside it.

"I suppose so. Why?"

"Well, see, me and the guys have this little group that gets together and plays ball every afternoon after we get off work. A lot of them are good enough to be in the majors. We are playing today, or at least we were before Clark Martin sprained his ankle sliding into second. Nothing too bad, but he's off it a whole eight days—" A spark shot across the young man's different colored eyes. "Hey, are you doing anything this week? I mean, I know we usually don't invite girls to play—in fact we never have—but I think the team would be alright with you. Heck, what does being a girl matter when you can catch better than half of them on a good day. So what do you say? The park? Today at one?" I sighed. At least he wasn't asking me to do something annoyingly feminine. In fact, he was opening a gate no other woman would walk. I grinned and picked up the menu.

"I'll be there. Now, about breakfast..."

I DID INDEED GO TO the park that afternoon. It was a grand establishment, the diamond well-kept in spite of all other filth in the world. 'The boys', as Frank constantly referred to them, were the finest example of America's melting pot as a foreigner could find. Dino Crocieti, the son of Italian immigrants and whose father was a barber just down the street, was an excellent outfielder.. John Logan, who went by Jackie after his baseball hero, was the catcher. Then there was Ned and Ben on first and second base. I was to take Clark's place at the third.

I will not dissolution myself in saying I am a grand player of the sport, but my knowledge of it assisted me greatly as I participated in throwing the ball with a strength that made a few jaws drop every now and again. We played, not for a want to demolish each other into the dust (though that did occur frequently) but for the love of the game. And when one loves a game as those boys did baseball, life itself may then be reflected.

They had done what the world had so often failed to do. They had created themselves out of the minorities to create a team that might have had a chance at the majors. And I had completed it as an incredible young man had completed the Dodgers. Only, this time, it was not the barrier of race being torn from its hinges, but the divide separating the strength of the male, and the assumed fragility of the female.

And I had done it in one, sound crack.

CHAPTER NINETEEN

SUNDAY PASSED WITH the ease of a winged chariot and Monday approached with an ungodly fury. Helios had biden me well on those days, for he was indeed out; streaking across the sky and banning clouds of impending rain. All was well in the world. I had managed to choke out the first, faint glimpse of plots for a series of short essays considering the advantages of bachelor life in comparison to an existence tied indefinitely to a man. It was a fine idea, I thought, and one I ought to have begun on that very day. However, I thought it best to gain the knowledge of a person who had earned a doctorate in that profession of bachelorhood.

And for that I needed Keane.

In light of his absence, I spent the next few days memorising the length and breadth of every street, absorbing the society I had left in my past and wallowing in the deep wealth of a library's walls. Even so, I grew exceptionally bored as time limped by, something I had not known to take effect until one afternoon when I struck out at bat for the third time that day. This would not have been a great surprise if I had not proved my merit the day before through several, well-placed homers. The boys said nothing, but the shame of my failings fell heavily upon my shoulders. I could feel them cringe as I stepped up to the plate for the last time that day, but it is so often in the dusk of our greatest failures that our finest successes take root. I hit a triple play and went back to the hotel exceptionally pleased with myself and ready for a long, luxurious, hot bath.

But of course, my wishes were not to be promptly fulfilled when the infamous hotel clerk came barreling at me the moment I entered into the lobby, his arms flailing like a madman.

"What kind of establishment do you think this is?" My shoulders immediately stiffened.

"I beg your pardon?"

"This is a respectable place, and don't think I'm not about to stand by and let you have a man up in your room. Yes, a man. He said he was your uncle from Stubenville, but no one's gonna pull a fast one on me. If he's your uncle, I'm your aunt." An uncle? It was true I had several relations from my birthplace; several of which were uncles, with only a few aunts.

Though it seemed I had another.

"Well then, *Aunt*, allow me to assure you that the man is indeed my uncle and I have asked him to come and review a great inheritance. He is a solicitor, after all, who studies the law, as well as . . ." What my association with the law began, the prospect of such a sound sum of money soon completed. The coward bowed aside and allowed me to charge up the steps, two at a time, until I entered the correct door and instantly came face to face with the light scent of cigarette smoke.

The man had dragged the desk chair to the furthest corner of the room and stretched his long legs out upon the carpet. I threw my jacket on the bed and grinned widely at my supposed relation.

"Hello, Uncle."

"Good afternoon, Lawrence. Or should I say Miss Fiona O'Brian? That was a fancy bit of trickery there, but nothing too challenging. Can it be that your imagination is falling short of its usual standards?" There was such a lightness to his voice—a rhythmic easiness—that quickly became the equivalent of a great howl of laughter. The latter of which, I quickly supplied.

"God, Keane, it has been exceptionally dull without you around." He cocked a grey eyebrow; a cloud raised over the watery blue.

"Has it really? I wouldn't have thought so with all that exercise you've been partaking in. I must say, it was rather a shock to see you playing ball with those other young lads."

"You were there? I didn't see you." But of course I saw little of anything as the baseball soared above Jack's head. "Baseball seemed a rather good use of my time."

"Indeed. However, I must object to you starving yourself 'for the love of the game', as they say. Were you aware it is nearly seven? No, of course not. Nevermind, we can find something suitable, don't you agree? None of your arguments, Lawrence. My nerves really couldn't stand such a lethal blow. You go into the washroom and get changed. I'll sit here and smoke, if you don't mind. Thank you. Off you go."

In the end, I did not bathe, but rather replaced my soiled uniform with a clean shirt and trousers. For once in my life, I even considered the addition of a bright red sweater rather than my RAF jacket, but fortunately came to my senses soon enough to veto the ridiculous notion. Keane was still smoking in the corner when I returned. Then, in one great motion, he stood and stepped fully into the dim glow of lamplight. This time the three piece suit was his, but, beyond that, he was a stranger. The dim blue eyes, entirely naked of their usual vividness, had been carved into his gaunt features. Lines had deepened into ravines, and all natural colour had been leached. I managed to hold my mouth firmly shut as he handed me my jacket and all but shoved me toward the hotel door.

The fresh air—or rather, the air exterior to the building—seemed to do him some good as he threaded my arm through his, but there was so much of him still kept at bay beneath his stony exterior. Every few cracks in the pavement I found myself unintentionally glancing up at that stolid face, firmly set upon the path of doom I hardly dared express. The dark shadows of exhaustion tugged relentlessly at his eyes, giving him the rather eerie effect of those men of war staggering along the battlines.

Men who would drop dead only a few metres later.

I thought these horrid, blasphemous things in the depth of a still silence. But even silence did not keep his eyes from catching mine as I stared up for what must have been the thousandth time.

"Do I not look acceptable, Lawrence? I did manage a quick shave and change of shirt before I came."

I washed my face and hands afore I come, I did.

"No, it's not that. You just look . . . tired." I felt my companion stiffen for a moment before again allowing his arm to relax.

"Is that really anything absurdly unusual for a human being? I have spent the past several nights playing an ungodly amount of checkers and serving as both doctor and jailer. In that time I have also been subjected to a man's constant attacks of shell-shock while smoking seldom and eating even less." My companion waved away my concern with a quick flick of his hand through the chilled air. "You needn't worry about James at the moment. I have a medical friend watching him until I return." Within the next few strides, Keane veered off into a nearby restaurant, wheeling me in tow. We were swept to a table and I sat quietly as Keane ordered a meal more than sufficient to subside the hunger of a giant. As the waiter strode away, my companion sat back from the table with his eyelids half closed against the evening lights. His despondent features strained more in this position, establishing a heavy knot in the pit of my stomach. I cleared my throat.

"I'm sorry, Keane. I suppose I didn't know everything—that is, I didn't think James would need—God, Keane, I'm sorry." He took a sip from his water glass before offering me a weary smile.

"It's hardly your fault. Come now, Lawrence, that look of hopeless guilt does not become you. There are already a sufficient number of people who spend their days drowning in sorrow. I knew an old woman in Cork who, having lost her only son in the war of independence, spent her days knitting. Nothing more than knitting. Everyday she grew older and uglier behind those needles and frowns. By the time she died, she was a hundred and ten with a wart on her nose." I chuckled, causing Keane to edge further from the brink of sleep's hand. "That's much better. It does me good to see you smile, and to do it often. Now, shall we continue this path to nowhere, or might we have a real conversation? How is your writing? Any new plots growing in that marvellous imagination of yours?"

"I've decided on a series of essays. About bachelorhood." I thought my companion would fall from his chair.

"I would hardly think a young woman could write knowledgeably on such a topic."

"I shall attribute your lapse of stereotypical thinking to a lack of proper sleep. Of course, a woman alone might not have *all* of the details that could create a respectable paper, but surely you could spare a few facts that may mortar the bricks together." He chuckled dryly, swirling the water around in his glass.

"'*A bachelor's life is a fine breakfast, a flat lunch, and a miserable dinner.*'"

"Francis Bacon. Though, I believe it is better to recall that, as a woman, there are those bachelors one ought never let too near.." I watched with no end of satisfaction as Keane made ready his stark reply just as our food was brought forth to the table.

"I see." He said at last as the waiter's arm withdrew. "Sound advice that, though not idealistic to the remainder of the population. What a place the world would be if people could say things straight out, rather than hiding themselves in lines of absolute dribble."

"You ought to tell that to Mrs. Caine."

"Mrs. *who*?" I proceed to explain the entire incident of Ruth Woodsworth and her brigade of prattling women, who found more value in life tied to a supposed husband than to live oneself. It would be amusing if it weren't so damnable to my half of the sex. Keane, on the other hand, listened intently as he shovelled laden forkfuls of meat into his mouth, nodding with every other word and asking questions when convenient. As the conversation wound on, I managed to explain even the most miniscule detail of my brief career as a female ball player, while making light of the fact the rest of the team were men. *Young* men. I did; however, bring to his attention the variety in that rag-tag team.

Keane eventually leaned back in his chair, his coffee half drunk and brow lowered in concentration. After a long instant, I had feared him to be nearing night's dreary grasp, but his voice shattered all doubt; coming warm and rich as the food which had once filled our plates.

"It is good, Lawrence, that you appreciate such freedoms in life. There are some who have not been granted with the gifts you and I have known throughout our lives. Are you by any chance familiar with the works of William DuBois?"

"Vaguely." I admitted. Keane shifted further against the back of his chair and tugged thoughtfully at his ear.

"You should make yourself aware. He is a most incredible man with ideas well established in a proper morality. I shan't be foolhardy enough to say that other countries in our world are innocent of the maltreatment of our fellow men, but America—America has that singular talent of ignoring the obvious and magnifying the superfluous. Lawrence, I am pleased to see in you some hope for your nation, just as Daniel O'Connell was for mine. We are only truly products of our nation's psychology for so long as we wish to be. But we must not blindly follow a cause we do not fully understand. To do so would be the start of yet another plague of war, and I pray I'll be long since rotting below the earth when that day occurs." His words, spoken with such conviction and enforced by years of wisdom, filled my mind as sweet nectar doth a bee's hive; instilling a renewed urge for work that might be praised by him who hath spoken.

Keane motioned our waiter and reached for his billfold.

"I think a brisk walk would be welcome before retiring tonight. That is, Lawrence, if you are free?"

"As a bird." My companion nodded solemnly.

"Good. And you wouldn't object to me taking an adjacent room at the hotel? I find the long working hours aren't quite so manageable as they once were."

"Object? Keane, between fueling the tongue of that damn clerk and scraping your remains off of the road after you collapse, I would prefer it."

I SLEPT EXCEPTIONALLY well that night, far better than I had those several darkened days before. The heavy blankets pinning me down to the mattress cradled me with a gentle warmth I could not place, but would not, in all sanity, reject. It was as if the entire world had been righted for my sake. Night had made victory over the day's exhaustion and I could rest in the knowledge that—for that night, at least—I could relax and know myself through the richest gift no human may ever bestow, but can take away when the idea suits them. Sleep. The tell-tale titterings of an overactive mind ceased until the moment that following morning when a solid knock echoed against my door.

I snatched my jacket, ensuring it was well-zipped before unlatching the wooden barrier.

"Good morning, Keane. I trust you had a good night's rest." It wasn't a question. Questions ought to be reserved for times when one requires an answer. My response had already come through my companion's impeccable appearance and the uncanny scents that accompany a visit to the barber. The heavy creases and shadows, which had marred his face the night before, had been lifted by sleep's priceless gift and a hot towel. His shoes had been freshly polished. His collar had the ideal amount of starch. And no doubt there was a new package of cigarettes somewhere in his pockets.

I caught the masculine scent of his cologne as he strode past into the hotel room.

"And a very fine morning to you as well, Lawrence. By God, I haven't felt so alive in ages. It's incredible what sleep can do for a man. The *'universal king of God and man'*"

"Homer." I noted, but I was not certain Keane heard me as he strode to the windows and flung them open in one strong swoop. A blast of fresh air struck my nostrils with its sweetness.

"Get dressed, Lawrence. We are going to breakfast."

"It may take me a minute." Keane turned and faced me, hands clasped loosely behind his back.

"Of course. But hurry. I ought to be back with James by eleven."

"Must you go back so soon?"

"Well, I can hardly leave him to his own devices after all our work, now can I? Why? Have I forgotten something?"

"No, it's just . . . well . . . it's odd not having you around to consult. And those lines for the play—" I let out an exaggerated sigh as I slipped into the washroom.

"Oh, those. Don't worry, you'll get the hang of it, right enough." His confidence was, if nothing else, vaguely reassuring to my bruised and battered ego. But it did not change the knowledge he was an olympic champion swimmer, while I was but a goldfish tossed out into the sea. I had not his grace or charm or chivalry or anything else I had long ago attributed to his infallible masculinity. I did; however, have a script pounded out by a typewriter and a basket of flowers to be sold in Covent Garden.

"HOW THE DEVIL DO YOU do it?" I interrogated as Keane cut into the eggs lying limp on his plate.

"How the devil do I what? Verbs, my dear Lawrence. The Lord made them for a reason."

"How do you play Henry Higgins as you do? How do you represent that character on stage so well? All I can get out of Eliza is a cynical flower girl whose hobby is to whine until everyone wants to throw her out the nearest window." My companion let out a deep chuckle and laid his eatery diagonally across the plate.

"Well, in this particular instance, I have the advantage of playing the man before in London. It was many years ago, mind you, but it doesn't take long to get back into character. However, I also have to completely rethink how I play the role, otherwise it would be like putting on an old overcoat. That would hardly be creative." I watched attentively as he quietly ate a bit of sausage before continuing. "You see, Lawrence, in the theatre you are working with human beings; one helping another to better themselves through a growth of personality, as well as knowledge and acceptance. Pygmalion is really a story that dates back to the beginning of civilization. To willingly overlook that piece of information is to make a mockery of life itself." I sighed and prodded half-heartedly at my own breakfast.

"You do make a good point for the man, woman-hater though he may be."

"Oh, I wouldn't say Higgins is a 'woman-hater'. He may be a little afraid of women, and I have a healthy respect for that. A fear of women is one of the wisest tools for the modern man. It gives women a sense of security and men a priceless sense of sanity."

I could have slapped him.

The audacity!

The cheek!

But, oh, the gentleness with which he said it. That vague grin that always made the world seem so dreadfully small and life so wonderfully full.

It was also one of his best defences against a solid smack to his jaw.

"Keane, I swear, if you say that once more, I shall create a character in your name and make it the most infernal, frustrating man ever to ruin the pages of a perfectly good novel. Stop laughing! I mean it!" I raised my head in cruel defiance to his show of hilarity until at last he threw up his hands; the sweetest show of surrender.

"Very well, Lawrence, I bow to your wishes. Perhaps in a few years; however, you will realise I was quite right in what I said."

"Perhaps." I conceded grudgingly. "But, even if I do, don't expect me to admit it." The restaurant erupted in a sharp bark of laughter which gradually softened into the fading edge of a hearty chuckle.

"I would expect nothing less from such an educated young woman. I must say, though, that you completely wasted your time with that degree in English. You ought to have studied law and thrown all the fat leeches in parliament out on their backsides. But no matter. Any degree would have suited you marvellously, and you made a logical decision based on your chosen profession. Logical impulsiveness is a fine thing to have. Cherish those impulses. Know thyself and you shall know the whole of the world."

And, from that moment onward, I knew Keane had been right all along.

CHAPTER TWENTY

"NO, NO, NO. THAT'S not even close to what I want. Walter, open your eyes you damn oaf. We have a show to put on here." The young man, always eager to oblige, jerked his scrawny form toward the other end of the stage, tripping over my shoe and nearly toppling over the wooden edge. Harrison's gaunt and pale face sharpened and a hand shot through the air with a screech of fury. "You stupid, no good, son of a fucking—"

"Lunch!" Keane bellowed, releasing all the people from the theatre in one deep lurch of his voice. All, that is, save myself and the director. "James, sit down." My companion demanded. Though his voice held not the viciousness so often used in the heat of anger, there was just enough bite to his English clip that the grown man fell easily into one of the theatre chairs and sunk a weary head into his hands. Keane too settled his long form into one of the cushioned seats, heaving a sigh that caused his ribcage to visibly retreat into the rest of his frame.

"James, are you certain you are well enough to continue all these rehearsals? It could be another week at least before your strength fully returns. Often a good deal longer." Keane's voice came not as some gentle hum of knowledge, but the gunfire of a cold, indisputable fact. Harrison jerked in his seat.

"And would loosing five thousand fucking dollars fix this damn body of mine any faster? Don't you see, Brendan, this is exactly what Cohen wants; to ruin me and let me die a penniless man. That is, if he doesn't kill me instead. I am nothing but a standing target. An old man. A—"

"Oh, stop being overdramatic." I snapped from my position still on the heavily-lit stage. "So you bought your Hydrocodone from this Cohen character. Fine. Surely Keane and I could afford paying that debt." In all honesty, I was not entirely certain of the amounts tucked safely away in my companion's various bank accounts, but Mrs. McCarthy had often hinted to an amount more than sufficient to any man. While this was, no doubt, a fine example of acute exaggeration, I knew my own accounts well and was by no means unaware of their bounty.

Keane glanced approvingly at me and gave a short nod.

"Lawrence is quite right. Name the amount and I will contact my solicitors immediately. Give us the devil's number. No, I will not listen to arguments. This is no time for fool hearted chivalry. Now, what is it? Six thousand? Seven?" The amount the director did indeed name was considerably more than that, but my companion did not so much as blink before drawing out his chequebook. To my surprise, it was Harrison who appeared more unstable with each stroke of Keane's pen, and not, I thought, out of some masculine embarrassment.

"Your offer is extremely generous—more than generous—but I am afraid there is more—er—weight to my problem than you could possibly fix. You see, I had this affair—"

Damn it.

Of course he did.

"I loved her, Brendan. Honest to God I did. We were young, reckless, foolish, and..." The director's head once more dropped into his hands. "There was a child." Keane's face remained stolid as the string of lethal bullets whizzed past his ears.

"A child." God, even his voice sounded calm—*logical*—as his eyes slowly absorbed the onslaught of information.

A child.

Damn it.

Of course there was a child.

Harrison sucked a harsh gasp between his slightly parted lips. I had feared the man had worked himself into an inconsolable state of depression when his voice again came, coarse, dry, and wavering on the edge of obscurity.

"He was born less than three years after my marriage to Marilyn. I couldn't tell her what I had done. What I had procreated. Our relationship was already suffering due to my other... various ailments. To know I had a child—a son—by another woman; that would have killed her." A heavy silence fell between us, only interrupted by the faint click of Keane's cigarette case and those first few wisps of tobacco smoke entering the air. It was him, my companion, friend, and wise mentor, who spoke first.

"James, while I do not deny your situation is an uncomfortable one, it is hardly an uncommon occurrence. You are not the first war-stricken soldier to find comfort in the arms of another woman."

"She was black."

Oh.

Keane's head gave a slight jerk, but I knew I was the only one to notice so small a discrepancy. He was not, nor had he ever been condescending toward anyone on the basis of race or ethnicity. In fact, I had watched him give various speeches regarding the importance of integration, and that all people—men and women, black or white—were indeed equal in the eyes of God, and therefore should be viewed the same by the various government agencies plaguing the United States. The country had sworn that all men were created equal; that a person's worth came not from their ancestry or heritage, but by birthright. They entered into this world, and ought to be given protected freedoms like their neighbour, their neighbour's cousin, and those so following.

What hypocrites.

I shifted my position on the stage, allowing my legs to dangle over the edge like an attentive youth fishing on a dock.

"So? Yes, that may throw the proverbial wrench in the works when it comes to the child, but I don't see why race is a problem." Why was race ever a problem? "If one may marry whom one likes, why would an affair be unreasonable?" Keane flinched angrily in his seat, dropping a small smudge of ash onto his trousers.

"Lawrence, may I remind you this is not England? There are different laws and mores here that are intended to be followed, however immoral and ridiculous they may be."

"But surely that damnable law about interracial marriage doesn't apply to . . . er . . . indescresions of the heart." The two pools of silver fire glaring up at me gave me an answer so clear I would not require a duplicate.

Damn.

Harrison snatched up one of Keane's offered cigarettes.

"The law might not come charging after me, but Cohen's fucking goons sure as hell did. Some just wanted to bring that son of a bitch his extra money to keep my information on the down low, but others—like that Smith girl—included their own personal prices in addition to Cohen's already inflated rates. She just wanted a part in this show, but others wanted extra green to line their own pockets. Can't say I'm sorry she died, but I tell you, seeing something like that makes you get off the white stuff faster than—" The director snapped his fingers through the air with such passion I almost didn't consider the blatant fact that he did not 'get off the stuff' by sheer willpower. No, that had been Keane who had supplied the ambition on his behalf. It had been Keane who had stayed awake for several consecutive nights only to stagger into my hotel room as the last fleeting glimpse of a man desperate for sleep and a hearty meal. As though I had said this aloud, my companion leaned back in his chair with a voice softer than the lazy, white clouds of smoke encircling his head.

"What happened to the child?" Harrison shrugged.

"I never knew." He never knew if his son was dead or alive. He never knew if that boy of his was making him proud in the cesspool of business or lying dead in some flimsy excuse of a grave dug just a few feet down in enemy soil.

He never knew.

But the fact that the boy had, at one time or another, existed, was enough to ruin him forever.

THAT EVENING, AS KEANE and I retreated from the theatre's battleground, I found him to be excessively silent; far more so than what was necessary when driving an automobile on evening's deserted streets. My questions involving this infamous Meyer Cohen were met with a wall of indifference mortared together with a near obsessive attention of the empty roads winding toward the coast. The last few birds of the air chittered along the telephone wires that struck through dusk's dimming haze. If they could hold their petty discussions, Keane and I could certainly have one of our own. I stared at the window a moment longer before glancing at my companion.

"You've been horribly silent ever since Harrison shared that rather unexpected lesson in the art of procreation. Care to state your opinion?"

"On procreation?"

"Most any subject would be some sort of an improvement, albeit an uncomfortable one. Keane, I swear, if you don't start answering at least a few of my questions about this Cohen fellow, I might just go and ask him myself." His entire body convulsed violently, hurling us dangerously near to the road's edge before he again dragged the hunk of machinery back toward a respectable path.

"You would—by God, Lawrence, only a desperate woman would do something so foolish."

"Foolish? I hardly think it is foolish to want some information about the enemy. No doubt the Navy trained you to identify German ships and submarines, else you might have been taken captive or . . ." I hardly needed to continue, for my point had sufficiently shaken both our minds into a reality neither wished to walk. Keane's entire form seemed stone against the moving horizon; a constant that would not be deterred. I reached into my pockets for the little package, lit a cigarette, and handed it to him. One, swift, long draw was all it took to see that tightness in his face relax into—not pleasantness—but acceptance.

"Lawrence, I believe you are misguided in your inquiry." I opened my mouth and was immediately silenced by a frigid glimpse of ice. "You are misguided because you really don't give a damn about Mickey Cohen, or perhaps not to the extent you intend me to believe. No, you have fallen into that constant state of curiosity."

"Curiosity? Curiosity be hanged! What would I have to be curious about?"

"Me."

"You?" I gaped openly at my companion, who wrenched the car a bit sharply around a right turn, allowing the centrifugal force to edge me closer to him. I caught that sharp scent of his cologne mixing with the dull brush of hair pomade and the vanilla of his tobacco. It was all incredibly familiar, as was that omnipotent glance in my direction once we were again steadfast on the road.

"Lawrence, at times you have the tactful qualities of an air raid siren. You think I am depressed. You think I am on the brink of becoming some crotchety old man listlessly looking upon my life with regret for not having done those little ceremonies expected of a man. I have not married, nor have I enrooted my lineage in this young generation. I was too old for this last skirmish against the Germans and their allies, and, even if I had a son, I don't believe I would have been like those other fathers and encouraged him to go marching into battle as some mighty proof of manhood. I have already walked that path, and I would be a fool to make him do the same. No, Lawrence, I am an ordinary man. I desire nothing more than a life well-stocked with books and the time to do as I please. Not once has a woman tied me to her apron strings or set me by the fireplace like a pet poodle with no more purpose than to drink himself to sleep for the sheer peace of it." I took his words like an old wine; the taste honed through years of thought, and yet the subject was not to my taste. I would be a liar if I said I had not thought of matrimony before in those years of my youth. I had even toyed with the idea when I found myself staring at the ceiling, rather than drifting off into sleep. The honest truth was that I did not want children. It wasn't that I minded having to watch other people's children, or that they were wretched little creatures like other people believed. I just didn't really want to be a parent.

A mother.

That was another problem.

I never found great trust instilled in some woman who cared or watched over me. I could not trust them. And yet I could trust myself. I could trust myself and this man at my side more than I could my own mother, if I had trusted her at all. It wasn't as though I hadn't made an effort to be a systematic child. I had tried several times. But that trust had been broken, along with my own mind, so many times that I had lost all grasp of what it meant to truly and honestly trust another human being. I was alone in the world. Alone.

Keane must have understood my silence, for he said nothing more as we wound our way toward the beach house; inching ever closer at a steady and relaxing pace complementary to the waning day. The light tap of his long, tapered fingers along the steering wheel gave music to my soul and sent my mind along a finer path well travelled in times of peace. The last few drops of sun caught Keane's silhouette and reflected it through the window as he stepped from the automobile and began that long, easy stride up toward the painted door. A key appeared from the depths of his pockets, strung to its cousins with a metal ring. He pushed the door gently open, took one step forward, and bowed to collect a sparse selection of envelopes from the floor; shuffling through them as he entered further into the house. Rubber seals were torn open carelessly and one article after another was flung aside until the handful of useless correspondence was flung across the floor. Only one still remained in Keane's slender hands, the white edges still unopened as he turned it over and over. He caught my curious glance and chuckled.

"From Bridget. Mrs. McCarthy must have forwarded it, God bless her." In the past year I had grown to believe there were no two siblings in the world closer than Keane was to his sister. He had played protector for much of her life, even when he was thousands of miles away fighting his own war.

The first war.

I watched eagerly as he methodically cut open the envelope's paper lip; tugging from it a letter that naturally would have taken him only a minute or so to read, but he took his time; those blue eyes tasting every syllable of the child-like penmanship before swallowing it all as a fine wine.

"I take it she and Sean are well?" My companion's attention slowly released the paper with a nostalgic smile.

"Quite. She has even taken up lessons in embroidery from one of the neighbours. Alice is also grand, if you cared to know." I chuckled. Alice was as much a friend to Bridget as any person could be. The only unusual aspect was her existence as a worn rag doll Keane had bought for his sister decades before. As he began folding the letter away, I started plucking the other envelopes from the floor. Most of it was rubbish, but one article succeeded to catch my attention where it had obviously escaped Keane's.

"Sofia Livens?" I asked.

"Mm? Oh, yes. She's the wife or something of one of the young stage hands. Never met her personally, though?" I skimmed over the card's contents.

"Looks like some sort of invitation." It was not by imagination Keane groaned.

"No doubt for something tedious and absolutely dripping with self-proclaimed scholars. Throw it away."

"The party is this Saturday at seven. Rehearsal ends at six." My companion, who had disappeared somewhere in the kitchen, now reappeared with his cigarette case at the ready.

"And since when has Jo Lawrence ever been a social butterfly?"

"Really, Keane," I scoffed. "I am *not* becoming infatuated with the idea. I was just . . . curious."

"Which was the downfal of the saber toothed tiger, wooly mamoths, and, eventually, the female sex as we know it. A pity."

"Well don't get your hopes up. There are those of us who know when to avoid tar pits in favour of a paved road. I mean, why would I want to spend my afternoon discussing nothing more interesting than the recent Hollywood wardrobe." Keane's eyebrow arched and his eyes twinkled with amusement even after I tried to brush the matter aside with my hand. "Besides, if you're not going, why would I want to go?"

"It might be good for you. Get away and be with people your own age. Antisocial behaviour is rarely good for your health, Lawrence."

"It may not be advisable, but it certainly saves one's sanity not going to those sorts of things." I protested. "Besides, you turned out alright." That at least earned a light chuckle from my companion.

"Kind though it is for you to say such a thing, and while I can hardly disagree, I think it would be best if you attended this party."

"But you yourself admitted it would be tedious."

"And how often do you heed my advice? No, Lawrence, you shall go to Miss Livens' while I see what I can do about Meyer Cohen. Perhaps, with some success, we will be back in England by the start of October."

Blast.

I didn't think I could survive another day in America, let alone weeks.

I threw myself almost violently into the nearest hideous chair like a rugby player diving for the ball.

"But, Keane, I don't *like* my generation. It's all about 'so-and-so' and 'he said' and 'she said'. Nothing is ever based on facts. Everything is according to another person who made a comment when they were roaring drunk that made some sort of sense to another intoxicated mind. I hate it." A cigarette slipped gracefully from the silver case. Though lit, Keane took the time to wave the burning object through the air a bit before drawing in great breaths of the white haze.

"You have not only described your generation, Lawrence. You have explained society as it has been passed down through the ages. There is something about being drunk that gives a person more educational accolades than a doctorate. Because they know to stagger around giddily, people expect them to comprehend life. We could hardly follow their example. If we did, we would all end up like James; slipping pills down our throats and enduring our existence through a dull haze. We wouldn't feel any pain, but . . . no amount of pain is worth a loss of joy, Lawrence. Never lose that joy of life—that hope for what is to come. If I have one regret, it is that my life has been plagued with events which have deadened the light of the world into a dim dusk." The fractured syllables—the raspiness of his voice—was something rare and, on the whole, concerning. I had heard Keane speak in slivers of his life, but the morose nature of certain events never broke into this sadness I now saw behind his eyes. Here he was, a man who loved life and the depths of society, and yet the world seemed determined to dislike him for wanting to understand the earth he was set to walk. He wanted to understand, so he did.

And that hurt him more than anything.

CHAPTER TWENTY-ONE

SOFIA LIVENS' HOME was not large itself, but behind it sat the popular point which warranted the dozens of people conducting themselves wildly outdoors on such a blistering hot day.

A swimming pool.

And so I discovered the singularly discomforting moment at the water's rigid edge in an absurdly boorish conversation with a boy a year or so older than myself with infinitely less common sense. What was his name? Tyler? Travis? Tony? No, Trevor. Yes, that sounded right. Trevor Stevens. God, what a bore. It would have been a miracle to find anything more than the latest football scores filling the area between his two pitifully large ears. I listened to the hellish numbers longer than I thought possible until the young man was finally called away to a swarm of giggling girls: girls who had little on their minds not inclusive to a life steamed with passionate romance and ending in a disappointing marriage.

Beads of sweat had begun to form along the nape of my neck and trickled downward to soak shamelessly into the cotton collar of my shirt. Had I known there would be swimming, I might have had the foresight to bring my bathing suit. But I had not known; therefore, I was stuck sitting along the edge of the pool in a hot cotton blouse and trousers that were just as uncomfortable as could possibly be imagined. The thick brown fabric clung to my legs and created great rivers of sweat to drip into my socks and shoes.

God, how appalling.

"It helps to put your feet in the water." My head naturally jerked upwards, forcing me to shield my eyes from the sun's devastating glare. The man towering over me was at least thirty, though I suspected slightly more. There was a distinct macherity to his face, as though he had seen the best the world had to offer and found it was made especially for him. His skin had been tanned to an even bronze with eyes so dark the pupils swallowed the irises whole. Brown hair sat ruffled on his head as a pile of twigs waiting to be caught alight by a careless match. It was as though he had just woken with no chance of going back to sleep; as if he had too much to live for to spend a third of his life in bed. That is, whatever he did at night, I did not believe it included sleep. I immediately hated him and liked him within the same moment. It was not his party, and yet he was Gatsby; roaming between the guests with nary a care in the world. I squinted up at him for only a second more before tying my eyes down toward the water's crystal, shimmering surface.

"I am perfectly content with my shoes on, thank you." There was such finality in my words I had hoped he would go off and leave me be like Travis—no, *Trevor*—had done. But unfortunately, he lowered himself leisurely beside the pool and outstretched his legs so the soles of his bare feet dangled over the edge of the pavement, hovering only a breath away from the water.

"I'm Sam Barker. Let me guess, you're Jo." My gaze flickered from the water for a painful moment.

"How did you guess?"

"You're the only one on Sofie's list I haven't seen before. Her parties are known as the hot weeklies. Same people. Same day. Same time."

"Oh." Stunning reaction that, a true accolade representing years of ceaseless dedication to the furthering of my education. I had a mind carefully melded to accommodate the most pristine words of the English language. Through Keane I had grown fluent in the more practical languages, as well as a brief smattering of Gaelic; absorbed more through moments of necessity than a formal drilling of the grammar. All this, and what could I muster?

Oh.

Bloody Marvellous.

I tried again.

"These things are weekly then? Sounds like an awful lot of bother." Sam Barker stared at me before letting his eyes wander aimlessly about the roaring party guests.

"I guess it could be, but it is really more a celebration of those of us who have nothing better to do. I throw a party every week at my house. A big smash. You should come sometime."

"What about work?"

"What about it?" I ripped all my attention from a bug skimming the surface of the swimming pool.

"Are you saying you don't work?" It shouldn't have surprised me. He smiled and slid his bare feet into the water where that bug had once been.

"Why should I? I have enough money to last me a lifetime. Two, if I feel like going around twice. No reason to waste my time in some old office. Don't tell me *you* work?"

"I'm a writer." He grinned.

"You mean like a magazine writer? I've met a few of those in my time. Had a lot more energy under the covers than—"

"I mean a *writer* writer. I'm a novelist." His face plummeted lower than the most acute case of disappointment, though it was not a reaction foreign to me by any means. At last he cleared his throat and squinted upwards toward the sun. "What does your husband think of that? You working, I mean." The ice ran cold and fast through my veins and my fists clenched into iron blocks.

"I'm not married." I cleared my throat; a painful action. "And if I was, you can be certain he wouldn't give a damn about my career as a writer. He would at least be supportive of women reentering the workforce." Sam Barker sat up a little straighter.

"So you're one of those feminists types. I should have known. Seems every girl is now. Babbling on about women's careers and all that. You should be thankful we gave you the vote."

By tongues of men, from lack of thought.

"I wouldn't say I was a feminist, but I wouldn't say I wasn't either. And as for women, you men should recognise us more. A friend once told me that everything is relative. I believe that includes our perspectives of others, as well as ourselves."

"Who said that? Einstein?"

"Probably, at one time or another, but he wasn't the one who told it to me. That makes all the difference."

I LEFT THE PARTY JUST as I had come; expecting nothing and gaining less. Something Sam Barker had said—if he had really said anything—struck me with the weight of the world. Einstein had indeed made some offhanded comment regarding the relativity of life, but Keane had mentioned it first on one of our sailing trips. I remembered it vividly; the tossing of the sea, the churning of the ocean, my companion fiddling with the sail, and the crisp English tones of his voice skimming effortlessly over the frothy waves.

"Never surrender to the stupidity of categorization, Lawrence. From where you stand, you shall always see a subject differently from another's eyes. The stars may appear insignificant flames from here, but we are but dust to them. Everything is relative."

I had only smiled then, a brief grin and some strand of words that meant so little now I can only recall they were incredibly well mannered and obhorrably dull. They were nothing like those great philosophical lines that poured from Keane's mouth as honey from a diligent hive.

Everything is relative.

Just as I became warmed by these three words, God lashed out his hand and sent great torrents of rain hurling down upon this speck of dust floating beneath the stars. The colour of life drained away into shades of varying grey; outlined with black paint dripping from the sky. That yellow California sun ran away to be replaced by half a dozen ominous clouds, scoffing at our lives sheltered from what we wish to ignore.

What fools we were then.

I hesitated, which is not an unusual occurrence when both sides of one's mind are occupied in a heated debate which marks the division between separate articles of one person. Some femininity that had survived banishment insisted I turn round immediately and call a taxi. Surely that was not too weak and womanly a thing. In fact, the more those damnable droplets found their way down my neck, the more reasonable that desire became. But the consequences of one's actions are so often worse than enduring some temporary discomfort. And the truth was I had no energy to return to the party and again submerge myself in a society of young people. I disliked young people as a whole and deplored them as individuals. Not all of them perhaps, but I had found a sufficient number of poor representations to soil the group as a whole. I really ought to have been thankful to the rain for chasing away the blistering heat and giving me a viable excuse to return to my own environment. I could no longer bear the bending and bowing to chivalrous graces and laughs that bubbled upwards like overpriced champagne. To endure such mental pain for so long was not only dangerous to one's sense of pride, but no doubt one's back as well.

Of course, it had occurred to me that I would need some sort of transportation back to the beach house; however, at that exact moment, I was suddenly and inexplicably content with being aimless. I travelled on the winds of instinct, sheltered by the colored canopies jutting outwards from the various storefronts as overstretched umbrellas. There is some virtue in being a wanderer. When you forget to worry about where you are going, you are not concerned about how you get there. I passed people desperately seeking shelter, yet there was a glorious feeling pent up in my soul, which was slowly released with every step along that mirrored pavement. So intent did I become on my imaginary axis, my eyes shielded themselves from my surroundings, only to have the blinders completely torn away by a strong hand maliciously clamping down over my mouth.

I lashed outwards; fists and shoes begging to meet unsuspecting flesh. Every jerk shot a dose of adrenaline through my veins. Heart pounding. Muscles screaming. Head whirling. A single glimpse of pinstriped cotton was enough to fuel my efforts further as my assailant dragged me toward the ominous alley. My fingers clawed at fabric sleeves until I heard the painful creaking of overtaxed bones on the verge of snapping. They were not mine, but that of the figure who's shoulder I now had twisted in a way that was believed anatomically impossible without complete separation from said limb to the rest of the strong body. It was a loud cough of a voice that exploded through my ear as the hand pressed further against my mouth. I recognised not the frozen rasps of words, but the words themselves held some familiarity. I had no choice. I fought harder until a great cannon fire shattered my eardrums with its close proximity.

"For God's sake, stop struggling before you hurt yourself." I slammed my heels into the sopping pavement and spun round with fists at the ready.

"Keane, if you don't want me to fight, it may be best to find another way to gain my attention. Brute force does not give a pleasant impression. Besides, you should be more concerned with injury to your own limbs before you begin analysing mine. I do hope your shoulder hurts for a while." An appraisal of the man crushed all hopes of ensuring some physical discomfort. His arms appeared fully intact without the slightest twinge of onsetting pain. But, where I was seemingly incapable of unravelling the muscles of a person's complex anatomy, Keane's necktie had been sufficiently disturbed from its infamous knot.

This; however, was quickly remedied by a few casual strokes of his long fingers.

"Well?" He lifted a grey fedora from the dirt at his feet, brushed the rim, and placed it rakishly on his head. "How do I look?"

"Ridiculous. Utterly ridiculous. If Mrs. McCarthy could see you now—with your hair slicked back and that vulgar suit—never again would she complain about your tweeds."

"I admit the style is rather... flamboyant." Obnoxious, more like. "And I can't say I am particularly fond of the cut of the jacket, but 'weeping may endure for a night, but joy comes in the morning.'"

"And what might that joy be? Nevermind, I don't want to know."

"You don't?" A greying eyebrow climbed high on his forehead. "And here I thought that adventurous spirit of yours would leap at the chance to enjoy those fruited seeds of prohibition."

"Now I really must decline. You aren't suggesting we *raid* some mafia hideaway to find what? Armed murderers?"

"A photograph. A rather *compromising* photograph depicting James and his maîtresse. Remember, Lawrence, ours is not a task of attack, per se. Merely an act of infiltration. But come, we mustn't stand out in the open like this." Keane's gentle fingers fell upon my arm and pulled me further into the dark shadows of the alley. I allowed my legs to follow his lead, and yet my mind had not yet fallen into his path.

"Let's say—hypothetically speaking, or course—I did go along with whatever it is you're doing. What the devil would I disguise myself as? A blasted fly on the wall?" My companion smiled; a boyish glow banishing the creases of his face to the unnatural gleam of his eyes.

I wished I hadn't asked.

CHAPTER TWENTY-TWO

ALL MY PRIDE—EVERY inch of disillusioned superiority—shattered in a single blast of teetering life meeting the solid wood of poorly crafted floorboards.

"Lawrence?" There was little true concern in the voice flickering over the creased edge of the morning newspaper, only a question created to stifle a bubble of impending laughter. I scraped myself off the floor, planted my hands on my hips, and glared down at the reclining man before me.

"Damn it, Keane, these blasted shoes have a heel two inches too high and absolutely no laces with which to keep them secured to my feet. I swear, if I sprain an ankle, you can be sure I will be chasing after you with a knife."

"I would very much like to see that; galavanting about with a sprained ankle indeed. You might at least like to create a threat which may be less ridiculous and more logical: one to strike fear into your prey"

"You're hardly prey. Besides, what good would I be to you limping around like an injured deer? None. May I please take them off now?"

"Do as you like." I did. I tore the shoes from my wronged feet and flung the offending objects on the opposite end of the sofa from Keane. The heels were a vulgar red with a polished piece scarcely covering the toe and heel and a thin strap buckling over the top of the foot itself. Oriental women had their feet bound.

We had ours bent and broken.

I threw myself into a chair, which had no doubt suffered worse abuse in its time, and began rubbing my scraped ankles.

"Why couldn't we stay at a hotel? This flat is hardly large enough to room a family of mice." The newspaper slowly folded in half and Keane thrust it onto the low table between us before standing; pulling me to my feet with him.

"We may turn to a hotel when our act has reached perfection, but not before. Walls must be torn and rebuilt with precision, and, unlike Rome, we only have a matter of days. Now," Keane towered over me, his greasy American brand pomade banishing much of the curl and wave from his hair. "Say it again. 'Buy me a drink.'"

"Buy me . . . a drink?"

"No, Lawrence, it is not a question of whether or not you want a drink, but if the person will buy it for you. And try to sound more American. Britain will forgive you under the circumstances. Again."

"Buy *me* a drink."

"No inflection on the pronouns. Again."

"Buy me a *drink*."

"No. Again."

"Damn it all! Buy. Me. A. Drink." My companion's arms jerked wildly into the air above his head before diving down for his cigarette case.

"No. No, that will not do. Tell me, what is this girl feeling?"

"What girl?"

"You, of course. Or whatever name you use for an acceptable alias." I sighed, folding my arms across my chest with my fingers gripping painfully into the flesh of my arms.

"Well, what name would you like me to use?"

"Blast it all, I don't give a damn what name you use as long as you respond to it." I thought for a moment, my mind reeling through the thousands of proper nouns to possibly fit the occasion. It had to be something unique (not Elizabeth or Emma or Mary), but still retaining enough dignity to separate my character between a woman who takes pleasure in life and one who makes pleasure a profession. At last I glanced past my companion's shoulder with an air I hoped to resemble nonchalance.

"How about I go by... Natasha?" So violent a reaction ought not ever befall the force of man. Keane's fists slammed into his pockets as the roar of machine gun fire spat from his slightly opened mouth.

"Like hell you will! That name is no better than the calling card of a painted woman! Choose something else! Consuela?" I scoffed.

"I hardly look like a *Consuela*. And really, Keane, 'like hell'? What an American thing to say. I do hope it isn't catching." My feeble attempt at humour met a wall of fire and was immediately burnt to ash as he stuffed the end of a cigarette hurriedly between his lips.

"Do what you like, but you are *not* using Natasha. I forbid it."

"You do, do you?" I felt the singing flickers of a flame edge upward through my face. "Well then I have half a mind to do it. What do you have against the name anyway? It sounds incredibly interesting. Exotic even. Italian perhaps?"

"You're wasting time. Say it again. 'Buy me a drink.'"

"I won't say that damnable phrase one more time until you get us out of this revolting apartment and into something more respectable. And don't you make me walk around in those blasted shoes. They aren't good for anything but sending one to the hospital. Besides, it's late and I'm tired." Keane dropped onto the sofa and ran his long, tapered hands up over his face and through the slick oil spill of his hair. I was particularly opposed to whatever that was he had started to grow over his lip.

"I know you're tired, and no doubt your nerves are raw and broken in places that, in time, might invite some form of infectious insanity. You have made it quite clear those shoes ought to be burned and that I will feel your anger if—God forbid—you are required to wear them again. But think of what we are accomplishing here, Lawrence. We will be freeing James from his past sins, at least in a mortal sense, and Cohen and his like will no longer have any hold of him for as long as he stays away from those pills. Think—*think* of what good we can do, not only for him, but those in the same position. We are liberating his son and lover—wherever they may be. Think of it, Lawrence. Think of it." I did. I thought long and hard over his words; words spoken with the unfaltering hope of a young boy who believed himself capable of saving the world. Or at least all of humanity. Then again, he had that face that never seemed to age; never seemed to grow old. There was always a youthfulness to its features. For as long as I knew him, they were there, though be they smoothed over my wisdom's sand. There was an aspiration to do such great and good things. Logic was a thorn viciously tearing through his flesh that his blood might spill onto the earth as a final plea for his dignity. I thought of it. I thought of those late hours when I heard Keane slip out the door and disappear until the early whispers of the morning. He would then sleep until lunch. A few hours followed rigorous study into our characters. Then the entire process repeated itself again. And again. And again.

Yes, I thought of it.

I sucked in a breath and gripped at the corners of my elbows with a vigour unfortunate to the fabric of my shirt.

"Keane, have *you* ever considered that you may have already placed yourself in danger. They have already tried to kill us once, not to mention their attempt to set the theatre alight. What makes you so damnably sure that no one in Cohen's circle will recognise us?"

"Lawrence, what they are searching for is a name, and those can be easily changed or adapted. Did you hear my lecture at Princeton? 'The mind better recognises titles than the strength of a single individual.' So long as we conceal our names and I am not attributed my intellectual status, all will be well. Now, if you would repeat that phrase once more, I believe we can both get some well-earned rest." I sighed, releasing my arms and throwing my hands above my head for exaggerated effect. But my companion would not falter. He never did; be it conviction or stubborn pride. When I feared he would insist I perform that poorly grammaticized line once more, I groaned, threw my head back, and surrendered the last few threads of my dignity.

"Wadda'ya say? Buy me a drink?" A light snapped to life behind his eyes, showering the blue pools with a twinkle I had seen rarely and welcomed easily.

"By God," He whispered. "I think you've got it."

"Have I? I feel ridiculous." My companion cleared his throat and rose to his feet.

"That is to be expected. You are playing a part so far beneath you it drags in the gutter. It will crush your pride and turn it into dust for the worms. But listen to me, Lawrence, if a few days—a week—it may all be over and we can again return to our lives knowing we have achieved something noble in our absence."

"Keane, if the rest of my costume is to be as hideous and demeaning as those shoes, I would hardly call this performance 'noble.'"

My companion smiled gently. Damn it. I knew that smile, as I intimately knew the words that were to follow. Those great souls of the Romans and Greeks never ventured far from his lips, though they had been dead from the minds and hearts that knew them best.

"'The noble man should either live with honour or die with honour.' And what could possibly be more honourable than saving another human being? It has been a point of recognition and promotion for thousands of years. In the middle ages, saving another person's life—especially one of considerable nobility—was an attribute of impending knighthood. In both recent wars we have seen that as well; heroes awarded medals for various shows of chivalry and courage in the face of something ought never to be experienced in a person's lifetime. Yes, Lawrence, there is nothing nobler than assisting in the mortal salvation of one's fellow men, or, in your case, women." He had a point. Of course he did. His mind was always as well tuned as Mozart's piano, honed to the finest degree that its performance might not be spoiled by some unforgivable moral fault. Such was the truth I had grown and flourished under through the passing years. And now I followed that same man in full knowledge we were soon to enter the den of lions.

IF THE WHOLE OF AMERICA had one vice, it could be most easily found in the basement of an obnoxiously large, red brick building thrust carelessly upon the earth. From what I could discern through the dismal shadows of evening, a white-washed sign dangled above the main doorway. Keane threaded my arm firmly through his, steadying my ankles from the damnable heels and my mind from forming an escape that might free me from my impending fate. We descended a flight of concrete stairs bereft of all light, save that which is born from natural necessity. There was a gentle brush to my arm, a breath of warning, and the creak of a solid door with shattered shards of laughter leaking out into the night.

It was not enormous, nor quite so elaborate as those great places spotted through the breath of Europe. The entrance was not small, but I noted a brief bow of Keane's lengthy frame as he led me forward into the chaos. That was the only way to describe it: the epitome of humanity's wilderness. Dizzying swirls of women, dripping with sparse fabric and lipstick, dominated the room as tornadoes do the great plains. Their winds of flirtatious whispers left only a path of admirers ready for a single night's exploits before turning to another pair of outstretched arms for comfort. I tugged self-consciously at the neckline of my dress; or rather, the lack of it. The thin material scarcely brushed my collarbone before dipping downward in a way that was neither tasteful, nor comfortable. Keane grabbed my freehand and gently tucked it over his arm that had previously secured my other limb. Though he was perhaps as fond of the confounded dress as I was, he at least needed not endure the humiliation of wearing it. To his credit; however, his masculinity compelled him to the facade of a cream-colored suit and thin, polka-dotted tie. His wavy hair was again slicked back against his head, which would be amended immediately after we recovered the photograph and retreated back into our lives.

The doorman, a grey-suited man with the solid outline of a firearm jutting out from his jacket, nodded to Keane as he pulled me into the seizure-inducing spectacle of lights and noise. I tried to overlook the occasional pair of greedy, masculine eyes dripping down to the inexpensive pendant dangling low beneath my neckline. I tried, but clearly not well enough, for we had only gone a matter of feet before my companion bent low over me with his lips a mere brush away from my ear.

"Remember to smile, Lawrence. You aren't dying."

"I might as well be. Do you realise how dipriciating this thing is? Oh, of course you don't. *You* don't have oversexed men ogling at your every move." Keane had no time to retort before we arrived at one of the several gambling counters.

Recent converts to the little casino were required to fill out some sort of membership card, which Keane had obviously done some days before under the name of Leslie John McCormic. I too added my own created signature while my companion exchanged thick wads of bills for a wide selection of chips; not just tens or twenties, but colored disks equivalent to that of hundreds, or even thousands of dollars. As I returned the pen to the man behind the marble countertop, my companion glanced over my shoulder at the spidery ink sprawled across the card and gently grasped my arm as we motored out into the whirring hive of people.

"Ingrid Shearer?" He questioned, his voice bearing the light glimpse of amusement which tended to be reflected in that infamous twinkle shimmering within his blue eyes.

"Well, I decided, if you had the gull to be Leslie, I could be Ingrid. Quite logical, don't you think?" His only answer was a throaty chuckle as we wandered aimlessly, students to the international art of lazy money-making. What might have been a large room felt incredibly confined as a constant stream of newcomers became woven into the fabric of the elite. The stench of cigar smoke made love with the unforgivable odour of cheap perfume. An adjacent room, considerably smaller but with better lighting, proved a haven for a throng of showgirls, who evidently performed at night, as well as day. Some strange man, floating quickly away from the docks of sobriety, jammed his elbow into Keane's side; muttering out some slurred question no doubt derogatory, if not to the whole of my sex, then at least the line of prissy girls kicking their legs shamelessly below the multicolored lights. Keane's voice fell dramatically from its English clip to something that might have harrolded from the ports of Boston.

"I don't care for bare bodies unless I love them." And so saying, I was again swept away into the throbbing clacks and curses at the heart of the casino.

It ought to have been disorientating, but I felt, if not steadied by Keane's presence, then reassured. I watched politely as he leaned low against the craps table, tossing the dice languidly, as though the hundreds of dollars wavering in the balance were mere pennies one could lay across the train tracks. Eventually, when his pile had become increasingly bountiful, I moved off on my own with no intention of making a profit. I drank little, but feigned more, lost enough at the roulette wheels to secure a book's imminent publication, and endured the sickening looks of half a dozen buffoons; illiterate to all but a deck of cards.

And yet I left the wheels with near five times my starting amount. With a motion that might have resembled some glimpse of intimacy, I moved across the room, slipped my winnings into Keane's breast pocket, and whispered a vague destination caused by the wine and other fluids of the day. Where the roguish elegance of the main arenas had been dulled by the idiocracy of human greed, the halls leading to the washroom were lined with enormous mirrors framed in lights. I gently pried open the lavatory door and allowed my eyes to befall upon a room large enough for a sizable convention. Unfortunately, that also meant there was not but open space between myself and the couple mashing themselves into the other wall. The bleach-blonde woman screeched at my entrance, and while I grasped desperately at the faintest glimpse of an apology, the man pushed past me into the noise, leaving his necktie lying limp on the floor, along with my profuse embarrassment. The woman, save the shot burst of understandable surprise, appeared unshaken by the entire occurrence. Instead, she patted the back of her hair and pulled the thin straps of her dress from where they had slipped from her shoulders. With a quick adjustment to the rest of her fawlty wardrobe, she made her own grand exit. The remnants of my horrified blush must have still flickered over my features when I again stationed myself at Keane's side behind the craps table.

"When the devil happened to you?" His rich chuckle was heavily diluted by a sudden uproar announcing yet another glorious win. I leaned hard into his shoulder.

"How the hell haven't the police found this place? It's hardly inconspicuous." Another chuckle shook my companion's chest and he nodded his head toward a man slouched over in a nearby chair.

"Why don't you ask that gentleman? No doubt, as commissioner, he should be able to provide you with a sufficient answer. And, as for the rest of your friendly neighbourhood policemen, the facade upstairs fends them off rather well."

"And what would that be? Some sort of church?"

"Close. Would you guess a temperance house?" I recoiled from him quickly as though he had landed a solid punch in my stomach.

"You're joking?"

"Hardly. Now, if you are ready to leave," Keane swept our combined winnings into his hands. "Would you care too . . . " I shook my head. Violently.

"You go and cash those. I'll be alright. Really. Meet you at the car?" He nodded and strode off toward one of the elaborate marble counters partially concealed by a few ecstatic men cradling some newfound success at the gaming tables. I smiled—my first real smile all evening—and slipped quickly toward the door.

The clean evening air struck me back a step as I emerged from the pit of filth. It always does one's lungs good to escape from that revolting cigar smoke. Keane never seemed quite so affected by the heavy smog of tobacco. But, then again, the state of his own respiratory organs was hardly commendable.

I closed the gap between myself and the automobile in a series of conscious, balanced steps. No question about it: these shoes were to be pried from my legs. My tortured feet liberated, I sank back into the black leather and contented myself with the silence as I awaited Keane's return. Other groups seemed ready to leave as well. I counted at least a dozen people rushing to their cars and speeding off into the waning night. Suddenly the driver's door clicked open and Keane practically fell into the seat beside me.

"Well," I sighed. "That was . . ."

"Exhausting? Yes. No doubt we shall both sleep past noon."

"By God, Keane, and you have done this every night for what? An entire week? It's a miracle you're not lying face down in a gutter somewhere." My companion eased our mechanical steed out onto the abandoned streets.

"Yes, well, it will all be over soon. Oh, and for heaven's sake, take a cigarette if you need it. Lord knows I do." I headed his welcomed advice, slipped my hand carefully into his jacket pocket, and brought out his silver cigarette case. However, rather than rows of white, paper-wrapped cylinders, it had been stuffed with coins sizable in both weight and value. I glanced curiously at Keane, whose eyes wavered slightly from the road.

"When one gains much, much must be sacrificed, eh, Lawrence? No matter. Try the glove box. There should be some in there." I opened the compartment and, true to his word, a package of the much needed tobacco lay casually atop a pile of other miscellaneous objects. I took one, rolling the paper slowly between my fingers before lighting it. What joy—what bliss—there was in that bitter smoke as the stale taste of vile sin was cleansed by the light brush of vanilla lingering through tobacco. Two long draws was all I needed and I handed the glowing cigarette to Keane, who immediately began pulling the life out of the flickering orange end. I dropped the coin-filled cigarette case into Keane's pocket as I started lighting a second from the open package. I took a deep, luxurious puff before passing it off to my companion. In doing so, I caught a quick glance at the rearview mirror.

"How long has that Continental been following us?" He hissed into his cigarette, sending a white stream of smoke over his shoulder.

"A little over a mile. Relax, Lawrence. I am hardly a novice behind the wheel."

"That may be so, but aren't they getting rather close?" Just as I stated what must have been obvious to Keane long before, the black automobile charged forward into our rear, knocking me forward with dangerous vigour. A few inches further and my head would have smashed through the windshield. My shoulders were suddenly shoved back into the seats as Keane heaved the accelerator against the floor. He could have been a racecar driver. In another lifetime, he could have been many things. However, at that moment, he was not more than an extraordinary man driving against insanity.

The other car struck again, harder this time. From somewhere behind us came the blood-chilling cry of a bullet that met a cannon in one motion. Our vehicle lurched to one side, then the other. In a matter of forced breaths, we were careening out of control directly toward the bridge stretched over a river. The stale taste of vomit caught in my throat as Keane desperately tried to steady the car, not so much by his fingers soldering to the wheel, but an iron will determined we not tumble into the cold river as a ball of mangled metal and fire. My body hurled forward again, the vomit inching forward in my throat. But the world wasn't moving anymore. The buildings remained stationary over the paved ground.

We had stopped.

The breath in my lungs caught for eternity before allowing me to break the silence with the first tentative hums of relief that had been held at bay by fear. Two men, both armed, stalked toward us with a purpose known all too well by those who have faced danger. Keane pushed open the driver door with his toe and, hands raised above his head, climbed out into the line of fire.

"Good evening, gentlemen. I trust you—"

"Cut the chit chat unless you want an extra hole in your head." The man's voice rattled like a tin of gravel, cutting the air with the constant abandonment of several consonants. Chicago, perhaps? The Bronx? The stomp of feet echoed through my ears as they moved ever closer to Keane.

"Where's the girl?" The second man was definitely from Los Angeles.

"Girl?" A gun cocked its warning.

"Quit stalling, old man. Dark blonde hair. Red dress. Damn dame walked in on me when I was in the middle of some important business with a partner of mine." Partner or lover? I thought—no, I *knew*—Keane would be ever the gentleman; denying everything to protect a woman's dignity for entering a lavatory and finding two individuals deep in the dance created for the two sexes. I climbed out of the car and two guns immediately swivelled to attention.

It was difficult at first to recognise the man in the blue suit. But then, when you find someone in as vulnerable a position as I had, their face is hardly the first thing you notice. To my imagination's utter shock, there were no unnatural markings spotting his face; no scars, bullet puckers, or acid burns. There wasn't even a ruddiness remaining from adolescence. There was nothing but hot, lethal anger. He looked me over with eyes that were scarcely human. In two heavy strides, he had caught hold of my wrist with one hand while the other pressed the barrel of his pistol into my throat.

"You little bitch. Why, I odda shoot you here and now. In fact, that's just what I'm gonna do." He shoved me against the bridge's cold rail with enough force that, had I been wearing those damnable shoes, I would have toppled over the edge head first. A gun was raised, cocked, and—

"Wait a second, Charlie." My makeshift firing squad turned to his partner, the pistol still jammed into the hollow of my throat. "Let the old man do it. The police know us, ya'know?" The barrel moved from my face and swivelled to face Keane, who had no doubt been concocting ways to take down both men in a matter of seconds. I waited expectantly for some gentlemanly remark that would save him from performing so distasteful a task.

I had never been so wrong.

Keane stepped forward, both firearms trained stiffly on his chest. A third gun was placed in his hands and he—my dearest friend and confidant—lifted the weapon until the leering metal paused in sight of my forehead. The man removed from his role as executioner glared at my companion.

"And how do we know you won't miss or make some other stupid mistake? Old fogey like you probably couldn't hit a cow's ass."

BANG!

A gaudy hair pin exploded just above my ear. My brain, though rattled, was somehow able to comprehend Keane lowering the smoking gun toward the ground.

"So?" The Charlie chap scoffed. "You might have been aiming for her head and missed."

"Really? Well then, would you like to see the other one?" Keane raised the gun again, steadied himself, and—

BANG!

Another broken pin fell to the bridge's rough surface. God, if I survived this, Keane and I were going to have a stern talk about these William Tell fancies of his. My companion rubbed the warm trigger with the pad of his forefinger, as if turning over several ideas in his mind at once.

"If I'm going to do this, would you mind if I at least did it in my own way. It would be a shame to shoot her without some ... enjoyment? At my age opportunities are scarce and certainly not cheap." The two adjacent men chuckled at the throaty inclinations of my companion's proposal and gifted him with a sharp nod. He handed the gun to the one nearest himself and rubbed his hands together; fingertips to palm, until I found myself inching back against the rail. Step by step he slowly approached, his eyes grabbing mine with an expression I had seen on the fiercest predators as they prepared to pounce upon their prey. When the distance between us had dwindled to nothing more than a few feet, he grabbed my shoulders and pulled me hard against him. His mouth clamped onto mine in something much too painful to be a kiss, and it certainly could not be favourable to even the most hopeless of romantics. Something cold slipped into the top of my dress, biting into my flesh as though warning of the imminent death to soon befall me. Just as I grew accustomed to the warmth of his dark suit or the burning danger of the situation, Keane pushed me back against the rail and returned to the men for the gun. As he checked the bullets, he turned slyly to them.

"You needn't be concerned. I have already proved I am an exceptional shot. Have either of you read Shakespeare's *Measure for Measure*? No? A pity. Well, I assure you gentlemen, Ingrid here will be as dead as the dear Claudio." I knew my fate then. I knew it and allowed my chin to rise as those thousands of soldiers set to meet their maker. If I must die in the United States of America, the least I could do was be British and hold a stiff upper lip. Keane raised the pistol to my chest, cocked the trigger, and—

PART FOUR

Death is the most terrible of all things,

for it is the end,

and nothing is thought to be either good or bad for the dead.

-Aristotle

CHAPTER TWENTY-THREE

BANG!

God, it made him sick. That final noise—that shout of metallic desperation—and she was flung backwards over the edge and down, down into the black river. He had played that scene over in his mind for more than a day now, and each horrid memory left his stomach lurching and his lungs gasping for a cigarette. He reached blindly for the nightstand, flicked on the lamp, and glanced at his wristwatch. She had given it to him a few months before on his birthday. It was a nice piece; gold, but durable, and made with fine craftsmanship. Yes, it was simple, but still endearing to its owner.

It was also three o'clock.

He rolled over onto his back and shoved the heels of his hands into his throbbing eye sockets. There had been times in the navy when he had gone with precious little sleep—none, in fact—but he wasn't a young sailor anymore. He wasn't even a young man.

Blast. How could it be three o'clock?

It wasn't that he minded getting old. After all, it was a part of life. You are born, you live, you grow old, you die. Oh, he had a while yet before that last bit. Decades, God willing. He wasn't ready to die yet, but she wasn't either. She was still young with her whole life ahead of her. She was incredible, and smart, and—

Bloody hell.

He needed a drink.

Brendan Keane—*Professor* Brendan Keane—flung back the bed clothes, refused to stretch away the dull ache in his neck and shoulders, and made a beeline for the amber bottle resting on the dresser. Rather than pouring himself a small dose to sip respectfully, he filled the glass to the brim and tipped the bottom up until the generous slug rushed down his throat. The fire of strong liquor was quickly quelled with familiarity. He repeated the process. Then, more at peace with himself than he had been for several hours, he poured himself a somewhat more moderate third and once more returned to the edge of the mattress. The creaking of springs perfectly correlated with the sluggish churnings of his exhausted mind.

Three in the morning.

The casino would still be open. It was always open. But did he really want to go back after last night? He would rather drink himself into a comfortable stupor. It may not be beneficial to his health, but it would be sleep. Sleep. That's what he needed. Sleep. Keane took a long sip from the glass and closed his eyes. By God, those puritans didn't know what they were missing.

Suddenly he leapt forward with new vigour. No, he would go to the casino. He had work to do, and some sentimental longing would not—could not—sway him. If she were in the room then, no doubt she would be shoving him toward the door and cursing up a storm.

God, he needed to get out of that room.

IN THE PAST WEEK, BRENDAN Keane had found himself incredibly competent in the game of craps. He had grown to accept the odds balanced upon the dice clasped in his fist. Chips changing sides had somehow become welcome to him. Him: professor of psychology and defender of the human mind. Was he addicted? No. Not yet, anyway. But, after the events of the night before, an addiction—if temporary—would be a welcome distraction.

Perhaps the endearment for the game came from the fact he had not, in total, lost any money. He had gained it. He could place a hundred on the table and walk away with an amount bordering the two thousand mark. From a single day alone, he could repay the sound total of James' debt. He could have done that the moment he knew the sinful numbers, but that had never been the problem. Of course, Keane was never above reproach when it came to affairs of the heart. He'd had his loves and his losses. He had even considered marriage on a few occasions. There had been those times when he felt himself a fool for not stationing himself at the altar with some darling girl well-bred in the niceties of society. But then, a man is so often inclined to get set in his own ways or become attached to the independence of bachelorhood. But James? Keane tossed the dice on the table. No, James was a different matter entirely. He thrived on feminine companionship to see him through the night. It was his safety net. It was James' hope away from the pills.

"Hi there." The high purr wavering at his shoulder came with brightly painted fingernails running along his lapel. A glance at the woman was all he needed to confirm she was just like all the other showgirls threading their way through the crowd. They searched out some lucky sap on a winning streak and sponged off some of the rolling dough. If those men weren't to their taste, there were always a few cads willing to share their bed for a night. "Hi." She whispered again, edging closer against his side. "Buy me a drink?" Keane spun instantly around, forgetting about the dice in his hand until a cigar smoking behemoth wrenched them from his crasp. He wasn't exactly certain what persuaded him to do it—sentimentality perhaps—that caused him to lead the woman over to the bar. He waited for her to be served some intricate cocktail before putting in his own order of scotch and water. When the glass appeared at his hand, he took in the feminine figure flaunting itself before him.

She was older than Lawrence by a considerable margin, but an exact estimate was muddled by the thick lipstick and eyeshadow smeared over her face. He sipped his drink. The scotch was adequate, but nothing so satisfying as a cold glass of whiskey enjoyed in the disciplined buzz of a pub along the Irish coastline, such as he had revisited just months prior.

The wonder was bright in her eyes as she surveyed the unique selection of characters. The way she tried to hide her curiosity behind half a pint of stout.

"So, you new around here?" Keane jerked his head away from the swirling liquor and peered down at the woman next to him. Her dark hair was carefully curled around her heart-shaped face. He shook his head.

"I started coming here a little over a week ago. Take from that what you will."

"Only a week? You're awful good at the table."

"Pure luck." The woman smiled and inched closer to him, her hand mere inches from his chest.

That self-satisfied grin on her face as she plucked on about a new subject. That had never been luck, her imagination. Certainly not. That was pure talent.

"Most guys don't come unless they brought their girls with them. Then again, there are plenty of those already here. Like taking a bag of rice to China. I'm Ruby, by the way. What's your name?" Keane ran his finger along the side of his glass.

"Leslie. Leslie McCormic." The woman wrinkled her nose in a way that could be described as nothing else but abnormally feminine.

"That's a funny name."

"Not if you were born with it. My middle name is John, if that is any consolation." In truth, it was not his middle name. John had been his father, and, from what he remembered of him, the name was hardly an improvement in dignity. Ruby; however, seemed satisfied with the explanation of his name as a whole unit and gradually moved on to just separate portions.

"I like the name McCormic. Makes me think of a real strong man just waiting to sweep a girl like me off her feet." Keane did his best not to laugh. By God, where were these sorts of girls in the war?

"Is that so?"

"Golly, yes. Why, gosh, it makes me tingly all over. But in a good way. Not like Mickey. You're more good looking than he is, the bald buffalo. That man sure knows how to throw a party, though." Ah. Now the rusted gears were starting to turn—tentatively—in his direction. Keane leaned against the bar, bowing his head ever so slightly as he took another sip of his scotch. And, by God, he could swear that the liquor was getting better by the second. He took another sip.

"I can't say I've ever been to one of his parties. But then, if he owns all this, they must be quite an event."

"Oh, sure. You should see what else he owns; diner clubs, jewellery stores, you name it. But Mickey's parties are just a smash. Bertie—a close, *intimate* friend of mine—got so drunk last time that Sam had to cart her home in his new car. Even Ellen Nelson—an old preacher's daughter, ya know—had to get bailed out of the slammer for running around the city buck naked after smoking one of Blind Benny's cigarettes. Though, between us friends, I don't think it was straight tobacco that made her swing on that chandelier. I mean, golly, I wouldn't go streaking past all those strangers just after a normal cigarette. Would you? Course you wouldn't. Oh, and then there was Helen Hewitt—we call her Helen Halfwit cause she's so gawdawful dumb—and Billy and Sid and . . . " The list was never ending, a testament to the degradation of modern society. Even so, Keane found it hardly necessary to conceal his disinterest in the many names on account, for the characters themselves were so ridiculously unique he could not help but find them interesting. However, when Ruby at last rose from the waters of civilization in dire need of breath, he pounced.

"And your Mickey is at these occasions?"

"Gosh, yes. Every Saturday. Would be a whole bag of shit—the party, that is—if he wasn't. But he doesn't have 'em at his house. Always has them at a friend's. Why? You wanna come some time?" Keane tipped his head thoughtfully to one side.

"Perhaps, if I were to get an invitation—"

"Oh, you don't need no invite or nothing like that. Guy Brooks just gotta give you the okay. He's over there playing cards, if ya wanna talk to him. Tell him I sent you. I'd go with you, but Guy and me ain't exactly on speaking terms, the son of a bitch." Keane downed the remainder of his scotch. (My, how good it tasted as it slipped down his throat.) A quick nod to Ruby was all he needed before he strode eagerly off toward a handful of men bent over their cards; smoking an endless supply of expensive cigarettes and cheap, fat cigars. It was not difficult to distinguish Ruby's former lover from the others. His sharp facial features were deterred somewhat by a trim moustache, but there was no uncertainty to him. He glanced up at Keane as he approached, but that was all. A glance. A decision. A single look that would determine whether the unoccupied seat across the table was empty or momentarily abandoned by another man, who would no doubt be conveniently absent for the entire day. Keane did not wait for a verdict.

He sat.

The reaction was lethal: thick, scarred hands diving into pockets that immediately inched upward. Guy Brooks hardly glanced up from his cards as he spoke.

"Put your hands on the table and the boys might just decide not to pump your gut full of lead. That's right. Now turn them over. Good. Alright boys, lay off, but don't make any sudden moves, Mister. See, these men are like hound dogs; jumpy. If you don't want bullets in your groyne—"

"I understand." Keane interrupted flatley. "However, Ruby did not send me to be shot."

"Ruby sent you?" The man's eyes shifted up from his cards. Ah. There is nothing like a familiar female to gain a man's attention.

"Yes. She said I needed your approval to enter Mr. Cohen's." The professor set his forearms on the table, leaning forward until his roman nose lingered somewhere above his intertwined fingers. His thin lips had been expertly set into the firmest, most commanding form of a smile. He had seen it himself on a few occasions by men being dragged off toward a firing squad; daring them to find the courage to shoot. But no handguns exploded through suit pockets, and Keane was still sitting by his own power when the man across the table gave his own predatory leer and laid down his cards.

"So you want to go to Mickey's? You know, some of them who goes ain't ever come back out."

"Quite. And if I were a child, I might manage a flinch." The daring words hung in the air for an excruciating moment before Guy Brooks let out a low growl of laughter.

"Ya' know, I might just like you. Tell ya what. You and me, we play a nice game of poker. One round. If you win, you get to come to old Mickey's."

"And if I lose?"

"If you lose, you pay me an even ten thousand and that wristwatch you're wearing. Would make a nice gift for some friend pushing up the daisies, ya know." Keane sat back in his chair and folded his arms across his chest.

"How about fifteen thousand, without the watch?"

"No cigar. Either the watch is in or the party is out. Got it? Now, if you ain't gonna put that piece of gold on the table, I'd leave now before Ricco here gets antsy with his trigger finger."

Keane unfolded his arms and carefully undid the watch's thin clasp; reverently laying the piece on the table's dark felt. That done, he intertwined his hands neatly before him.

"Will we be using those cards, or shall we get another deck?" The man across the table grinned; placing his neat stack of cards further toward the table's centre.

"Why get another deck when I've got a perfectly good one right here?"

"When I play for high stakes, I like to be certain the odds are even between both parties. Get another deck. And I will check both yours and the new one before a dealer shuffles." Guy Brooks' smile faltered slightly, but that did not deter him from sending one of the other men after a dealer and another deck of cards.

All fifty-two cards seemed unmarked; no gravy stains or little tears or creases in the corners. This deck—though identical to Guy's—looked new, as though just purchased that morning. Or was it close to afternoon? Did it matter? Keane rifled through each rectangle with special attention to the aces. In long, clean motions, he had lined all four of the little devils on the table, running his long fingers over each edge and side. In the ancient mythology of the Greeks, there had been three old fates to weave the tapestry of human life. But here there were four to either raise him up to heaven or damn him to the pits of hell. Four paper fates leering up at him as he replaced them one by one into the enormous pile and mixed them in with the others. The dealer—a nervous young man with a twitch in his right leg—slowly shuffled the cards; pausing only to allow a passerby to cut the deck before continuing with the ritual. At last the time had come. Keane leaned back and tugged at the tailored edge of his shirtsleeve just above where the wristwatch—*his* wristwatch—had been clasped. When each of the two men had been properly dealt, the younger swept up his cards, checked them, and casually laid them face down again with a nod toward his opponent.

"You're out of your league, old man. Better shove over that ten grand and gold now, cause there ain't no way you've got something better." Keane too laid his cards to rest, leaning over them with an expression attributed to the wake of a fine jest.

"Isn't there? Well, if that's how it is, you wouldn't mind making the stakes a bit more equal, now would you? I'd say five thousand ought to do it."

"*Five thousand*?" The man scoffed. "You're bluffing."

"Then match the bet. I have over twice that amount laying out in front of me. And you did say my hand couldn't possibly overpower yours. Of course, if you don't wish to match, I could easily make it even another way." Keane wrapped his fingers around the gold band of his wristwatch and tugged it away from the table's centre by a fraction. When that caused no reaction, he strengthened his hold and pulled it back to his side and made to clasp it once more over his wrist when the rustling of paper bills stopped him. Ten, crisp, five hundred dollar bills inched forward across the felt surface, and the gold wristwatch was unceremoniously dropped once more in the middle of the table. What confidence was lost in the heated exchange disappeared as the other gambler turned his cards over, one at a time, revealing three eights and two fours.

A full house.

Guy Brooks instinctively reached his hand out toward the heavily laden pot, but Keane—ever the thespian—had already begun to lay his own cards face up. A jack and one . . . two . . . thre . . . *four* aces. The young man's face fell to an ashen white before slamming his fists onto the table, demanding the deck be counted.

There were fifty-two.

Again the supposed victim attacked the table, knocking both the used and original decks together until the entire corner of the casino was littered with playing cards. Even if it could have been guaranteed that no card had fallen into some nook or cranny undetectable by human eyes, the havok exploding over the table would have ruined all chances of ever again accounting for all one hundred four cards of the combined madness. It was in this chaos Keane clasped his watch back into place, swept up his winnings, and left the casino; shoving the hefty bills into his pocket besides his five original cards: a seven, a king, a four, an eight, and one very lovely queen.

CHAPTER TWENTY-FOUR

KEANE FOUND A LONG—THOUGH late—breakfast, washed down with several cups of smouldering coffee, could dissipate the symptoms of an exhausted mind, as well as body. The diner was not nearly as competent as Mrs. McCarthy, nor was the food to the same calibre. It had been three days now since he had enjoyed a proper night's sleep. Four nights and three days. His head felt increasingly sluggish, with only a minor jolt of stimulation as he forced another cup of coffee down his throat. The gears, corroded through long hours of use, gradually began to creak into motion; stuttering momentarily with the thought of having to endure the party that night, and, no doubt, well into the morning. At least his insomnia would be put to good use.

Keane slammed down the empty cup, placing his paid bill and a sizable tip beside it. There was no use in going back to the hotel, but he gave the taxi driver some vague instructions in that general direction all the same. As he sank back against the seats, he became all too aware that the dull ache, which had planted itself in his bad shoulder sometime that morning, had flared through his muscles; pausing in the centre of his back. His eyes too felt a strike was suddenly necessary. The optical muscles stabbed into his weary skull relentlessly until he had staggered up the stairs to his hotel room and drawn all the curtains tight against the light.

Damn.

When had there been so many windows?

By the time Keane had called down for some strong liquor and reclined against the chaise lounge along one wall, he could have sworn one of Lawrence's baseball friends had spent the past hour swinging a bat into his back. Every inch of his body was sore, throbbing in pain, or about to buckle from exhaustion. The alcohol did little to alleviate any of these, but it did give him some sense of lost dignity.

Dignity. Always dignity.

Damn dignity. He was going to bed. At least there he would be able to endure the inconvenience of age and war wounds without feeling like some pitiful old man. Yes, he consoled himself as he undid the knot in his necktie, he was tired—*overly tired*. That was his problem. That was the only problem. He wasn't old enough to be feeling decrepit. After all, he had only just turned fifty-four, and that was most certainly not old enough to allow his aching form to control every aspect of his life.

Dignity. Always dignity.

Keane chuckled dryly to himself. What had his father ever known about dignity? More to the point, what had he known about growing old? He had at least died in the best of health, while his son was now cursed to endure—not so much as the spoils of age—but the incompetence of the world. A world that, twice in his fifty-four years, was unable to find some peaceful solution to their differences. Keane toed off his shoes and laid back against the bed; the soft whisper of springs welcoming his tired body.

Dignity?

What the hell did the world know about dignity? What did anyone know about dignity? The only other person who even thought about the term was—

Keane writhed as a sudden blast of excruciating pain burst through his shoulder, interrupting his thought as efficiently as would a bullet.

A bullet.

He had only fired one bullet; one skilled squeeze to the trigger that had pushed her over the edge, as soundly as if he had physically shoved her.

BANG!

He could feel everything about that moment as it surged upon him through another wave of sickening pain. The pistol had been cold in his hand, the trigger but a thin slip of metal beneath his forefinger. There had been little kickback from the weapon, but it was enough—more than enough—to jerk his mind to the reality of his actions. A thin yelp echoed through the air, followed by an overpowering splash. Everything in him—every instinct he had accumulated and honed during the war—screamed for him to jump off that bridge after her. He could swim. Of course he could swim. It had become second nature after all those years of training.

And yet he did nothing.

No, he did worse than nothing. He stood there. He stood there like those young men who refused to march into the swarm of bullets, though they already wore the uniform. He stood on the deck, cowering from a fate that was possible, but not sealed above his head. Yes, he stood there as the two men cackled and patted his shoulder before they drove off. And then he too left. Alone.

But hadn't he done all he could to ensure her protection? Not entirely. He had tried to prove himself; shooting the pins out of her hair. She hadn't flinched. Of course she hadn't. She had trusted him. And yet, she had not rebuked his boldness when he kissed her. No powerful slap sent him staggering back to that pit from whence the other men came.

Virtue is always admirable to the foolish, and fear never coveted by the good.

KEANE AWOKE. THAT was a miracle itself, for no one can awaken without first sleeping. Now *there* was a miracle.

He had slept.

It took a bit of effort to tug his mind out of the much needed rest enough to realise the room was dark. Or, if not dark, then dim. The sealed curtains were no longer illuminated by the sun's rays, but merely glowed a tired amber. Even the pain in his shoulder had subsided into a somewhat more bearable stiffness. Keane carefully propped his back against the headboard and glanced at his watch. A few grains of satisfaction multiplied into a running stream as he realised he had been able to enjoy more than five hours of uninterrupted rest. A solid seven hours, in fact. Seven long, luxurious hours of the purest sleep known to man.

Keane ran a hand through his unruly waves of hair, allowing his fingers to then detour along his jaw, only to find it marginally concealed beneath a rough stubble. When was the last shaved? That morning? No, not that morning. He had gone to the casino again that morning in a vain attempt to lose some of his earnings.

Keane slowly pulled his frame upright and sat along the edge of the bed, relieved when the action did not cause any new spasms in his shoulder. He took his time stretching all the knots out of his weary muscles. How glorious it felt to be free of age's spindly grasp.

A few hours later, after a long, hot bath, not to mention a shave and hot towel from the hotel's barber, Keane felt considerably relieved of his mortal frailties and ready to endure however many hours of celebratory life as his infamous host found necessary. Stuffing the pockets of his new suit with a generous amount of paper bills and cartons of cigarettes, he climbed into the first taxi that presented itself and relaxed into the leather seats. Through the waning light, he squinted at the passing surroundings in the event he may need to drive or—heaven forbid—lead a harrowing escape from the realm of armed fools and gambling simpletons. It was a never ending battle, to which Keane had become incredibly bored.

The long, gravel path led upwards toward a towering mansion, which had been seemingly built up from the ground by God's own hand. Enormous decorations of marble outlined the house as pillars stolen from the minds and hearts of the Greeks. Overpowering blasts of music exploded through the cool air. Keane recognised the tune. (A similar was in his own collection; a purchase of Lawrence's.) To arrive at the heart of the party itself, one was required to enter an elegant foyer and lead into the back gardens. A series of tables groaned beneath platters of meats, fruits, cakes, sandwiches, wines, hard liquors, lemonade, and a few pyramids of cigarette cartons still in their packaging. A well-stocked band played energetically in one corner of the garden; creating the music, rather than merely presenting it through a phonograph's flat mimicry. Lights had been strung from polls until the entire expanse was illuminated with their gentle glow.

It did not take long to notice how the guests had divided themselves into separate groups, with only a dozen or so flitting about like lost butterflies. Many of the females were much too young to be entirely distinguishable from those sauntering about in similar bright dresses that were both too high and too low, which, he supposed, was the point. Keane was able to spot a few faces he recognised from the casino, but the majority of the guests were no more than figures whirling about the world in one, enormous, purposeless moment. He began with the pulsating conversations of the young things; nodding vaguely at ideas that were certainly modern, but not quite distasteful to his pallet. Many of the subjects included the ever popular debate of a woman's inclusion into the ever changing world, something he agreed with on the whole. Perhaps a decade ago he might have been more leery of sharing such new opinions; especially with people half, if not a third of his age. But that had changed, hadn't it?

Seven years before.

When he had finished his second cocktail in their boisterous presence, Keane ambled on toward the scotch-drinking businessmen. Within a matter of painful minutes, he found himself sufficiently aware of the miraculous recovery of the country's various markets. Having learned enough about the stocks themselves to become quite sufficient in the world of investments, he then moved onto the next group. Then the one after that. Then the next. Soon he discovered he had explored all of the party's nations except for the handful of young men smoking along the far wall of the house. Perfect. He could use a good smoke.

Keane tugged a package of cigarettes from his pocket, casually set one in his mouth, and approached the soft, sparse sentences passed between the unsociable of sociables. Each suit had been carefully tailored to its owner's frame, which ranged from tall and stocky to a youthful figure, who, even with a hat, scarcely rose as high as Keane's shoulder. It was by the latter of these he stationed himself, his back digging into the mansion's brick exterior to prop up the rest of his long form. Puff by puff, draw by draw, the cigarette grew smaller between his fingers until he had no choice but to grind it beneath his heel. Before he could reach for a fresh one; however, an open case was offered to him. He took one gratefully, lit it, and glanced down at the considerably smaller guest next to him, who was busy on their own cigarette. A silence settled between them; comfortable, yet enshrouded in a tense combination of nerves. It was the other who first gave in to the fleeting glimpse of conversation.

"Strange, isn't it?" The voice was quiet—scarcely carried beyond the smoke—but bore none of the rough traces one might expect. Keane's match paused just before meeting the end of yet another cigarette.

"I beg your pardon?"

"Don't you think it strange, all this for a few hours? A man with all that money would spend it on a battalion of top of the line cars. Not this." The frustrated character waved a hand out toward the tittering masses, as if to make the senseless words somehow more meaningful. "I mean, why a party of all things? Why not something more substantial? More sustainable?" Keane exhaled thoughtfully; a long, soft billow of white smoke spiriting upwards toward the heavenly stars. Some say the balls of hot air worked miracles, but he often thought the miracle was that things of such beauty and might would stay to illuminate their inconsequential, fleeting lives.

"I suppose . . . " He took another draw, releasing it more leisurely than the last. "I suppose there are those who enjoy the company of others; overzealous though they may be. Some might even find the lifestyle of an extravert necessary to their existence. After all, not everyone can be so dedicated to hidden glories of life. Wouldn't you agree, Lawrence?"

CHAPTER TWENTY-FIVE

SOMETHING HAPPENED when he said my name, something I did not expect. Every inch of me was split between pounding my knuckles into that Roman nose of his or embracing him in some utterly feminine attempt to drain myself of the fear I had endured for the past several days. In the end I did neither of these, settling the difference by pulling the cigarette case out of my pocket and thrusting it mightily into his hands. He did not open it and enjoy its restocked contents, but then, I never thought he would. For all his blustering and bellowing about my own curiosity, his was often just as fierce. The silver glimmered between his fingers as he turned it over and over in his large hands; each time pausing to rub his thumb over the obvious dent defacing the front cover.

"Never was I so thankful for your excellent marksmanship." I muttered shakily. "You were right. You didn't miss." Rather than make some vain comment about him never missing or that he was in the war, after all, Keane held his precious cigarette case towards one of the overhead lights and grunted softly.

"I was a bit off to the right, I believe." I chuckled, a dry, nervous noise.

"I didn't give a damn about perfection, just so long as that bullet hit the case and not me. However, when you shoved that heavy thing in my dress—"

"—Yes, I imagine that was a surprise. You didn't keep the bullet, did you?"

"Not unless you want to go swimming in that river." Keane crushed out his cigarette and reached for another.

"God, no. I would have demanded you destroy it, if you had."

"Demanded? My, what strong words. Thank God I can swim with the same strength, or else you might have found yourself '*groping for trout in a particular river*'." Even above the roaring music and increasingly intoxicated crowd, I couldn't miss that rich chuckle floating just above my ear.

"So you enjoyed that *Measure for Measure* bit? I thought you would." It was my turn to smile.

"I must admit it took me a second to realise why you chose that particular play, but mentioning Claudio was a helpful addition. At least then I didn't think you had gone *completely* mad."

"Ah, so you think I am still mad then?"

"Are any of us really sane? Besides, 'we're all mad here.'" Keane paused a moment to enjoy a firm draw of his cigarette before nodding thoughtfully.

"So Lewis Carrol's cat has returned, has it? He's quite right, though. Sanity is only a dilution created by the vain to describe those who follow their morals, and not their pocketbook." Another puff of smoke dwindled lazily from my companion's slightly parted lips before his eyes flickered away from that nostalgic glimmer and into the alert shards of ice. "I don't believe I asked what brought you here, did I?"

"No, you didn't, but I can answer that simple enough. I was looking for you. It took a few visits to that casino—calm down, Keane. For heaven's sake, you look as though I just admitted to some scandalous affair. I do appreciate your gentlemanly concern, but it *is* 1948, after all. Now, where was I? Oh, yes. It didn't take much really. I just had to ask around at the gambling tables about the tall man exceptional at craps. That took me to several people, but it was Guy Brooks who eventually led me here. You left quite an impression on that Ruby woman, by the way." Keane stood a little straighter against the brick wall.

"Did I?"

"Yes, you did. Should I be the one inquiring about some illicit affairs? No? Well nevermind then." I leaned back against the house, leaving a respectable amount of space between our shoulders. All the other guests were content demolishing the feast laid out on the tables, with an unwavering attention to the alcohol. At some point, Keane excused himself and strode off toward the buzzing masses. He eventually returned with two sparkling glasses.

"Scotch and water." He announced, carefully handing the first to me before taking a sip of the other. If there was one thing I had learned about liquor from my several years with the man, it was that water could enhance the flavour of even the most abhorrent scotch, and, when drunk in small sips, might even rival Keane's madeira back in Devon. This scotch, though arguably one of the finest I had ever tasted, still did not hold the sweetness or flavour of that exotic wine. I set my glass on a window ledge lingering between Keane and I.

"So, what made you come here? I doubt we will be able to find those photographs tonight. And even if we did, what would we do with them? We could hardly sneak them away beneath our jackets, or shove them in our socks." Another chuckle floated through the air.

"How I have missed your vivid imagination, Lawrence. No, I hadn't made any tonight. However, if we could find an excuse to go into the rooms, that might be enough for a temporary search." I lifted my drink again, pausing uncomfortably before the rim even reached my lips.

"Keane, I may have the perfect excuse. When do you wish to act?"

"I believe sooner, rather than later. Why? What are you concocting in that infamous brain of yours."

"In your absence, I have spent the last several hours drinking cups of watered-down tea, a rather abhorrent cup of coffee, and now some excellent scotch. There comes a time when a human being's anatomy can not consume any more fluids without doing something about those already in their system." I was determined to sound perfectly at ease with the situation, but, as a woman disguised as a man, using the facilities was the absolute last thing I wished to do.

"Of course. Yes. I see your point." Keane glanced at my suit—or rather one of his suits tailored for the occasion—and the battle between gentlemanly humility and immediate necessity began. "I suppose, if you would take care of that, . . . er . . . predicament, I could just look through the other rooms for that material. That seems reasonable considering the . . . that is, the circumstances dictate we must . . ." Rather than finishing the jumbled strings of words, my companion downed the rest of his drink before leading me toward the ornate entrance.

As I rather cursely explained the situation to one of the uniformed servants wandering the halls, I caught Keane slipping through a pair of sturdy oak doors centering the hall. Making a mental note of the exact placement of the doors—as well as the directions of the lavatory—I sped off in steady strides to fulfil my own mission.

It was not long before I finished, washed my hands, and struck out again toward the hall. I found the more glamorous the rooms became, the more my mind wandered. Everything was new, be it a replacement for an original piece or just released to the public markets. Even the ominous oil paintings—no doubt older than the owner himself—still appeared incredibly bright and vivid. So enchanted was the ornate interior, had I not come to my senses once more, the search for Keane might have been entirely forgotten. The polished knobs were eerily cool in my hands as I eased myself into a room that largely resembled an extravagant lounge that had been casually dropped in the centre of a study. As the doors clicked behind me, I found myself staring at my companion. Blatantly. His long, slender form had been casually draped onto the rolled arm of a sofa. The gaudily fashionable hat he had been wearing lay beside him, the dark brim a shocking contrast to the pale green. In his fingers dangled a glass of cut crystal; half filled with some dark liquor I did not recognise. I was about to hiss something sharp—and no doubt insulting—when there was a soft squeak to my left. A single step. A squeak. A blink. A flash like that of a camera. And then I was smacked in the face by the exact copy of those photographs; grey shapes and shades smeared across hundreds of newspapers. Only, this was not a copy. This was the original. His balding head was level to mine, if perhaps a hair higher. The tell-tale signs of boxing had flattened his ears against his head, but, where most athletes were slim or heavily muscled, this man was round. Not fat. Round. His form was really quite agile, but his face was considerably circular with the lower half distorted by a pair of lips tightly drawn into a scowl. I pulled the loose threads of my thoughts together as best I could and nodded respectfully to the man: a man who had power over life and death.

"Good evening, Mr. Cohen."

The mobster, a legend in every right, eyed me for what boiled into years of incarceration. His dark eyes dragged warily up and down my form for a weapon's imprint. He was sceptical, but he had a right to be. Anyone who made a living spilling another man's blood had to be careful. He could not afford to be overeager. That is, he ought to remain cautious, lest his business offices sink away from a half-dozen of casinos to a box six feet below our feet. At last his eyes returned to my face and the first, firm glimpse of a smile played at the edge of his mouth

"You got manners, kid. I like that. Any kid with some polish can't be all bad. What's your name?"

"Devon. Devon English."

"Well, Devon, you're welcome to take a seat by Leslie there. Go ahead and take your hat off too. You'd see better." In the corner of my peripheral vision, Keane tensed, preparing to jump to my rescue at the moment the brim slipped from my head and a thick mop of hair dangled down to my chin. I did not know how Cohen would react to seeing a young woman galavanting about in a man's altered suit. No doubt it would be something new. Perhaps he would even find it amusing. But he would not get the opportunity, for a mentor's influence carries into the oddest of times, and, just as Eliza could not break from Higgin's lessons ground into her skull, I could not escape Keane's.

I pinched the brim of a fedora purchased the day before, and swept it theatrically toward the ground, exposing the masculine crop of my hair curled and pomaded to the finest male fashion.

Cohen's amusement flared into a grin, but my own humour was not fulfilled until I noticed Keane's left hand clinging to the material of his jacket. His grip did not lessen as the Los Angeles crime boss strode toward the doors.

"I'll be right back. Help yourself to a drink if you want it. I heard Sam stocks some pretty good scotch." And like that, he was gone, his footsteps echoing quickly through the hall. My spine tensed as I sat next to my companion.

"Where did he go?"

"To wash his hands." Keane answered quietly, now cradling his glass of whiskey between both his hands.

"Oh. Does he do that offen?"

"Constantly. I have seen similar cases before. They can scrub their skin raw and still not feel clean. It's an obsession; something they need to do to carry on with their daily lives. Perhaps someday we will lessen the impulses, or make them more acceptable to those small minded busibodies of society. Were a miracle to do away with the symptoms completely . . . ah, well . . . I've seen worse habits in my time." Like John Christie.

John Christie.

Of course, the police had no evidence when we met him, but it was cemented in Keane's mind that the man was a murderer: a man obsessed with, not so much the need for killing, but a need for corpses. Cold, rotting bodies to lay motionless with eyes unseeing to the world. He would steal the breath from them;

waiting until they succumbed to a gas-induced stupor before strangling them into an eternal sleep. In some cases he even dared fall to the realm of commanding the empty body into tasks which made even Keane grow pale and ill.

I had been more than glad to return to Devon at the end of that week.

Mickey Cohen did indeed return soon after, along with the gentle scent of soap. The transformation from those alleyway tales was breathtaking. It is never pleasant to find yourself in the company of such a powerful man, and yet I found myself unusually at ease in his presence. However, I would have been a fool to doubt this man would hesitate to kill one or both of us if he felt his life threatened. You would not think so to look at him. From where I was sitting, Meyer Harris Cohen looked—dare I say it—normal.

The small man perched on the edge of an ornate writing desk, but he did not reach for the scotch, nor did he grab a cigar from the box. He merely sat there with his hands folded over one knee.

"So, Kid, where'd you get that mark on your forehead?" As conversation starters went, it was a good one. He knew where it was going and, like most everything else in his life, he had full control of the situation. No man can ignore the signs of his trade ingrained upon other human beings. I cleared my throat and ran a hand through my heavily pomaded—and ultimately shorter—hair, which no longer concealed an inch long scar just above my ear. I brushed it self-consciously with the pad of my thumb.

"A boxing ring in Cleveland."

"No kidding? I did some training over there when I was fifteen. Good sport. Gives us small people a chance to be scrappy." There was a lilt to his voice—an amusement—that caused me instinctively to smile. He was perhaps a decade older than I: a decade to create that wavering line where white and black bled into grey. One instinctively wants to walk toward what is morally right—safe—however, there are also times when the good is muddled by change. For a timid, taunting moment, I found I might even *like* the murderer looking down upon me. Keane jerked those thoughts to reality in his feigned Boston tongue.

"Mr. Cohen, I would be remiss if I did not pay you a compliment. I went to one of your tailors for a suit, and found the work far superior to my own back in Massachusetts." The mobster leaned back a little with another easygoing grin.

"Yeah, they're a good group of boys. I see 'em just about everyday and their work just gets better every time." *Everyday*. Good Lord, this man probably never wore the same suit twice. "So, Kid, you come from Ohio then, or were ya just passing through?"

"When my father came from Ireland, he moved to Steubenville. I was born there."

"I have a few friends from Steubenville. I also had a girl once who was Irish. The only thing wrong with her was she made the mistake of fallin' for in love with a crazy young punk, such as I was." Again that confident humour shone through the man's clean-cut exterior; tipping the balance away from my hastily gathered hatred for him. It is always easy to hate someone everyone claims to be bad and evil; however, when you discover there may be some good in a person, words mean little. Actions mean everything.

Cohen's eyes jerked quickly to Keane as my companion reached back into his pocket; the mobster's gaze calming as a billfold appeared in his hands, rather than an automatic pistol. Was Keane even wearing his gun? He opened his wallet.

"Mr. Cohen, I have a friend named John Harrison. I understood he did some business with you over the past several years." Two brown eyes gazed lazily at Keane.

"I do business with many people. Could you be more specific?"

"He had rather a sizable debt to you over a considerable supply of hydrocodone. I would like to pay the difference on his behalf."

"I don't know nothing about no Hydrocodone." Nonetheless, Keane pulled out several five hundred dollar bills, folded them neatly together, and handed them to Cohen. To my surprise, the shorter man stuck the sizable wad in his jacket pocket without bothering to count them. The doors swung open again just as the tips of green dove into hiding, and a fourth figure entered our sombre gathering. Cohen's seemingly ever-present smile only grew larger.

"Boys, meet the real host of this party. Sam Barker." I wanted to hide; to dive under the sofa and disappear from the world. That, unfortunately, was not possible; therefore, I simply rose to my feet while we were introduced by the king of Los Angeles.

"Sam, this here is Leslie McCormic and Devon English." As the young man and I shook hands, I used more muscle than strictly necessary for two newly met individuals and arranged a somewhat tired expression on my features to match the obvious shock facing me.

"I take it you've met my twin sister then. Don't let the names fool you, she is English at heart. Or at least she would be if she hadn't insisted on taking on that infernal pen of hers." My feigned masculinity completed the tailored facade as Sam Barker wrenched his hand from my grasp with special attention to his aching fingers.

"Devon here was a boxer in Cleveland." Cohen announced, as if my achievements had as much right to his pride as it had to me all those years ago. It wouldn't have mattered if I had won or lost. We had a connection. In the underworld, similarity was everything. It was family.

"I'd believe it." Sam muttered, stretching his hand before turning to my somewhat less popular companion. "And what is it you do Mr . . . McCormic, wasn't it?" Keane once more lowered himself upon the sofa.

"Oh, a little of everything, I suppose. Gambling. Travelling. Philanthropy." The last grabbed Cohen's attention.

"Seems we are in the same business, McCormic. Come round here on Tuesday, if ya want. Sam usually has in a few people from all over town. They state their case. Ya know, philanthropy." Mickey Cohen's claim to help the less fortunate was not a great surprise, though I doubted Al Capone would have done something in its like. With Cohen, his generosity seemed to be as commonplace as his ruthlessness. His sense of survival somehow spread to helping those who could not survive on their own accord. Everyone was human until they crossed him. Then they were dead. No, it was not his answer, but Keane's that really sent me reeling.

"Tuesday you say? I don't think either of us have anything definite planned. What time? We'll be here."

"Good." The mobster grinned, standing up from the desk. "Now, I'm afraid Sam and me better be getting back to the party. You two will stay a while, won't you?" Keane assured him we would as all four of us walked toward the door. Sam immediately struck up some boorish conversation with my companion, while Cohen pulled me aside as we emerged into the hallway. I had come to expect many things in my life, but having a one hundred dollar bill thrust into my palm was certainly not one of them.

"You're alright, kid. You're an honest, hard working kind of guy. I like that." And with those words, accompanied with a solid pat on the back, Mickey Cohen—king of Los Angeles and lord of the underground markets—disappeared into a buzzing crowd of celebratory guests.

CHAPTER TWENTY-SIX

"LEAVE IT TO YOU TO find a friend in the mafia." Keane chuckled as he pulled a cigarette from his case. He looked more like himself now than he had when he appeared at the party. His wavy hair was washed loose from confining pomade and now dangled at the tips of his ears as blonde-grey curls. A dark blue dressing gown had been wrapped loosely around his athletic form. A white, silk pyjama shirt stuck out over the collar; a new purchase for the fictional Leslie McCormic, no doubt. I sighed and tipped my head over the back of the settee.

"This is a nice hotel. Exceptionally nice." And indeed it was. Not quite so elegant perhaps as those grand, old establishments in Europe, but far superior to all in which we had stayed on this journey thus far. The carpeted floors were more reserved in colour. The decor was less vulgar than most. Even the upholstery on which I sat was more of a faded blue of yesteryear, rather than some audacious pattern of ill-matched stripes.

Cigarette dangling from his mouth, Keane casually lifted my hat from my side and tossed it onto an ancient basket chair. He sat himself in its place, but looked at the floor beneath his slippers, rather than me. His voice; however, bore the quiet directness I both admired and loathed.

"Will you be alright?"

"About what? Cohen?"

"Come now, I know women in an emergency; all sobs and smelling salts. Heaven knows I keep enough handkerchiefs in my study to save an entire regiment of emotional females over the menial trials of life." I replaced the first tinglings of laughter for a frustration that was never far beyond my reach.

"Really, Keane, if you think that low of me—after the past few hours especially—we might as well introduce ourselves as the strangers we are. What on earth have I to be weepy about?"

"Why your..." His voice fell to a whisper. "... Your hair."

My hair.

Ah.

Admittedly, it *had* been a cause of some discomfort over the past few days, but I hardly thought one's physical annoyances were cause for hysterics. Not a tear had been shed over the loss, though it did take a bit longer to recognise me in the mirror when I gave a damn enough to look.

My fingers tread self-consciously along my pruned, reddish-blonde curls. It was not a fashionable colour by any means, but one I bore with an arguably foolish pride.

"I take it you don't like it then?" I tried to sound vaguely disinterested with whatever his answer might have been; however, somewhere between my vocal cords and mouth, the words took on a tone that seemed uncharacteristically melancholy in comparison. Keane looked at me then; not hard, yet acutely. His eyes carefully ran from my brow, back to the top of my head, and returned to an unidentifiable place near my temple. His cigarette had shrunk considerably.

"I can't say I dislike it, though it will look a great deal better when that grease is washed out. It still goes past your ears a bit, which is good. And you needn't worry about the play. If it doesn't grow miraculously by then, wigs were invented for a reason."

Blast.

The play.

I had forgotten about that.

"I did what had to be done." I defended feebly as Keane tipped my head forward with his forefinger to inspect the hair curling at the nape of my neck.

"Indeed you did, and, considering the circumstances as they are, it is a rather fine job of it too." My pride flourished.

"I did most of it at the beach house with a pair of cooking shears." My companion ran his thumb over the finely trimmed ends.

"Most of it?"

"I went to a barber to finish it. I wanted something modern enough to keep some length, and we both know I pay little attention to fashion. It did get a bit awkward though. He insisted on giving me a shave. Something about him having never cut a man's hair without one." My companion's amusement was reflected magnificently as glimmers danced through his ice-blue eyes. I squelched the impulse to grin and stared down my nose at the dark, cream carpeting. "You know, Keane, I believe I can appreciate the luxury of a hot towel on one's face, but to have someone holding a razor so close to your throat." I flinched. "It's ridiculous." At that he did not chuckle as I thought he might. No, he laughed. His rich baritone erupted so close to my ear I started convulsively at the deep tremor. So rare were those great shows of humour that were constantly in wake of his presence. To earn a chuckle—however brief—was a joy.

A laugh? An honour.

I must have drifted off soon after, for the next recollection was based upon a hushed voice, not at my ear or side, but lingering over my shoulder.

"As much as I relish your company, Lawrence, I fear a scandal would ensue if the hotel's staff found your bed already made." My mind slowly wrapped itself around his words. A part of me had thought Keane's melodious tember only a part of a dream. It would be a very nice dream, rich with sails and sea salt, but a dream nonetheless. Then, when inevitable realisation at last occurred, I leapt up to find him leaning over the back of the sofa, a waggish grin positively glowing on his familiar face. How blue his eyes were; how deep the laugh lines running and crinkling along the side of his face. I rushed back into my own room just as an intricate mantle clock made some muddled declaration of the hour. Clothed in all but my suit jacket and a pair of brown, polished shoes I had bought sometime in the last forty-eight hours, I flung myself into bed.

I had not thought myself tired or prone to more sleep than I had already enjoyed on Keane's sofa, but it was not long before I found my mind swinging in the belly of a great ship, where lanterns creaked and swayed above my head and a first mate called down that all was well.

All was well.

WE AVOIDED THE CASINO for the next few days, fearing a more bountiful harvest from the gambling tables and finding the time better spent regenerating our energies. Breakfast and lunch we took at the hotel by having it hauled up to our rooms, rather than enduring the inconvenience of spotting ourselves at two different tables. There was little between us that was incredibly private to our lives, save our pasts, which were entirely separate and infinitely more complicated than our unusual companionship. I knew little of Keane's own life. Exceptionally little. I had heard stories of his days in the navy during that first war, as well as his doctorate from some Irish university I had momentarily forgotten, and yet it was not until a few months before I had found he had two siblings and a history that existed long before I.

He knew something about me as well. He knew of my unfortunate American birth, doubly cursed by any maternal lineage, and torn over the rocks of an unusual child scorned by all. At that point, I had come to suspect Keane was more aware of my tragic history than I was of his.

We never discussed these things during meals. Or if the subject did occur, it was just as quickly brushed aside by a wave of a hand or the arrival of our waiter. It was only on the eve of that Tuesday morn that Keane or I dared venture away from our played roles into those two people who had met all those years before. Two lost people: a greying man whose life had followed little of his direction, and a young woman searching for a direction to follow. As usual, his bluntness was preceded by no unnecessary pleasantries. It simply shot across the table as Keane balanced a piece of steak onto his fork.

"Lawrence, I will not be joining you at Mr. Barker's tomorrow." I paused to return my knife from where it had fallen from my plate.

"You said we would go. *We*, Keane. Not *me*." My companion peered down at me as though what I had just said was an idea never considered in the minds of humanity. He shook his head, chewed thoughtfully on his steak, and cut another browned square before continuing.

"It cannot be helped. As it happens, my presence has been requested to attend a gathering of psychologists tomorrow."

"And you didn't feel it was convenient to tell me until now?"

"The telegram only arrived this afternoon." He pulled the paper from his jacket and gently pushed it across the table. "It cannot be helped." The words were all there, carefully written with the official stamina which could have made even Freud weep. I gently refolded the telegram along the creased edges. No, it could not be helped.

Keane pulled out another, thinner paper, which had been folded only once, and slid this too in my direction.

"I suspected you might need a large sum of money tomorrow." I opened the check, allowing my eyes to wander slowly along the neat curls and strikes of Keane's handwriting, though it was signed to an account number as foreign as the alias signature scratched across the bottom. Perhaps it was not the finest example of prime calligraphy, but it was beautifully done with an endless amount of manual dexterity and the great male ego. I gasped.

"Ten *thousand* dollars?"

"If it is not enough, I have authorised my bank to release to you any amount." I grabbed his long, dry hand and thrust the piece of paper into his large palm.

"Keane, I have my own money. I have plenty of my own money. More than any I would ever need. I can use that. I—" His other hand fell over the check, gently pinning my fingers easily between his palms.

"Do you realise how much I have won day after day behind those infernal craps tables?" He leaned forward and whispered a series of numbers that made my head spin. Then, as the wheels of reality still wobbled along the razor edge of shock, I was half aware of Keane paying our bill and climbing to his exceptional stature. He was Zeus; his thunderous bolts thrashing downward and thrusting life into even the fallen. "And, Lawrence, I do mean *any* amount."

I FELT WELL ARMED AGAINST the elegant fortress up to the very second the door opened. Then I felt nothing. I was numb; awash with that which I did not know. Men in elaborate suits stood idly in the enormous foyer, with glasses of pale liquor in their hands and international forms of tobacco crushed between their teeth. There were cigarettes from the hierarchy in France, clay pipes from the highlands of Scotland, and thin twigs of cigars from . . . India perhaps? I refused the last of these when presented to me and took out a package of Keane's cigarettes. There is a safety—a comfort—in that which is familiar. I could only hope Keane would forgive me for taking less of the smoke into my lungs; allowing thin tails of white to rise from the cigarette's smouldering end. It was better this way, for I stood there with the gentlemen for the better part of half an hour, and a person can only inhale so much of the stuff before finding themselves hopelessly infatuated with the infernal things. Sam Barker's butler appeared and escorted our dull band of heavy billfolds into a large sitting room dominated by a loathful fireplace so abnormally intricate, one questioned whether it was of any practical use at all. The colours were again conservative, but there was no subtlety in the vast amounts of wealth this man held. One by one as we passed through the door, each man received a cordial nod and firm handshake from Mickey Cohen. His cream-colored suit had been replaced by one of a moderate grey. It appeared equally expensive, but not nearly so obnoxious as the bright necktie dangling from Sam Barker's neck as he drank a glass of champagne by the fireplace. Suddenly there was a strong hand grasping mine and shaking it firmly as two old friends meeting after a long separation.

"So ya made it, Kid. Good. A man who keeps his word is one I can trust." His dark eyes flickered briefly over my shoulder. "Where's McCormic?"

"He couldn't make it. Last minute business deal. But he gave me a check on his behalf and said he would get more if he needed to." What I had worked so diligently to lose from my American habits now returned in full force. Granted, I was glad to have them as I played this fatal role, as long as I was able to brush them once more beneath the carpet when I was to return to Harrison's theatre. Cohen smiled and patted me on the shoulder before nearly sprinting off toward the hallway. Only once had I seen a man so desperate to wash his hands; a germaphobe tucked away in the hills of Switzerland. However, as Keane rightly observed, this was different. There was a separation, for Cohen seemed not so concerned about falling ill as he was to commit himself to the practice of scrubbing his hands raw.

Sam Barker positioned us in a circle along the various chairs and settees, rather like a class of overgrown children smoking and drinking and talking and laughing. And all about things that would not matter the next day. The young host seemed to enjoy this intimately, as though he had done something profound for this gathering of businessmen. There were all sorts of money; old money, new money, and even those who had the slightest possibility of stumbling into money somewhere along the road. The man smoking those horribly Indian cigars stood lazily on the other end of the fireplace, slurring out some drowsy words about how he hoped the little meeting wouldn't take too long because he had a girl waiting in some motel. She charged by the hour. The rest of the group cackled their approval of his situation, and I—a person who had created a sound sum of money by setting myself far away from society—suddenly regretted having not been made by God to be more sociable. At least Keane understood at least a little of humanity and was able to enter and exit each scene of life with the same gentlemanly grace I admired. I had none of this. Looking back, I could understand it was in part because of my youth, and a person must never feel guilty for the small selection of years they set aside.

And yet I did.

As many of the other men muttered jokes and profanities, I felt increasingly ashamed to have been young and not quite having swallowed enough of my own life to understand the great moral travesty of theirs. Just as my mind had defensively numbed itself from words demeaning to my concealed femininity, Mickey Cohen entered the room.

And everything stopped.

Well, perhaps it didn't stop, per se, but a ripple of silence swept over the room; engulfing all language in his presence. It took several minutes to realise there was another man behind him. It was even longer before my mind was able to comprehend that the man was a priest.

I was Catholic. I had been born Catholic. And, in the end, I would die Catholic. But such did not mean I was unaware of those other religions. In my travels I had feasted with Arabs and Monarchs, celebrated the Passover with a Jewish family, and prayed in tongues I knew not. I was the first to stand when he entered the room, and the last to sit when he bade us to do so. He introduced himself as Father James Kennedy. The long, black cassock he wore jerked stiffly as he spoke.

"Mr. Cohen has kindly invited me to speak to you fine gentlemen about an orphanage our parish has run for the last seventy years. It is a good establishment; large enough to house over two dozen unfortunate youths. We educate them in a few classrooms we were able to build into the house itself; however, our congregation is not a large one, nor do they have the funds necessary to sustain such a program."

A general succession of nods and sympathetic murmurs arose from the other men. Mickey Cohen smiled. "Right, so what'll it be? Jack, you go first. Name your donation."

"Six hundred dollars." Cohen's smile faltered and he wagged his head.

"That's not enough, Jack. I know you can do a lot better than that. Now, say it again, but a better number."

"Three thousand."

"Much better. Stoney?"

"Sixty-three hundred."

"Good. Hank?" And so it went; one after another. If the chosen amount wasn't to his liking, Cohen had the man raise it until it was at least an honest man's yearly wages. After the first victim; however, he had little trouble coaxing a generous donation from each man. At last, it was my turn.

"Well, wadaya say, Kid?" Cohen asked; his smile more expectant than it was threatening.

I named the amount.

The men gaped at me. The priest's eyes grew wide. Mickey's smile only broadened.

I stood and edged over toward the stunned priest, taking out Keane's enormous check and adding an equally abundant amount of paper cash. In total, our twenty thousand completed the deal with a sound sixty thousand dollars, which Cohen promptly doubled. One hundred twenty thousand dollars, and we had only been there only a little over two hours. In the time to follow, Sam Barker and Father Kennedy retreated from the house and the drinks and tobacco returned in full force. A few of the business men wandered off to the billiard room, leaving me to face a man I found as equally curious as I did frightening. He had killed men, no doubt: shot dead in cold blood. Perhaps our greatest similarity is that we had both seen death. His suffering; however, had been planned by a murderous heart. Mine was the wicked hand of chance. He motioned for me to sit on one of the low armchairs while he took his natural perch along the edge of a sofa. One was never to doubt his dominance in a room. Perhaps he had been a king in the east, but here he thought himself a god.

"So tell me, where'd ya get all that dough. I didn't make that much boxing even on good fights." I pulled out a cigarette and rolled it between my fingers. I was beginning to understand Keane's adoration of the little things.

"Boxing isn't all I did. Writing can make a pretty penny, 'specially if you have a good story." The cigarette nearly fell from my hand when I instinctively dropped an 'e' from my words. My midnight hour was drawing near. Soon the illusion of English heritage would fall away even from myself, and a rotting pumpkin would forever take its place.

God, this needed to end.

Soon.

Mickey grinned calmly; folding his meaty hands over his legs and edging eagerly forward.

"So you're in the media?" I waved a lit match in some vague attempt at casual ease. Casual ease. Can one ever find comfort in the presence of a murderer?

"Something like that. Saw you in the papers a few times. Good stories, those. Keep it up and you'll be as big as Capone."

"Bigger, Kid, if fate pays its dues." And I suspected it often did. "You gotta take what you can when you can. No questions. No hesitation. Just take it."

Carpe Diem.

Seize the day.

CHAPTER TWENTY-SEVEN

I DIDN'T BOTHER ENTERING my own hotel room, but instead went next door to Keane's. He was unceremoniously hunched over the little desk never made for a man more than one and a half metres, let alone two inches over six feet. I threw myself dramatically onto the sofa and tossed an arm over my eyes.

"Brendan Keane, you are an awful, horrible man and I hate you terribly." My companion tried to swing his long legs around to face me, but the quick motion became a slow, methodic task of extracting his knees from beneath the wooden table and stretching them out straight as he twisted his torso in my direction. His thin, silver spectacles he occasionally wore slipped along the bridge of his nose. "I hate you horribly." I announced again, with a little more theatrical conviction than the last time, before allowing my voice to falter and fall to a whisper. "I hate you for what you have done to me. I find cigarettes are bearable: even, heaven forbid, enjoyable. Especially compared to Indian cigars." The chuckle began as a thin wisp of understanding, growing louder as the full weight of my words settled over the room. Keane's voice only bothered to appear when his laughter sputtered between a few short breaths.

"I don't believe I've ever smoked Indian cigars."

"And, if I have any say in it, you never will. Here," I reached a hand into my jacket pocket and threw the package of cigarettes at Keane's chest before laying back and dropping my hat over my face. "Take them, and may you have more luck with them than I do." The package disappeared beneath a pile of papers etched in his handwriting as my companion stood; gradually working the knots out of his shoulders. There was the soft thud of agile footsteps blended with the rustle of those horrid first drafts. He pinched the hat from my head, glanced down at my face, and dropped it again.

"Have you eaten? Doesn't matter, lunch or dinner. Did you have either? I thought not. Come." I let my hat fall to the floor in time to catch Keane's reflection in the mirror as he did up his waistcoat buttons and shrugged into an elegant, dark jacket. The simple necktie, which had been dangling from his neck, had been replaced by one infinitely more obnoxious in both colour and pattern. It fairly exploded from the dark contrast of yet another new suit. Modest, but expensive. Dark, but not depressingly so. I caught the first breath of a sigh as he adjusted his lapels and did up the jacket's bright buttons. "I shall be glad to return to my tweeds." He announced with a final glance toward the looking glass as he cajoled me out the door.

As I had come to expect carefully chosen restaurants accentuated with fine dishes and old wine, it was rather a shock when Keane vered off the paved walkways toward a small deli. I waited outside and watched the infamous oddities of the world up until the moment my companion reemerged with a paper bag clutched in his hand. With the other set of fingers, he casually steered me toward a nearby park. The first flickers of evening had just begun to shift along the green grasses. As Keane farely knocked me onto a poor old bench, the results of our last visit to the point of imagined paradise had ended in frustration, irritation, and confusion. But that couldn't very well happen twice. Certainly not. We were—in all eyes, save our own—two men. Two normal, ordinary men. Keane tossed the parcel onto the bench and lowered himself beside it, peeling away the paper wrappings to reveal two grand sandwiches, well off with slices of thick beef and cheese. While I tore into mine ravenously, my companion was infinitely more patient, chewing thoughtfully as though each bite was an algebraic equation to be meticulously solved. He had barely made a dent in his meal when I paused to mop my hands on the oily, white creases of the wax paper.

"How was the business meeting? Any unusual psychiatrists?"

"None." I started a little, believing he was joking, or at least trying to coax me toward some tempting jest of fate, which might finish with some hilarious tale of a mad scholar with long, wild hair and a funny moustache.

"None?" I repeated. "Surely there was someone. Never have those conventions occurred without some exciting tale. How could there be none?" Keane glanced at his sandwich then squinted up toward the darkening sky, and I immediately knew whatever he was about to say would have little to do with the subject of psychoanalysis or dedicated intellectuals.

"Strange how easily things can be hidden, yet they are so bloody difficult to find." I almost choked. He had not fallen from the country of conversation, nor even the continent.

He had fallen from the earth.

"What the devil do you mean by that? I'm not denying that there may be some truth in that statement, but what does that have to do with meetings and—" I stopped, catching the tilt to my companion's long head and the glimmer as he glanced at me from the sides of those two twinkling oceans. I shut my mouth hard and, once my poor abused teeth had ceased their rattling, I opened it again; my voice slowly unfurling itself into a single, coherent sentence.

"You didn't go to that business meeting, did you?" A cigarette appeared at his lips.

"Lawrence, would you believe I spent the better part of this afternoon within a mile of yourself."

"You couldn't have. I would have recognised you." Would I? Was I able to recall every muddled face wandering about in the tobacco haze? Scars may be replicated and added just above real skin. Facial hair may be glued. Theatrics could go unnoticed.

"Not if I was a floor below you." Keane stated simply, his voice muffling slightly as he held the cigarette in his mouth as he fished about for a pack of matches. "There is no doubt in my mind that those photographs are somewhere in that house; however, *where* is something I am having a bloody hard time finding." It was difficult to imagine my companion having a 'bloody hard time' of anything. There had never been a failure to him. A *real* failure. Something that was so horrible it made me hate him. It is incredibly—*damnably*—hard to hate someone who makes the world a bit more logical. A bit more secure. A bit more substantial.

Beyond Keane, it was insanity.

KEANE AND I HAD MADE plans to return to the noise and bustle of the casino late that night. As usual, this theatrical debut required another one of Keane's new and extravagant suits to be whittled down to accommodate my smaller, and far less masculine, frame. It also meant a great deal of poorly concealed sulking from my generous comrade. I adjusted my silk necktie.

"Really, Keane, if you are going to be so intolerable about this, stop buying such expensive suits."

"Leslie McCormic would *not* wear anything less than the best." My companion declared with a villainous wave of his comb. His jacket had been laid neatly over the back of a chair, leaving him in his white shirtsleeves with black suspenders crossing his back and climbing over his shoulders. God, even *those* must have cost enough to feed a family of seven. The comb dove toward his head. "Devon English, however—"

"What about Devon? Wouldn't he wear nice clothes as well?"

"A former boxer?" A rough scoff tumbled to the floor. "Surely you jest." I finished tying up the laces to one shoe, pausing briefly to glance up at my companion's back.

"Come now. They could be hand me downs from some well-off friend." Keane swivelled around like an office chair, with the same grace as well oiled wheels. I couldn't quite tell if he was smiling, or about to run me through with the jagged teeth of his comb.

"*Hand me downs?* My dear Lawrence, I hadn't even gotten to wear that suit before you hauled it off to the tailor's."

"Good. That means no one can suspect another man is wearing your clothes. Now wouldn't *that* cause a scandal?" I bent down to tie my laces, ready to be pummelling by every selection of verbal insults, or the possibility of something that carried more force. Keane, being a gentleman, would never dare hit a woman, although I was not certain how far those rules of chivalry came when applied to me. One does not create a seven year friendship with one of the opposite sex and follow all social expectations.

But he again surpassed all logical expectations when he merely shot a single, sharp 'Ha!' and once more leaned over the mirror to smooth the last silver wave of hair into place along his temple. He was a magnificent actor—incredibly so—but I had known him too long to miss that brief smile in the reflective glass.

To every dawn there is a sun, and to every dusk there is a star.

It had been planned that we would arrive in separate taxies; Keane first, then myself a little over thirty minutes later. Were two actors, such as it were, to enter upon a stage together; mouths agape with carefully pasted words. His name could not be tied to mine by more than a mutual acquaintance. Our paths were not to cross more than a few times; muddled together until they were of no particular importance. When I at last arrived at the casino, it did not take more than a few glances to find my companion, for I had learned that such places made dynamic masculinity obvious and cowardice the dirt of humanity. Good or bad, moralist or villain, there was a sense of impending danger among all the gamblers.

They could win or lose everything.

I didn't bother laying any bets or catching any cards in fear of winning more money than I already had. It was a shame how much I had collected in my visits, though I suspected it was only pennies in comparison to Keane's growing treasury. Every now and again I recognised some finely dressed man or scarcely dressed woman. I recognised them, but rarely knew their names. I didn't care to know. The only person I had met more than a passing glance was Sam Barker, who had settled himself at one of the card tables near to the bar, but not so awfully close that a visit might gain his attention. As one of the brightly dressed staff mechanically walked passed, I gave him some polite instructions before shoving off toward the bar.

It is a pleasant thing to allow the world to shift around you without having to lift a finger to make it so. Wheels turned, cards were dealt, and money was frequently passed from hand to hand; lingering only when some fortunate chap struck a thin vein of luck before blundering it all back into the eternal abyss of odds. I ordered something strong enough to dull the pain of life, but not anywhere near the border of intoxication. That done, I moved again toward the only space of the room where there really wasn't anything more than frustrating conversations to rattle the sanity of life. It was an ocean; thousands of fish swimming up against each other with long strings of incoherent words to tie those loose pieces of fabric into a quilt so gaudy it was repulsive. A quilt of life. A quilt of memories. And all of it beneath an eternal fear.

A fear of sharks.

It was easier to find Keane manoeuvring through that crowd than it would have been for him to find me. One can always find achieved greatness, but a young fledgling clinging to success may be lost to the darkened depths of time. The only thing to set me apart from those around me was the simple fact I had no intention of becoming like them. I had not been born anything wonderful or worthy of life's breath, but circumstances—horrid circumstances that strangled me from any hopes of a pleasant childhood—made me willing to fight until I had nothing left to believe in.

I met my companion at last and wordlessly pulled him to a slightly less claustrophobic part of the room in direct sight of the bar and card tables. It was a placement perfect in every form; however, even in perfection, there is always that daunting question to be asked.

"Keane, do you trust me?"

"Lawrence—"

"Do you?" My companion gazed down at me as a teacher whose student had asked whether the world was round. An unquestionable assurance.

"I believe you know the answer. I have always trusted you." I knew he would say some such declaration, but it was one of the rare times in my life where reassurance was vitally necessary for those wild whips of ideas flitting through my head.

He trusted me.

He trusted *me*.

God, how daunting a thought to have a soul—noble and, I often believed, infallible—to rely on one's own shoulders. It was a burden too monstrous to carry.

I jerked my thoughts into something more coherent. He trusted me. That was good. *Very* good. But of course, there was a test: an obstacle.

"Then I need you to hit me." Keane's shoulders went rigid.

"Good God, Lawrence. Are you certain?" Are you certain I should hit you? Are you certain I will not hurt you? Are you certain you have a plan? I turned my chin up a bit and pointed to my right cheekbone.

"Right here. And make it a good one, not some halfhearted fling of a mollycoddle." My companion took a sharp indraw of breath, and for one sinful moment, I walked in the footsteps of Thomas. It was not until a crushing blow sent me hurling backwards that I believed. I had the foresight to move with his knuckles, but the hand still connected with a crack. I took my stance, fists raised and feet balanced. I had rarely lost a match in my boxing days, and those were only when I had been shoved into the ring with men three times my size (not to mention eight stone heavier). This was not quite so unequal as those other bouts had been, though I would have shuddered to challenge his tall, guard-like frame under any other circumstances. It was a dance, taking turns twisting our heads as the other's bare fist approached, while trying to ignore the blood pouring from cuts and a sore nose. It was not until the staff peeled us apart that the fighting ceased. It took two men to drag Keane off to one side, while only one came to take me away. I suspected I would be the one thrown out onto the streets. I was a new addition to their world—practically a stranger—where Keane had ingrained himself into their lifestyle nearly a fortnight before. Of course I would be thrown out. I suspected it. I knew it.

But even Peter, having cut off Malchus' ear, did not know it would grow back.

And yet the saviour of the world was not who healed my wound.

"Let the young one stay, Jimmy." A voice sauntered through the crowd. "It was the old man—McCormic—who took the first punch. He can come back tomorrow once he cools down." Sam Barker appeared from the crowd and the fist at my collar immediately deteriorated into my own sweat. The salt of labor mingled intimately with the blood on my face, causing the sparse stripes of red to smear into the boisterous shouts of murder. A handkerchief—reeking of common perfumes, watered down for economic purposes—was shoved into my hands, along with the instructions to wipe my nose. (So that was where the blood was coming from.) Another gruff voice declared that I looked like shit. I was not inclined to disagree.

Sam pulled me along to the bar and ordered something that was infinitely stronger than I would have chosen myself. I poured a good dose of the vodka down my throat, coughed, and finished the drink, having learned the good of it.

"Alright?" He asked. I nodded and smacked the drained glass onto the counter. The sudden thrash of noise shook the pain tingling at the base of my skull. I was in no condition to embark upon a conversation that must be created upon carefully planned falsehood after falsehood. Sam Barker; however, was uncomfortably eager to open the gates and let the horses run rampant through my brain.

"That was quite a fight. What about?"

"I don't see it is any of your business what happens between that son of a bitch backstabber and me." It was a careful blend of anger and curses. So perfectly mated it caused my stomach to lurch. The man in front of me ran a finger along the rim of my glass.

"You forget, I could have you thrown out of here on your ass."

"*You?* I thought Mickey owned this place. You know, that you only work for him sort of thing." Sam Barker shot up indignantly.

"I don't work for anybody if I don't want to. Just like you ain't working for that other guy you hang around with."

"Me? Work for that bastard? Not on your life."

"See. I'd bet you are fuck'n furious for showing you up in front of all the men around here. Well, ain't' ya?" What was it with Americans and that dreaded contraction that ought to have been thrown the instant of its creation? I ordered something weaker from the bartender. I would need it.

"You have no idea."

"And you want to get back at him. Right?"

"O'course I do." Henry Higgins would have washed my mouth with soap, but the man leaning mere inches from me appeared to be drinking every word of my Americanisms with a daunting vigour.

"Then, tell me what the fight was about. C'mon. He had to have done something."

"*Something* my aunt fanny." I choked out. "He told me he wouldn't pay for . . . for my part of our little business arrangement, even though I've been the one risking my neck for our customers. Owes me half a hundred thousand, and says I'm not seeing a lick of it." The mention of such a large sum of money meant nothing to the wealthy young man. No, his attention wavered on only a single word.

"Business? What kind of business?"

"The kind the rich can afford, the poor despise, and the soldiers need; Hydrocodine, cocaine, opium, and . . . other things." I had seen the devil countless times throughout my years on this earth, but they might have all been the angelic Lucifer in comparison. Gone was the carefree Sam Barker I had met at the edge of a clear, rinkling swimming pool. Gone was the conviction he did not work. All of it—the entire American dream of idle glory and glamour—had dissipated into dust equivalently worthless and common as pyrite. There was nothing special anymore about his relaxed demeanour, his countless wealth that steadily grew, or even the house he kept well populated with the figures as popular with society as they were with police records.

Sam leaned forward, his dark hair spiking ever so slightly at the temples to the point they might have been confused for horns.

"Do you have any photographs?" I shrugged, pushing the man's serpentine resemblance far out of my mind's invasive reach.

"No. No, I don't. But I could make some—photos, that is—and bring them to you here. Or at your house."

"Do that. Who knows," He grabbed the glass half filled before me and threw the entire thing back with no loss of conviction to its mercies.

I will drink, and right freely, just because you tell me not to.

"And who knows," He began again. "We might get your money out of that old Leslie McCormic after all."

CHAPTER TWENTY-EIGHT

THERE IS AN EVIL IN powder. It has been so for centuries too numerous to count. Some powders may reach your eyes and blind you from the world; forever to stagger through darkness. Some may stain men's lips as they make pale the brothels of Paris. And others—those sprinkled throughout the poor and rich alike—create a world no mind would dare build alone, and those addicted to its force would never willingly release it. And there I stood, entranced by the mystery of it all, with white grains spread before me on the hotel table. Each was a piece of sand; many among its members. They were the sands of time. They were the boundary between logic and fantasy. Love and hate. Strong and sickly. Life and death.

How bountiful the harvest of sins.

And yet, I did not hesitate to dip my finger into the white pile and drop a pinch onto my tongue as Keane entered from his own bedroom.

"Lawrence, I must congratulate you on a plan well enforced, but perhaps you should refrain from tasting the sugar." And sugar it indeed was; sweet to the tongue, but deceitful to the eye when presented in a blurred, grey form darkly engrained onto a photographer's paper. I reformed the bountiful pile, only for the miniscule pieces to tremble out of place as Keane set three identical bottles on the table mere inches away. "These are the last of James' collection. I had thought I had found the entire stash weeks ago. *Seithí olc go maith.*"

Evil hides well.

I nodded and backed away from the display. Evil does indeed hide well, but that in plain sight disappears easily within mortal ignorance and insecurities. Even we were secluded carefully from light. Dark curtains had been pinned over the more fashionable drapes, and a string of red light bulbs had been flung around the hatrack near trays of various chemicals. We had left the lights on, but once the photographs were taken, there would be not but darkness, spotted with eerie red eyes leering at our shoulders.

Within an hour, we were inspecting a set of dripping photographs strung across the washroom door frame with an old shoelace. I had seen Keane tromping about the cliffs of Devon with a camera slung around his neck, but so often I had passed it for one of his many hobbies. How wrong I had been. Every line—every granular outline—was perfectly clear in the darkened grey; most certainly not the work of a mere hobbyist.

As the photographs dried and were slipped into a manilla envelope, the necessity of the crimson glow waned away. Keane turned on the lights, revealing an open cigarette case and lighter at the ready. I waited patiently for the rich smoke to begin straining at the thin end before tearing down the dark sheets and winding the strings of red bulbs over my arm. My companion, shirtsleeves still rolled above his forearm, sat thoughtfully in an armchair with the brief streams of white unfurling into the air.

"*By failing to prepare, you are preparing to fail.*"

"Of all the works of Benjamin Franklin, you might have chosen something more optimistic." I countered coolly.

"Optimism? Come now, Lawrence, is there really anything optimistic about our situation. Here I am, willingly throwing my reputation to the wolves for bait while you talk about some vain positivity of this world. But then, I admit you must have some nervousness—"

"Damn right I do." I dropped a clothespin to the floor with a taunting chatter. "It's indecent how calm you are about this entire lie. These men are killers, Keane. *Killers*. Not door to door salesmen looking to make an extra income to send some spindly tike off to university. *Killers*. Murderers. Cheats. Liars. And—God, hand me that cigarette." I snatched the glowing object from his fingertips, took a long draw, and handed it back to my infuriatingly amused companion.

"You could light your own. Heaven knows I have plenty." I shook my head, rubbing the sore spot taunting me from the base of my neck.

"What? And be a smoker?" I waited for his chuckling to filter away before begrudgingly seating myself on the edge of the sofa nearest to himself. "I suppose I will have to move hotels then? Keeping up appearances and all that?" A hiss of bitter tobacco smoke jutted into the air.

"Or you could simply change floors. There is a great psychological distance within a few flights of stairs." A great distance for both the prey and hunter alike, and, at that moment, I was not entirely certain which we were.

I sighed and accepted the cigarette as it was passed between us.

"I don't believe I fully considered the consequences of our little skirmish. I did not think that we—that *I*—would be abandoning you, and—"

"My dear Lawrence, you are hardly abandoning me. You are only appearing to society's eye that it is the case. As for considering consequences, you did not have time to look beyond the exact moment." He stubbed out the last ends of his cigarette into an ashtray and began the slow, methodic ritual of starting another. His long fingers slipped one from the silver case, tapped the end mere millimetres from the bullet's dent, and pressed it between his lips. Lighting the cigarette was a faster affair; the sulfuric hiss of a match, an orange glow, and, at last, smoke. Keane had spent the entirety of that time carefully formulating his words. Perhaps they had meant to be amusing, but the humour had dried over into the thin crust of fact.

"I would be a stubborn old fool if I did not admit to the existence of danger. There is always some danger in life. Any one of us could be knocked from life at even the most inconvenient moments. Tell me, Lawrence, in those glorious boxing days of yours, did you retreat to the corner when your opponent *might* take an offensive stance? Of course not."

"But there should be another plan, in case I . . ." Fail? Is that what I was so damnably afraid of? Failure? Certainly my pride has sustained enough incidents that it was of no general consequence; however, mine was not the only life relying on my actions, just as pushing myself backwards over that bridge's rail was as much for my benefit as it was firm knowledge that Keane was safe. As long as he was alive, James Harrison still had a chance at mortal redemption. Surely the man deserved a chance at that? He had ridded himself of unnatural demons, enduring withdrawal and nightmares forced upon him by the bountiful faults of mankind. He had waded through the shadow of sorrow and hopelessness.

Was I really afraid of failure?

Keane stood and moved to sit on the table; leaning forward with that same storm-like intensity I had seen when the ocean lashed powerfully at the cliffs of Éire.

"Your insecurities astound me, Lawrence, though I shall more readily categorise it with your youth than character." A long, thin hand stayed me from any remarks. "However, understand that I have known you for more than seven years. I know your strengths better than you do and accept your faults with more mercy than you would ever allow yourself. I have seen your stubbornness and perseverance hone your intelligence into a fine diamond incomparable to any other megre stone. Your knowledge of the world far surpasses those twice your age, and Lord knows you make it quite clear that you are the most valuable jewel of females in the world. I have seen all this in the full awareness that the strength—the coal—was there from the beginning.

I tell you this that you may feel secure in the knowledge that, if you truly feel you cannot do this task, I will accept that without any ill feeling toward your person. You may return to England now, and I shall join you before the Holidays. At the very least, before the new year." I shifted uneasily on the sofa's suddenly sharp edge.

"That long?"

"It is inferior, I admit, but what are a few extra months in the game of life? The worst you could fear upon my return would be a collection of those unfortunate American mannerisms."

"And the play?"

"As you said before, there are hundreds of young women in Los Angeles who would do most anything for such a role. While they may not have your natural talent, one can hardly be too particular in these dyer matters. As usual, the decision is entirely your own. But, Lawrence, whatever you do, I am behind you all the way." I stared at him for an excruciatingly long moment; absorbing his words as a new wine. The initial melancholy overtones were gradually smoothed by a surprising amount of sentimentality. He was risking his reputation—his life—by producing the photographs tucked away in the envelope. He was opening himself to a blackmailer's sword for the sake of a friend. Were I to make a mistake—some unforgivable error—he, or I, or both could be killed. Should it be me, it would be a tragedy easily dismissable by the world. My novels were more set toward the young intellectuals of the age, rather than drabble for the sake of society's ignorant consensus. Few people recognised my name, and less my life. I would not be missed by most. Should it be Keane; however, the scientific world would no doubt stutter and crumble at its loss. Though his name might not be known at a carefree party, his theories had begun to shape and mould the world so magnificently he could be viewed as nothing but a genius. The world would not mourn me, but it would cry for him. He was risking everything. How could I give nothing?

"Even in the most horrific of storms," I whispered shakely. "A rainbow can be found." Keane smiled gently, a warmth running over with satisfaction.

Suddenly, my face was pinned to his chest and the strength of his arms enfolded me in his embrace. The world stopped. Life was nonexistent. Time disappeared into the scents of cologne.

And—for perhaps the first time in my tattered and torn life—I became the child I was never able to become. Innocence washed upon me in a wave of security.

And, like a child, I began to weep.

PART FIVE

People do not lack strength;

They lack will.

-Victor Hugo

CHAPTER TWENTY-NINE

"THESE ARE *great*." Sam Barker nodded, thumbing through the stack of black and white photographs pinched in his claw-like hands. "Just great." He praised again and laid the evidence of worldly economics on his desk as some report strong enough to warrant his attention. "So, how much do you want to get out of the old bastard? A hundred grand? One fifty? Two hundred?" I shifted in my seat across the polished wood.

"Two hundred thousand seems an awfully large amount for a debt a fourth of that."

"Do you want to get back at the coot or not? Besides, you'll be paying me a good cut of that. Seventy percent." My head swam with the numbers and my tongue felt thick with the constant use of purely American syllables. Either way, there was no end of grief.

"Why the hell would I give you seventy percent? You'd be getting a hundred forty grand easy."

"But I'm also using *my* funds to get *your* money. I'm doing you a favour here, not the other way around." It certainly felt the opposite. He was risking money. I was risking lives.

I was risking souls.

"I will give you thirty percent."

"Sixty."

"Forty."

"Fifty. And don't think I'll go any lower than that." I relented.

"Fine. Fifty then. I suppose we should spit into our palms and shake on it to seal the deal, or something like that." The young man jerked ever so slightly, appalled by my lower class sense of humour.

"I don't think we have to do that, but maybe a contract would be a good idea. I'll have a friend of mine draw it up and you can sign tomorrow." He paused with his hand wavering over the layer of strewn photographs. "I guess you would want to hold onto these until then?" I nodded vigorously, swept an arm around the stained collection of supposed sins, and carefully stacked each one before slipping the entire pile back into the envelope. The whisper of lies rattled my ears, yet I was not so affected by it to do something endangering the cause.

"I think that would be wise. How do I even know you could keep these things safe? We wouldn't want anything untimely to happen, now would we?" I had hit it; the doubt never to be expressed toward that great male chauvinism. Sam Barker leaned back in his chair with an expression that was neither pleasant, nor reflecting any intimidation. It was the predator sizing up its prey; establishing a list of weaknesses pliable to his wicked hands. His eyes flickered, and I began to fear he had seen through my cropped and pomaded hair or the tight bindings concealing the epitome of womanhood. Gradually he relaxed back into his chair and I into my mind. Of course he had not seen. He could not have. One is always so accepting of the oddities of the world, the obvious falls away into oblivion.

"Of course." Sam Barker consented slowly. "Of course you would want to make sure your investment is safe, and I assure you that I have one of the most secure houses this side of Fort Knox."

"While that is reassuring, I find it hard to believe that a person who throws so many parties would be able to hide anything." The young man—millionaire and mobster—laughed with the same gentle features as a shark about to engourge itself.

"I have Mickey here, don't I. You don't have *him* over without a few precautions." As if the man in question had just entered the room, Sam Barker stood and strode quickly to the door, swinging open the enormous panels of wood without so much as a squeak of inconvenience. A quick shout for the butler brought the shrivelled, ancient man from the woodwork. He was old—easily over seventy—with only a thin lip of wispy, white hair curling around his wrinkled head and a face gaunt and sunk well into his skull. His teeth were all there, though perhaps not those naturally his own. The expensive uniform had been made for a man a good three stone heavier and a bit more at the midsection than the man before me was. He was a withered excuse of a human being; better fitted for fish bait than an example of masculinity. I had seen wrinkled old women in better shape; and that, I thought, was saying quite a lot.

"Yes, sir?" God, even his voice was raspy; scarcely audible above his laboured breaths. His employer seemed not to notice.

"Wilson, take Mr. English here to the lock room and show him about. He will be making an investment and wants to make sure it will be secure." The butler croaked out another polite answer and turned to usher me along. After nearly tripping over his slow, frail frame several times, I moved beside him, carefully measuring my quick, strong strides to match his prehistoric shuffle. It was a miracle that the man worked at all, or didn't fall to his death when climbing those polished staircases.

"Have you worked for Sam long?" I asked informally, desperate to interrupt the grinding inhales of breath at my side.

"Yes, Sir. Since he was a very young man, it was. Eight years or more." I guessed the 'more'.

"And you like it?"

"It's a job, Sir. A little rough on the old bones once and a while, but I can't complain. Can't complain." The butler paused his shuffle a moment, as though struck with a thought strange to his increasing age, but soon continued onwards toward another flight of stairs. "Don't like his friends much. Down right scary, if you asked my opinion. But I can't complain. Can't complain."

When we at last reached the top, I faced a hall almost identical to the one below. The paintings were different—more expensive—but the woodwork and papering were the same. I could not discern the pattern, but it was yellow. Horribly yellow. Obnoxiously yellow. The sort of colour that tears into your eyes at the brink of morning when you do not wish to awaken, or that final taunting as the sun dipped low upon the horizon as the evening turned to night. Yellow. Wonderful yellow. It was vivid with life, glowing as would a pile of the purest gold that had fallen to the earth from the stars above. Gold: splendid, glorious, sickening gold.

And then it hit me with a blare of trumpets.

"Midas." I announced, the unexpected echo of my voice startling the poor butler. "That's what this house makes me think of: King Midas." His lips curled back into his face. It took me a minute to realise it was a smile, rather than a show of canine anger.

"Guess it does that. Can't say there's too much of a difference between the two. Mr. Baker has the golden touch with everything: girls, friends, money. Mostly money."

"No difference at all." I added silently. Or at least, there was little ill comparison in the business sense. Sam Barker had ties to the mafia. What of it? Seemed everyone in the United States did in those days. And yet, I had not thought him so much a part of Cohen's operations as a willing follower. An assistant tied not by either character or work ethic. Sam Barker made no desperate grasp for success, while success coursed through every inch of the great Meyer Cohen.

Suddenly, with an alarming clatter of polished shoes thumping along the floor, Sam Barker's ancient butler fell against the wall.

I was ready to lunge forward to scrape the poor man off the extravagant paper, when the certain panel of the hall *moved*. A portion about five feet high and three feet across groaned and stiffly slid forwards into the rest of the wall before swinging inwards as a door. The old butler, having dusted imaginary bits of loose plaster from his jacket, beckoned me forward into a pool of darkness. I could not see but black past the end of my nose. It was a stifling darkness; pressing upon the ears and mind until one felt strangled by the mass of emptiness. I had expected an array of white electric lights to blind me at any moment.

But it was not angelec lights that came.

It began as a taunting blip before spreading along the walls and ceiling; dozens of red eyes glaring at me with malicious intent. Yet it was not I upon which they leered so devilishly, but hundreds of photographs in different stages of development. Some were seemingly innocent (two people chastely kissing in a doorframe or a group photo carefully positioned), while others were increasingly morbid and certainly something scandalous, should it somehow leak into the press. I had seen some such articles before and, while never having participated in the act of lovemaking myself, knew the general sense of the idea captured repulsively by a camera's lens. Good Lord, there must have been thousands of poor souls captured under Cohen's hand.

In the corner was an enormous safe that ran from floor to ceiling and halfway across the wall. My voice echoed about my ears; light with a forced hilarity.

"What's in there? Dead bodies?"

"No, Sir." The servant chuckled dryly. "Tell the truth, I don't know what's in there at all. Don't even know the combination. Mr. Barker tells us very little, but it's a good job, and I can't complain. Can't complain."

SAM BARKER HAD GONE out by the time the butler escorted me back down to the office, and I immediately saw myself out. I leapt into the open arms of a taxi—checking first that it was not Keane huddled behind the wheel—and was carried back into the rushing rivers of Los Angeles life. A quick wash and change of clothes was all I needed to feel myself sufficiently drawn back to my resources, and not one in the Devil's employ. To seal it; however, I felt the best solution could be found in sacred stones. I chose a modest necktie and shoved out into the streets; walking rather than whistling for a yellow chariot. The pavement was not particularly crowded that afternoon, nor the air quite so filthy as the day before. It was as though a pure life had fallen upon the streets. I could see as far before me as I could behind me.

And yet it was not until I had walked several blistering blocks that I first became aware that I was being watched. Or at least, it is quite an unnatural coincidence that, at the exact moment I leaned against a building and dropped to tie my shoe, two men a few yards behind me were required to do the same. I followed a different path then; diving into taxis for a street or so, changing automobiles, leaping into most any shop and store, and occasionally searching for a back way out. The men were not particularly hard to lose, but when they disappeared, two others came.

Always two.

Always armed.

Occasionally there would be a car following me with a bit too much accuracy to be strictly natural, which only proved a large sum of money hiding behind the muscled facade. Twice they came much too close to me. Three times they coughed when they oughtn't have. And no less than six times did they curse to the other when I disappeared behind them. It took several hours to finally break myself away from them, but break away I did. At last, as the final wisps of daylight played at the horizon's purple edge, any burly, overgrown figures to whom I had become unfortunately associated, crumbled into the earth.

I had succeeded.

As the nectar of momentary relief fell upon me, I dropped back down a street and walked the distance to my initial destination. It was the belltower that was first to appear; the rest of the mortored stones following close behind. An enormous window of stained glass showered the pavement in spectrals of vivid light. The steps were perfectly distanced from the street to the ominous oak doors; holding the church well above the immorality of passersby, while still remaining a welcoming figure in the darkness.

The sanctuary was enormous, vast stretches of elaborate representations of all spiritual feats of the divine lord. White doves raised themselves towards the great bowl-like ceiling with their wings spread outward in peace. The high altar had been carved in a stony mass of white, and decorated by a simple, green linen cloth. Saints had been depicted splendidly in every window; staring dejectedly down at us mortals left to walk the turning earth.

I moved to one of the front-most pews and took my place in prayer before the tabernacle. Even to those who do not pray, one must admit there is a peace to it. Now, among the saints and angels, I recalled not the glory of these things, but a time churning with suffering and death. It was a time where Keane was forced to carry his nephew's body in a long, wooden box down the Irish countryside to the cemetery. He did so dutifully and without complaint. His back remained rigid throughout the entire affair; his face filled with quelled emotions. Keane had known his nephew well, it seemed. He had known him through the joys of boyhood, troubles of adolescence, and the pains that create a man.

After all, even murderers are family in the end.

Thomas too looked upon the brink of death's door; his once heavy frame whittling away to a frail stalk of a man. Any relation to Keane's strength and endurance had disappeared, but even my companion, stiff and sure against the world, seemed a good deal older as he and five others lifted the young Michael Keane upon their shoulders. Shoes on snow crunched the funeral march down, down into the graveyard. And there the young man lay even now, adjacent to his grandparents, lest he felt alone.

But this is not what I remembered.

I remembered the final words; the frozen fistful of earth as it was thrown against the coffin's lid with a rattle of finality. Finality. It was finished. A life had officially ended.

Michael Keane was dead.

Thomas left then with his wife Catherine, his frail form desperately supported by her steadfast strength. The death of their son seemed not to affect her as tragically as it did her husband. Or perhaps she had not yet accepted the fact that he had gone. Or had she indeed accepted Michael's death as easily as she would soon accept Thomas'? In any rate, the solemn priest too moved off toward the sparse group of mourners, leaving Keane and I towering above the hole.

The hole that swallows man.

I had not expected my companion to say anything, not from a lack of heart, but one that often does not reveal itself in great flows of emotion. Many times I had seen him draw into himself; tucked away in his books or a selection of exhausting lectures at some respectable university. No doubt he would smoke much, sleep little, and eat even less. It was a shock then to hear that rich baritone, carefully built upon rough Gaelic and smoothed by the King's English, as it flitted outward into the air like waves gradually rolling unto the shore. With each meticulous word, the power grew until every syllable smashed downward into my mind with all the force of the world.

"*Go dtreoraíonn na hinggil tú go Paradise; go tiocfaidh na mairtírigh chuna chur romhat agus tú a thabhairt go dtí an chathair naofa, an Iarúsailéim nua agus síoraí.*"

May the angels lead you into paradise; may the martyrs come to welcome you and take you to the holy city, the new and eternal Jerusalem.

I recited the words myself then, in that Californian church; allowing each word to mingle with the lost incense and float before the stained glass windows. The saints seemed little impressed by the pitiful whisperings, for they had said hundreds of such words in their own lives, but I was not particularly interested in being a saint. Children wish to be saints, and men wish to be gods. I, being neither of these, wished to be only mortal. To live life and be glad of it. I wanted to live knowing my weaknesses, follies, imperfections, and all the things that so kept me tied to this earth. One doesn't have to like or approve of their own faults, but they must at least know them. I repeated the prayer a second time, though again my mind wandered to my missing companion. He had made it quite clear when I had left that I would not know where he was, and I did not try to find him. That did not mean I did not search for him casually in the face of every butcher or baker or taxi driver or business man or most any other person. But he was not there. I said the prayer again. Then again. And each time I finished wondering if I was truly distracted, or if I was subconsciously repeating it for him. For his safety. Or . . . or could it be I was saying it to be more like him? It was possible. I often wished to march through life with the same billowing force that changes tides and makes mighty ships crumble at the helm. I recited the prayer one final time, and at last entered peace.

A peace that was immediately broken by a pair of heavy footsteps behind me and a cold, commanding voice whispering down a thousand curses of destruction.

"Mr. English, I could shoot you now, or you could come with me. Since I haven't already put a bullet in you, I hope you know which one I like better. I may not be a religious man, but killin' someone in one of these places gives me the creeps."

The simplicity of the words, matched with the stale taste of a cheap film, gave the entire situation an odd sense of hilarity . . . up until the moment a gun's cold barrel settled into the nape of my neck.

And yet, my voice did not waver.

"What right do you have to shoot me?"

"A friend of a friend who wants to talk to you. And he doesn't like waiting, if ya get my meaning."

"And if I do not wish to go?"

"Then I shoot you. There. In your head." There was the creek of the pew's backing as the man leaned down on it; the frozen metal pressing further into my skull.

"This is a church. You would not shoot in a church."

"I would if I had to. You have sixty seconds to decide." A full minute wasn't necessary. I stood gradually, the barrel following me with a lethal hesitation. At last, when I was on my feet, I turned slowly around. He was not as menacing as the many villains I had the misfortune of facing, but a part of my mind screamed that he had killed before. Another life ended. Another coffin was buried. If he had already ridded the world of at least one human being, why hesitate to kill another?

But the gun did not shatter the sacred silence of the church, and no glass exploded into deadly shards. But the gun did not stray from its lethal poise.

"Come on. The car's outside." I calmly stepped into the aisle, considering briefly the weight of his words. Keane had been run down by an automobile in Ireland; left bloody and bruised on the side of the road. We had nearly been killed in another automobile upon arriving in Los Angeles. Now, I was to trust my life to the metal confines of yet another car.

How ironic.

My polished shoes hit the glimmering floor with a heavy solemnity, each step ringing as a march to an eager firing squad. The shouts of doomsday did not scese as I stepped out into the street and approached the black, elegant car waiting impatiently at the edge of the pavement. The door was opened and I was shoved inside by a heavy hand on my shoulder. Shock. Pain in my back. A sudden realisation that I was not alone. I wrangled the first glimpse of a smile and nodded to the man adjacent to me.

"Good to see you again, Mr. Cohen."

CHAPTER THIRTY

THE AUTOMOBILE'S BURLY driver turned the machine off of the main roads and into those sparse streets running alongside one of the parks. I saw some of the boys—Frank's boys—playing baseball on the diamond. God, how I wished I was with them. I wished I was still playing a game, and not the roulette wheel of life. Why had I left? I left to help Keane. And why did I leave Keane?

To get yourself in a devil of a mess, I finished silently.

For that was what this was, a devil of a mess. And I had put myself in the clean middle of it. Rather, I had pinned myself shoulder to shoulder with one of the most lethal men in all of Los Angeles.

"I trusted you, Kid. Why'd ya have to go off and do something stupid?" I fought the urge to shift in my seat. Surely he did not know of our plans. Surely he knew nothing of our identities, our pasts, our follies. He couldn't know. And yet, I found him rather like the wee man down below. Though he may not be God, he could still be omnipotent.

"Stupid? What do you mean?"

THWACK!

A sharp ringing in my ears erupted with the hot iron of blood in my mouth and a singeing fire spreading along my left cheek.

"I ask the questions. You give the answers. Got it?" I nodded. "Good. Now, what's your job for old Jack?"

"I don't know a Jack."

THWACK!

My face was now melting with the brutal strikes of a trained fist. Cohen may not have had the finest reputation in the ring, but, by God, his right jab was enough to make a grown man weep. And we were sitting down.

I took in a steady breath and tried again.

"I don't know any Jack, and that's the truth. The only people I know around here are you, Sam Barker, Guy what's-his-name, and Mr. McCormic." My jaw tightened in preparation for another attack, but Cohen appeared to be considering whether another strike was necessary.

THWACK!

And then it hit me. Not the man's fist, but a sudden mental jolt I cursed myself for not having undergone sooner. Jack. Old Jack. The Capone of Los Angeles.

I leaned back against the seat, the whirring of my mind created a confidence I had lost through the soreness of my cheek.

"You mean Jack Dragna, right?" Cohen's fist did recoil slightly then, a timebomb to be set at will.

"Thought you said you didn't know him?"

"I don't." I explained rapidly. "Not personally, anyway. I have just heard of him a few times; street corners and the like." The fist remained a constant, the beating sun burning a desert's dusty skin.

"You're sure about that."

"Quite sure." My words were a gun, piercing his flesh with a bullet of silver truth and forcing crimson anger to wash outward into the leather seats of the automobile. He sat back easily, and yet he still retained eye contact as he nodded toward my face.

"What are you doing messing around with Sam Barker then? If you were a woman, I might think it was something harmless. But you're a man." And so was the great chovanistic pride of the male sex. Had I been truly myself at the time, rather than an American refugee having returned to play the epitome of the country's stupidity, I might have mentioned some off-handed statement regarding Mrs. Cheveley. Mrs. Cheveley: a vile, infamous woman who tried to ruin Robert Chiltern's position in public life. Though they were but characters born into a world carved at Oscar Wilde's hands, I loathed her. And yet she was perhaps one of the few examples I could properly compare with the moral-less ideals of Samual Barker. Cohen was gambling on chips that claimed I was not a woman. But I knew the truth.

I was not a man.

And Barker worked for Dragna.

I SLIPPED INTO THE hotel with a white scarf draped over the lower half of my face despite California's singing heat. After gathering up whatever mail had been left for me at the desk, I desperately retreated up to my room, away from the piercing eyes of the public. How could Robert Chiltern adore public life the way that he did? It was almost indecent how his ambition churned the desire to stand before Parliament with decisions that could cause people to love him or hate him alike. I could not live such a life. I could not throw myself at the mercy of society. I could not do so for one dastardly reason.

I didn't give a damn.

I peeled the scarf from my face, eyed the long patches of dried blood, and tossed it into the bin. My purpose was to pose as an up and coming mafia man, not a bloody scrapper who ought to be locked behind bars in an asylum. Fortunately the swelling, while painful, was more a discoloration than an unseemly deformity. As I ran a hand gently along my throbbing jaw, the faded type spotting the top telegram leapt upwards from the page.

Dearest Devon,

I ought to be disappointed in you, nephew of mine, for you haven't written for much too long for your dear old aunty. You can find the return address on the label. I'll be waiting for any news. Are there many postcards in Los Angeles? How many? Are they expensive? If the are, your uncle can always send more money.

Yours Sincerely,
Aunty Bek

IT WAS ALL I COULD do to not throw the typed note on the table with helpless peels of laughter. I had long ago associated Keane with many things, but Aunty Bek was something far beyond the grasp of my own imagination. To most anyone it would seem the same sentimental dribble of any old Englishwoman, but beneath it all was that constant thread of humour which was always reflected in his rippling blue eyes. I could almost hear his rich, baritone timbre catching each syllable and translating it into something more meaningful than even a saint could decipher.

Dearest Devon...

Dearest Lawrence.

You can find the return address on the label...

I am stationed at that address.

Are there many postcards in America? How many? Are they expensive?

Did you find the photographs? If so, are there many more? Is it possible to buy them?

Yours Sincerely...

Aunty

Brendan Edward Keane

Bek

Having never been able to imagine Keane in a family role as I could an intellectual one, the prospect of an aunt, though ridiculous and impossible, was only mildly more shocking than finding him an uncle a few months before. In truth, he was a son, brother, uncle, cousin, brother-in-law, and no doubt half a hundred other things that were equally outlandish. The list had grown the longer I had known him, flourishing further as the list of unattended roles grew all the shorter.

He was not, nor had he ever been a husband. That I knew for certain by his own mouth, as well as that of his brother, Mrs. McCarthy, and the rest of the neighbours and townsfolk of Devon. He was the infamous bachelor; a Henry Higgins without a doubt.

In this way I was myself certain of another fact.

He did not have a son.

He had no children; no little brutes or heirs to his throne of intelligence. There was no offspring to whom he might share his valuable attention. There was no one to fight over his vast wealth accumulated over the years. I had so long ago learned that this was not so much due to some hatred of hereditary youth as it was the same logical reason Brendan Edward Keane—*Professor* Brendan Edward Keane—remained a bachelor.

He just never married.

And that, by his own morality, meant no children.

There was no one for him, save a long suffering housekeeper who did as much to clean his house as she did to soil it with her strong tongue. There was nothing between them but the most tirelessly forged business atmosphere of an employer and employee. Whatever friendship that might have been sowed through such a long association was purely second nature. There was Keane. There was Mrs. McCarthy.

Oh, and there was me.

That was something anyway.

I slipped Keane's rather unusual letter into its envelope and tucked it into the edge of the hotel dresser, took out a piece of stationary, and strode over to a typewriter I had borrowed from a wealthy drunkard down the hall. As I sat down behind the dark, metal keys, I immediately took upon the mantle of my character; the beloved (damnably American) nephew.

The incomparable Devon English.

And so it began.

DEAR AUNTY BEK,

You would be shocked to know just how many postcards this one shop has. Hundreds, at least; so, there is no need to send any money. There is stationary for letters as well. Everything is here; old and new.

Yours sincerely,
Devon

Two days later, a second envelope arrived for me at the hotel; this time bearing a stamp from San Jose.

Dearest Devon,

That is marvellous news to be sure. A variety means victories for smaller establishments. Would it be possible for me to visit soon? Or would it be prudent to wait a while until you send for me?

Yours Sincerely,
Aunty Bek

I posted my own rendition of the pitiful excuses of literature that very evening after dinner. As it happened, I made it a point to visit one of the restaurants suggested by Keane himself. The man may be many things, but subtle was perhaps not one of his accomplishments. His voracious temper was not to be ignored either, as well as a strict, undemonstrative nature. Sentimentality was seldom shown openly, and certainly not by physical attention. There had been those one or two instances of contradiction; a kiss or embrace when words at last failed, but that was all. It was all it had ever been. A friend's compassion. A friend's comfort. A friend.

Because that is what we were: friends.

Weren't we?

Dear Aunty Bek,

Is it wise to make the journey? You know how dangerous such a venture can be in this modern world, and I certainly wouldn't want you catching a cold at your age. A cold today, pneumonia tomorrow. It is your decision; however, and I bow to your irrevocable judgement.

Yours Sincerely,
Devon

WHETHER OR NOT KEANE received this letter—or if it died from malnourishment of literary substance—I did not know for several days. Nearly a week, in fact. It was in those long, horrid hours reeking of tedium that I tied Devon English ever closer to Sam Barker, while building bridges into the infamous world of Mickey Cohen. One by one the pieces were set, as separable as chess pieces staring down the carved figurines stolid on the other end of the board. As I found myself shoved into the mobster's automobile on several more occasions, my mind reeled further and further into the dark chasm of confusion. Sam Barker seemed neither a friend of Cohen's as the parties implied, nor was he a distinct enemy. I could gradually sense the armouries of Lexington and Concord drawing distinct positions in the earth; daring one another to fire that first shot that might be heard around Los Angeles. The gunpowder was stored. The guns had been cleaned and cared for by the failures of prohibition and the addictions of a thousand men. The crates of economic explosives had been stacked neatly inside the armoury of powders.

All that was left was for some poor unfortunate buffoon, spawned from America's pit of moral-less idiocracies, to light the match.

THE CRIMSON SHAW

It was an immeasurable comfort to find a worn and yellowed envelope in my hands one afternoon as I carried my tense and aching body up to my hotel room. Though the words were not long or profound, they rang out with more reassuring glory than a thousand church bells swinging joyously in their steaples.

Dearest Devon,
I am coming.

CHAPTER THIRTY-ONE

PATIENCE MAY BE A VIRTUE, but allow me to state most clearly that it is one of those virtues created by those with wealth who have nothing to wait for. That, and it is a virtue of which I lack entirely. I walked on air for some time; playing the casinos with no real eye to whether I won or lost. (Though, by the cries of intoxicated admiration, I was inclined to believe my winning streak had not yet wavered from its harrowing plight.) Three days this occurred: three days wreaking of a lifestyle that would make any priest wince and every stockholder green with envy. I was a wealthy woman in my own right, though my novels seemed to have not yet been swallowed by the American markets. The gambling tables only served to fuel my ego. I watched the cool profit from my latest paper-bound feat nearly double in those three days. Hours, which might have been spent painstakingly wiping ink from my hands with the sweat of my brow, were now being spent making a comfortable living off of nothing but fate's seemingly endless generosity.

After each indulgent evening, I returned to my hotel room with the expectation of some street vendor or cab driver to suddenly materialise from the pale, papered walls and sweep away an intricate disguise to reveal a man I had come to know far better than even myself. And yet, every evening, I ate with silence, walked with separation, and allowed day to slip into night with not but darkness. It was only after the night that the day once more arrived.

I had started my way to the casino, winding between the allies and taxicabs as I had learned to do, when I was struck with the realisation that it was unnecessary. It was useless to dodge from those constant shadows for the sole reason they had disappeared as assuredly into the night as the solemn ghosts of one's mind. The street was not busy.

It was not even crowded. No. No, no, no. That could not be. That was simply—simply *impossible*. If neither side had believed it necessary to follow me any longer—oh, God! I heard it then; flooding my senses with fear.

Sirens.

I ran.

I sprinted along the streets toward the mechanical screams where oily smoke belched into the already hazy air. I dogged between people as though they were not but stationary wax. I continued foolishly, recklessly, and full of horror. And there before me my worst nightmare lay; shattered shards across the pavement in petrol reddened with blood. Keane's car—or rather the one he had been borrowing from James—now resembled those unfortunate declarations of modern art. The bonnet had been smashed in. Glass windows shattered into knives, which had stabbed maliciously into the leather. The other automobile was in considerably better shape, or at least eligible for repair. The owner swarmed about as an injured bird; squalking over every dent and scratch as though his own flesh had been so abused. Off to the corner, lying by a stray police man who seemed to have a weaker stomach than one in his profession ought, was a motionless bundle swaddled entirely by heavy woollen blankets. I took in the approximate measurements of the parcel. An inch or two over six foot. Slender frame. A few wisps of grey hair stuck out from beneath the dark wrappings.

I must be quite clear that, female though I may very well be, I had never fainted in my life. But I would have at that moment had it not been for a strange desire to run. Adrenaline pulsed through my legs, insisting the reality splattered red before my eyes was not but a delusion gifted by the devil, and so enforced by those under his employ. It began as a slow, vicious retreat; each step burning through me as a steam engine hissing to go faster. I needed to escape. To hide.

To disappear.

I slowly backed into an alleyway without peeling my eyes from the horror of life. So much lost, and nothing to be gained. My shoulders bashed into several people, all voicing either concern or intense irritation. At last I was able to turn my back on what was to be the final scene of my short, and arguably useless life. That was what my life was. Useless. Dim in comparison to Keane's accomplished career. Had it been me—had I been the motionless corpse impaled by glass—he would have survived. The world of psychology would have flourished. My life would have been worth something.

But it was not until I began to run from life that it began chasing me with heavy footsteps. My imagination had always been something beyond mortal control, yet the echo as I careened wildly along the hidden streets did not cease, no matter how hard I willed it to be so. In fact, the louder my own heart rattled through my ears, the greater the intensity of my rival's pursuit. I wanted to scream; to spin around and shower them with an assault of carefully acquired curses harrolding to all across the earth. (I had, in fact, acquired a rather celebrated arsonal of German profanities during the war.) But there was no time to stop. No time to think. No time to breathe. No time. No time. No time. And when an unfortunate stagger lost that precious time, and his hand grabbed my wrist with a shattering twist, I did the only thing I felt logical to the occasion.

I lashed out with my fist.

I have always had a strong arm, and I admit I relished the sudden freedom as the hand instantly released me and flew upward to his cheekbone. A solid punch was always as valuable to me as my decidedly unladylike temperament. Had there been ropes around us and a clear mat, rather than brick walls and dirty streets, my assailant might have recovered his dignity and retreated deftly into the shadows, never to be seen again. But boxing rings are never supplied when convenient. He staggered back, one arm outstretched behind him, while the other still covered his face. He did not see the crate. His legs hit it with enough force to send him down against the pavement with multiple curses that ended with a rather familiar surname.

Mine.

I leapt forward when he did not move, fearing the worst brought by my own, bloodied hands. His legs remained bent and propped up on the overturned box of wood; however, where I expected a skull bashed in and a thin crimson stripe to be trickling from a slightly opened mouth, he had laced his fingers behind his head and stared up at me with a rather ironic smirk. His eyebrows had arched high on his forehead.

"You know, Lawrence, I believe you have just reminded me of one of the multiple reasons I have remained a bachelor." Considering his precarious position, completed with his hat lying upside down a few feet from his head and the ill grace of his motions as he extracted his long legs from the crate, whatever disapproval he might have conveyed through those exceptionally blue eyes was strictly irreverent.

"Good lord, Keane, I am so glad to see you." Keane maintains to this very day that, in some fit of "unfortunate femininity" I tackled him to the ground and "bloody well ruined" whatever dignity remained after flinging him backwards over that crate; however, I must accuse him of acute exaggeration. He was standing—or something very near to that—when I flung my arms around his neck. It was reassuring not to be pushed away, and twice so when the action was returned. His arms embraced me, awkwardly at first, then tight enough to warrant some bruising along my rib cage. It is in his stubbornness that he denies this, and in my own that adamantly assures you it was so. What a strange sight it must have been—immoral and scandalous—to have seen two masculine shadows drawn tightly together in the lights of dawn. All the strength I had clung to so ferociously in the past several weeks now drained into pavement beneath my shoes. I allowed my head to be pulled even closer into his shoulder. It was a comfortable silence between friends, for that is what we were: friends. Close friends. Old friends.

And yet, as I hesitantly considered excavating myself from his embrace, the words rushed from my mouth.

"Keane, I really am so wonderfully pleased to see you. That is, when I received your letter that said you were returning, and when I saw that accident and no one was following me and the blood and the body, I thought—"

"Yes, I can imagine what you thought."

"Can you? But of course you can. Please don't explain how it happened, though. Not now. I—I just want it to be over." The constant thud of his heartbeat was overpowered briefly by that rich, deep chuckle I had so horribly missed.

"The mind is willing, but the heart aches at the consequences, eh?"

"You needn't make it sound so repulsive. I admit that emotions may not be my forte in life, but it hardly means I am a heartless piece of stone. But why couldn't you have secured a more practical entrance?"

"What? And have this touching scene in the midst of a busy street? The purpose of our plight is to rid the world of Sam Barker's filthy grasp, not add to his collection with a possible affair of two men." Keane reached up and touched the side of my head with a sense of mourning. "You will grow your hair back to its former length after this, won't you? At least before it was long enough to be delightfully feminine, while this . . . Lawrence, you will always make a better woman than a man. Always." I fought a thousand urges ranging from some snappish comment to something damnably emotional. The latter never having been a select choice of mine, and the first perhaps not the most prudent of plans, I settled on allowing my brain to notice the thin, dark shadow spotting Keane's cheekbone.

"Oh, God, you're bleeding. I'm sorry. If I had known it was you—"

"You would have no doubt had the same reaction." My companion countered easily, releasing me enough to wipe his face with his handkerchief. "One ought never apologise for their strengths, just as one should not succumb to a constant fear on the chance it might invoke a weakness." I smiled grimly.

"That rather sounds like something Mickey Cohen said when he was asking me about Sam Barker. Of course, it did take a bit of time to persuade him I was more loyal to him than I was to the young millionaire." The stained cloth paused just below Keane's left eye.

"Why the devil was it necessary to state your loyalties?"

"Because Sam works for Jack Dragna and—heavens, Keane, what's the matter?" I instinctively grasped my companion's arm in the fear he might have hit his head harder than either of us suspected, but he waved me away before my fingers had clung too tightly to his suit jacket.

"God," He whispered, his voice near inaudible over the ideas being flung throughout his head. "God, have I blundered? Quickly, Lawrence. We must act quickly, or we may be too late. Come, put on your hat and we shall go to the hotel. There may be rough work ahead, and danger too, make no mistake. Breakfast can wait. There is a fixed amount of hours before dusk, and we must—I repeat myself—we *must* be ready. Come, Lawrence. Come. There is no time to waste. I fear there will be blood spilt tonight."

CHAPTER THIRTY-TWO

I STARED AT MYSELF in the mirror. Or rather, I gaped at the figure who consequently resembled the person I thought to be myself. Grease paint had been painstakingly applied to my face and neck, stopping at the black, high-necked collar of my shirt, which was tucked into trousers of the same mournful colour. Keane, in his endless generosity, had loaned me a pair of thick socks to go beneath the pair of rubber-soled shoes a size too large. I had drawn the line at darkening my hair for the occasion, and therefore willingly settled for a tight-knit cap one might find at the docks. Overall it was mildly ridiculous, some occurrence of an overactive imagination. I resembled the darkest point of humanity; a common criminal disreputable to the equally common man. We are all thieves in some way. We all wish to steal from society its many failures to better illuminate our few successes. Even the great moralists steal from the rich to improve the salvation of the poor. I was then merely a representation of that belief, and therefore acquired more dignity through my unusual costume than a king in his chains of gold.

A sharp rap shot into the wood door separating the washroom from the spacious hotel room. When I did not answer immediately, Keane thrust his head inside, causing the figure in the mirror to start visibly.

"Good lord, Keane, I thought you were a proper gentleman. What if—what if I had been indisposed?"

"Then you would have shouted to high heaven when I knocked. Are you nearly finished?" The mirror person leaned dangerously close to my face, inspecting the pale slivers of skin still visible just below my eyes.

"I should say so. This blasted stuff really does smell awful though." My companion gave a sharp bark of sardonic laughter and leaned casually against the doorframe.

"I believe the 'stuff', as you so eloquently call it, was made for practicality, not to appease your aromatic senses. Come here for a moment. Your neck and ears are still exposed. Yes, it goes on your ears, though I assure you there is a greater chance of discomfort than actual harm." Keane took the tin from his pocket, tipped my head back at a precise angle, and began to smear the nasty substance along my skin. It was a thick, slimy affair that would have been quite unbearable if he had not undergone the same ordeal himself. The dark paint had been rubbed completely into his eyebrows and well into his hairline. Our clothes were much the same as well, though his guernsey was tight against his torso, while mine remained loose and unshapen. His gun and holster had been strapped over his left shoulder, while my penknife was safely folded in my pocket. I had offered to carry a second firearm, but it was decided to be unnecessary and impractical.

It also meant I could not shoot Keane if I had half a mind to do so.

Not that I would, of course.

A small amount of water soluble dye had been washed through his hair to conceal the light shades of grey at the temples, turning them soot-dust black. He appeared as a chronically depressed mime, with paint to conceal his expressions rather than encourage them. We could slip into darkness as shadows and not let the shadows follow us. I was; however, extraordinarily pleased that he had not had the damnable stuff on when I informed him of the concealed darkroom, else I was to miss the brief glimpse of shock as it melted gradually into an odd combination of amusement and intrigue. But there was no time for such amusements then.

No time.

That afternoon had been packed full of exchanged information and a few hours of sleep to compensate for those precious nocturnal moments to be missed on that harrowing night. Keane had secured an automobile sometime earlier that day, and, at precisely the stroke of midnight, we leapt into the mechanical steed and started off toward the castle. Our tires trembled over the dodging roads; spotted with rocks and the mutilated corpses of unfortunate animals born without foresight. Twice I feared a punctured tire, but that dutiful little car kept on steadily at Keane's skillful hands.

Approximately two miles down from our destination, he drove off of the road into a patch of sparse trees (the thin edge of a forest, I thought) and jumped out from behind the wheel. He paused only to grab a canvas bag stained charcoal grey. We pushed the car further into a space that had been cleared that very day, proceeding to line the metal with nature's discarded shrubbery. It had been agreed we would not light our torches unless it was vitally important to our task. Instead we stayed within arms reach of each other, communicating with brief brushes of our hands rather than endangering ourselves with speech. We were the wavering outline of some childish comic illustration; me with my black little cap and Keane with the sturdy bag slung over his shoulder.

We jogged quickly through the brush, dodging across abandoned streets, and continuing on through the feeble representation of nature's brethren. Eventually sparse arteries of the city gave way into a clear stretch between us and success. When at last we came half a mile from the enormous house, we realised our deepest fault and stopped immediately.

"Keane, is that . . . music?" My companion leaned forward slightly and winced at the faint blair of overzealous brass.

"I fear so. Appealing, isn't it?"

"I should say not. What should we do? Turn back? There is tomorrow, I suppose, though I can't say I relish the thought of having to apply this grease to my person for a second time."

"We have come too far to retreat."

"Keane, be logical. We are hardly dressed for a party and our presence—our coalition—would spoil all that we have worked to achieve." His blackened chin jutted up a bit and he immediately seemed to add another inch to his towering stature.

"You seem to be under the impression I shall be seen. Yes, *I*. You stay here and—"

"Why can't I come? As you said, we did come this far."

"Lawrence, there are over a hundred people at that house; at least half of them armed."

"Is there more to that statement; because, I am already aware—"

"Damn it, it will be dangerous!" The volume of his voice had not changed, but the sudden burst of intensity threw me back on my heels with a staggering blow. My voice, when at last it came, was exceedingly cool and cold against my throat.

"Say that once more and I shall not only disappear, but do so permanently. Never have I heard such nonsense of my inability to face danger. I am going with you. Or have you forgotten that *I* know which floor the darkroom is on?" Keane glared down at me with half-lidded eyes, his lips drawn tight in a line until they began to pale into the natural colour concealed beneath the grease. Had it been in better lighting, I might have caught the tightening of his spine as his shoulders rolled back defensively; every inch the commanding sailor. But there are consequences to power, and I had named them eagerly and without remorse. Should he push me away, I would leave. His will slackened. My victory was fast coming.

"Very well. But stop wasting imperative time with this idle blather. I assume you feel up to a bit of a climb?"

We stalked forward, staying well into the shadows on the side of the enormous mansion opposite the uproarious party. Dangling above us was a scattered row of windows, many open, with only a few panes of glass shimmering beneath the ominous moon. Keane dropped his bag silently to the soft earth and pulled from it a long stretch of sturdy rope with metal claws sweeping outward at the end. I staggered back a step as he dangled the heavy bit by his legs and swung it up, over his head until it arced through the window frame.

"A grappling hook?" I hissed. "For God's sake—"

"Only to the second floor. Third at most. Ready? Fine, now up you go." I dug the toe of my left boot into the building's brick exterior, pushed quickly, and managed to get both feet jammed into the wall with minimal effort. It really wasn't much of a climb, but the process was excruciatingly tedious. With each step I was forced to let go of the rope with one hand and swing my arm up a ways before grabbing hold once more. More than once I had to consciously force the muscles of my hands to open and allow me to dangle dangerously above the ground. When at last I scrambled over the window frame, crouching painfully on the polished floors, the rope grew taunt once more. It did not take long for Keane to scale the building, though I dared to glance down from my safe perch a few times to check his progress.

Damn the man.

Of course he made it look effortless.

In no time at all, he was sliding his long legs through the window frame and pulling the rope up after him, winding it skillfully into a heavy coil before shoving it into the bag and slinging the entire bundle over his shoulder with an exasperated glance in my direction.

"By God, Lawrence, stop that staring and start moving." We cautiously began our ascent up several flights of stairs; our footsteps giving a far gentler titter than what was natural. No mortal man had yet become aware of our presence as we reached that long hallway. I recognised it at once, the paintings ever so slightly more majestic than the others. Oak doors appeared every now and again between the paintings, but, as with my first visit to this particular floor, I had not paid them much heed.

And then it struck me that perhaps I ought to have noticed.

"I . . . I think it is a bit further down. Further. Yes. No. Oh, I should have marked it. What a foolish thing not to at least memorise which painting it was near. I wish I had bothered to do that much." My companion's answer came over his shoulder as he ran his fingers along the wall in search of a fault when there was none.

"If wishing made it so, the world would not have need for well-kept minds. You said the butler fell into the wall. That would create scratches to the floor, would it not? But look, there are none. Barker's staff have cleaned them away as assuredly as they would have a smudge of lipstick to the wall papering. Those with any sense would have discovered our plot immediately. There now, stop that blasted self reflection and—" Keane pushed himself back from the wall with a flicker of satisfaction before ramming his shoulder into the yellow paper. The same eerie growl erupted around my ears, forcing me back with fists high in horrid fear we might have awakened one of the monsters below. But ours was not above a whisper in comparison to the roaring music outside or the flat mimicry of a phonograph some floors down. As the hidden doorway lurched forward further, my companion settled his gloved hands at shoulder width across the panel, tested the weight, and opted for a sturdy push with his right arm. The door swung forwards into the darkness. He did not stagger back, but he did pause for an instant with childish wonder before lurching to life and thrusting himself into the darkness. Here he again made a full turn of the room with his illuminating torch. No doubt our presence caused the ruin of a hundred photographs in that moment, but that was the point. Wasn't it? Had our very lives not been teetering in the balance of our actions, I might have expected Keane to let out a low whistle as he examined the drawers and glanced at the enormous safe. As compensation, he whispered while he sized up the metal jail of all things sentimental and compromising.

"My God, all these souls captured by that man's greed. How many men died with his hand to their throat? Lawrence, I have made an unforgivable blunder. I have underestimated your words to believe these great masses were only a few boxes easily disposed from the earth."

"We can return some other time. We can liberate the others once Harrison is safe. We can—"

"—We cannot. How could we know what a wonderful thing it is to be safe while others lay in deathly petrol? No, Lawrence, we must act now and quickly." Keane dropped his ear to the safe's surface and silently began the tedious task of spinning the dial back and forth until the mechanism announced it was time to move the other way. I feared my thudding might spoil his work, but it did not. He pulled the door open and came face to face with shelves and shelves of letters and envelopes bound with string and ribbon alike. With a great sweep of his arms, he began knocking the piles to the floor, covering the wooden panels with misdeeds held woefully above man. In his example I took to the photographs, adding them atop the letters without care to where they landed. Surely these would not fit into Keane's canvas sack. They would not fit into a dozen similar bags. Soon, all the papers and sins had piled upwards to our calves; a pure snow created from evaporated murk. Keane shoved me out into the hall before dumping the trays of chemicals, once used for the development of man's horrid deeds, out upon the white. In moments he was beside me on that marble floor and shoving a cloth into my hands.

"Over your mouth and nose." He demanded curtly as he grabbed one of the chemical stained letters from the top of the loathsome stack and brought an inexpensive lighter out from his pockets. I started.

"Keane, you can't be serious." But, by God he was. The well-mannered little flame sprang up with life along the paper's edge. He worked from back to front until a great monster billowed before us; belching thick, black smoke as the man with the cigar had done upon our arrival. Was that man one of Dragna's men as well? Suddenly a hand was on my arm, dragging me along the hall until my feet remembered the great thrill of running. But we were not running away. No, this was not a retreat.

This was to be a victory.

Down the stairs we flew, lower and lower. We must have been on the second or third floor when the first gasps of fire started up among the servants. But there was nothing to be done. The great orange flames spread faster than either Keane or I might have imagined, clawing along the papered walls; swallowing the paintings, and grinding along the floors. Rugs sprang into forests of smoke. Doors became fringed with an unnatural glow. Even the great tiles became black and charred, soon to be nothing but pieces of the past.

We reached the first floor when we first heard it; that great wine of strength easing from an old man's bones. It came slowly but grew louder until it was a scream not to be ignored. Keane dragged me by the arm to the nearest window where one could see automobiles filled with horrified guests retreating in dark veins of death against the smokey sky. I nearly grabbed for my companion's collar as he leaned far out of the wooden frame. When he threw himself back to our side, he held my shoulders tightly and pulled my face to catch his.

"We have to jump." He shouted above the growing screams and moans. I tried to pull back from his grasp, but he held me all the tighter by the one opening between life and death. The flames were behind us now, so close I could feel their heat singing the skin of my hands and melting the grease from my face. I watched the lethal fingers claw upwards toward the electric lights and further through the wall toward the lines. But what lines were these? Surely not—oh God—

"Listen to me, Lawrence, we must jump. The shrubbery will break our fall." That wasn't what I was concerned about breaking, and the arm at my back, turning my face down into the darkness did nothing to steady my throbbing nerves. "With me, Lawrence. One . . . Two—"

A sharp smack to the back of my head strangled whatever chances of hearing the announcement of the third number . . . had there been an announcement. My body was suddenly swallowed up in a singeing heat and I had the vague recollection of an enormous hand hoisting me up by the collar and flinging me forward into the world, just as assuredly as I was to be taken from it.

I began to fall.

I CAME TO IN IMAGES; stages mauled and clouded by a battered brain and eyes unwilling to bear witness to any more destruction. Eventually I became aware of a few distinct factors.

I was lying on my back.

Someone was leaning over me.

And we were moving fast.

I must have announced the coming of my conscious state—a none so subtle curse, no doubt—that made the figure over me chuckle dryly just as a shower of painful shards fell upon my sorry form. I recoiled automatically and awoke, for the most part, immediately. But a hand—no, an *arm*—pinned me down.

And, of course, I fought it . . . until the moral screech of an oncoming bullet whizzed past my ear. I shouted then, and was suddenly aware I was shouting for Keane. Greater still was the realisation it was indeed his arm I was fighting to defy.

"Quiet, Lawrence. By God, I knew you had a fine pair of lungs but this is not the time. No, don't sit up. Can you turn around a bit?" It was excruciatingly painful to do so, but I managed to roll onto my side and make more room for Keane to face the back of the automobile and aim something out of the rear window. His pistol. It was then, through the shattered glass, that I saw the faces; faces carved from a stone's anger and glowing with the eternal fires of Hell. A burly man had been shoved behind the wheel, while Sam Barker, worse for wear and charred by ash, leaned out of the window with something oddly metallic and—

BANG!

Something flew through the metal through one of the side windows only milliseconds after Keane dove down on top of me in a hurl of shouting toward the front.

"We need to lose them!" I wrenched my neck up to catch the driver's face and found the infamous Meyer Cohen twirling the wheel between his hands.

"Can't go much faster than this." He huffed, screeching around a turn. "Already pushing ninety-four." At that very instant, something that vaguely resembled an explosion erupted below us and the roaring ninety-four immediately dropped to a depressing zero. Cohen was the first one out of the automobile and dodging into the alley. Keane was second and dragged me into a close third; firing every so often behind us. It occured to me that Sam Barker was the only one at our backs. He was the only man to represent Jack Dragna, who, though I myself had never met the man, had become our adversary. Our advantage lengthened gradually, or victory eminent... until—

BANG!

I was shoved behind a stack of crates just in time to see Keane's body jerk and fall to the ground in a pool of blood near his head. The world stopped dead only for my life to return in a blazing force. In a deaf shriek of adrenaline, I threw Barker to the ground in a flying tackle, knocking the gun out of his hand and against the cold ground. I worked rhythmically, pounding my clenched fists into his chest and face without noticing the crimson blood pooling over my knuckles. The pain in my body gave way to strength. I continued harder—maddly—until the young millionaire was barely conscious. It was then I took up the gun and aimed it down at his fogged eyes.

"You shot him." My voice was cold and dangerously foreign to my ears. "You shot him. You sent a man to kill us when we arrived and, when that didn't work, you shot him."

"Look behind you. I missed. He's fine." It was true. I knew it was true. I heard Keane's steady breathing behind me as he slowly rose to his feet; the red puddle turning black and oily in my vision where grease had been smeared from my companion's face. But I didn't care. I could see it as clearly as though it had already occurred. The deep crimson red of his blood coating the street in rust. It made my stomach turn, but he had not shot Keane. The bullet had missed.

But he could have killed him.

It could have left him contorted and cold against the stones. Still. Silent. Dead. But Barker had not shot him. He had missed. Like Michael, he had missed. And yet, even my companion's resonant voice did not pull me from the abyss into which I was gradually sinking.

"Lawrence, you do not want to do this."

I did, in fact, *want* to do it. I wanted to give the dangers we had faced some finality. I wanted to give all those lives he had ruined some salvation beyond the mere knowledge his hold was destroyed. As by God's own omnipotence, the first solemn yelps of a police squadron entered into the world, approaching steadily. But it was Keane—a man who, in himself, could be considered omnipotent—who fished together the bruised edges of my conscience. His hand, long and dry, rested lightly on my shoulder. Were I able to feel the presence of my guardian angel, I would have thought it very much the same. The fingers brushed at my collar bone as his voice appeared; thick with an emotion I was unable to understand.

"Joanna."

The gun fell from my hand, and with it, my desire for revenge. Sam Barker was arrested, just as Leslie McCormic and Devon English disappeared from the world.

PART SIX

The rest of the story need not be shown in action . . .

if our imaginations were not so enfeebled by their lazy dependence . . .

-George Bernard Shaw

CHAPTER THIRTY-THREE
September, 1948

THE APPLAUSE WAS DEAFENING, enveloping the stage in an assured vanity as Keane and I stepped forward for the curtain call. The audience leapt to their feet in a whirl of whistles and cheers when the entire cast joined hands, swung our arms up, bowed, and retreated behind the curtain.

And like that, it was all over. Every line. Every movement. Every wonderfully exhilarating little joke that had been skillfully thrown forward by Shaw. All of it. We had done a total of twenty-one performances; far more than I would have thought possible for a small Californian theatre, but the fact was we couldn't close. Newspapers gave only the highest praise for our little group. (One even dared mention the physical similarities between Keane and the late Leslie Howard.) Tickets were sold like gold with a full audience for each and every performance. And so it was with some regret, as I wiped away the thick smudges of makeup across my face, that I realised the close of some great moment of my life. Worse, I had no fathomable idea of what to do next. I slipped into a pair of dark trousers and a cream shirt before turning once more toward the mirror. A dark wig sat on its stand: a reminder. I ran a hair through my slightly lengthened curls.

One could not help but notice the healthy glow surrounding James Harrison's features as he burst in. His strength had returned tremendously with the banashing of the Hydrocodone, but his soul had been truly freed on the day Sam Barker was tried and charged with, not only blackmail, but attempted murder and the arson of the Caldwell Theatre. The burning of his own home, as surmised by the great Los Angeles police force, was an accident: consequence of the rowdy parties.

"Jo, dear, you were absolutely wonderful! Wonderful! I wish you could convince that old fool to stay around longer. We could make a fortune."

"Old fool?" Keane entered smoothly, his eyebrow raised in the perfect combination of amusement and dignity. For a moment I thought he was still dressed as his professor counterpart, but the tweed was far more expensive than that used beneath stage lighting. "I do hope you don't mean me, James. There is that saying about being kind to messengers, is there not?"

"Messenger?" I asked.

"A certain beautiful woman sent me to inform a Mr. James Harrison that she is waiting just outside the stage door." Harrison wagged his head slowly, as though it was an old play scripted between the two in the times of their youth. A joke.

"And did you tell that 'beautiful woman' I do not sign autographs after ten in the evening? It is eleven, you know?"

"I did, but I'm afraid Vivien insisted." Harrison's head jerked up, straightened his tie, and made some unintelligible excuses before racing wildly toward the stage door. I glanced at Keane.

"Vivien?"

"His wife."

"Oh." Surprise quelled to amusement. "I thought you said once that you never interfere with 'matters of the heart'?" My companion sighed heavily, but the steady glimmer in his eyes was anything but morose or depressive.

"*A h-uile riaghailt, tha eisgeachd.*"

To every rule, there is an exception.

I chuckled lightly as I finished doing up my shoe laces. Keane was one of those men who didn't mind the rules, as long as they had acceptions when necessary and understanding toward the common man. He was full of paradoxes and, though private and guarded, was so full of life it was impossible to not appreciate it in his presence.

Keane plucked my leather jacket from where it had been haphazardly strewn over the back of the makeup chair and gently tossed it to me.

"It's a bit late for dinner, but no doubt we can find something suitable for such an auspicious occasion."

EVEN THROUGH THE CASUAL quiet of night the boisterous applause lingerd as Keane and I exited the theatre for the last time. At the bottom of the steps, he tucked my arm securely through his and pulled his hat securely over his head. His grey curls had become plastered into style with an overabundance of pomade. Everything about his exterior had been smoothed into place for the audience's understanding. Only I had the honour of seeing the gears within the machine; the light within the lamp.

The true Keane.

"Do you think he will be alright?" I asked solemnly, much to my companion's amusement.

"James? I should say so. They say the best thing for a man in trouble is a wife to clean the mess. And with a successful string of performances—as ours indeed were—Vivien could hardly turn him away now." Keane paused and cocked his head sideways for a moment before continuing our slow and steady walk down the street. "I can't say I'm fond of Shaw's ending, though."

"In Pygmalion?"

"Precisely. There isn't any finality to it. And for the man to insinuate that Eliza runs off with that Freddy character. Ridiculous."

"Perhaps Shaw merely wanted to note Eliza's independence; that she could be on her own without requiring Higgins. Feminism is rather a fine thing, if used in the right contexts." An eyebrow climbed upwards above a glimmering ocean.

"And what might those 'contexts' be?"

"The liberation of women from masculinity. We can go to school—university, if we like—and do just as well in the world as any man."

"And you believe that is why Eliza didn't marry Higgins?"

"No." My answer surprised me slightly; not the answer itself, but the conviction with which my voice shot quietly through the streets, bounding between walls and lampposts until it was lost as a fleeting whisper. "No." I started again. "She didn't marry Higgins because he didn't ask."

Nothing else was said for an excruciatingly long time as we walked up and down the streets. If a taxi stopped, Keane waved it on and we continued around another corner. We paused briefly at a bar for a quick drink, but soon set out again for the streets. Los Angeles really was quite pleasant at night; the quiet tones of life at rest. No evil can come in rest. No greed, nor lust, nor any of the other mortal frailties can appear in the wonders of sleep. One was only to close their eyes and dream. And it was in dreaming that realities gave way to the life all wished to live, but never could the sun again rise to its throne in the sky.

At last, when my body had begun to feel the exhaustion of the day, Keane's warm and rounded English floated seriously above the fantastic world painted meticulously about our heads.

"You realise how potentially disastrous this entire thing is. I am a man set in my ways and can—I have no doubt—be terribly rude and incorrigible. Verbally I am as tactful as a sailor, but, of course, you are aware of this. I dare say you also know how infuriating I can be. I am afraid I am unlikely to show you much romanticism—" Whatever polite drudgery might have been scattered upon the world next was immediately cut off as I threw my arms about Keane's neck and slammed my lips to his. When my mind at last whirred to the realisation of what I had done, I tried to pull back and regain the brief strands of dignity left between us, but I was faced with an obstacle far greater than I had ever thought worldly possible. His head dipped further to mine and his arms forbid more than an inch's space between us. When the time came when we could either remain in our precarious position or breathe, we chose the latter; stepping back from one another with Keane's blue eyes drilling down upon my face and my eyes staring holes into my shoes. At least my voice bore some traces of the confidence I no longer felt.

"You know, Keane, you're bloody awful at proposals."

"I could get down on my knees if you like." Keane's voice wavered slightly, as though he expected me to actually suggest such a ridiculous thing.

"Don't you dare. Very well, I will marry you . . . on one condition."

"And that is?"

"That I not be required to take your surname." For a long moment Keane stared down at me, almost appalled by the audacity of my declaration, but gradually a few drops of reasoning surged forth into a waterfall of the richest, most wonderful laughter in the world: laughter so great it shook every inch of my soul and sent it soaring to a height I had not known existent until that moment. At last, he took my arm and threaded it through his so tightly I could not help but be aware of his warmth.

"I agree to your terms, Lawrence, though my name is yours, should you ever want it." Without another word, we journeyed back to the hotel and I slept in my room that night, safe in the knowledge that, though the union was inevitable, we were two forces. We were strong individuals. Together we were invincible.

I laughed then; laughed as I never had before. Yes, the union was inevitable. That was certainly no joke. I was not Jo Keane.

AUTHOR'S NOTICE
Meyer Harris Cohen

IN HIS LIFE, MEYER "Mickey" Cohen became known as one of the nicest killers of the mafia era. His generosity was only outweighed by his ruthless ambition. One must understand; however, that, unlike the systematic assumptions of the mob, Cohen was a philanthropist, suffered from Obsessive Compulsive Disorder (requiring him to frequently wash his hands), and lived his life nearly illiterate. The latter of these he worked to improve constantly, but there was one other fact to truly create an interesting king of Los Angeles.

Meyer Cohen had trouble adding numbers.

Money was not counted, but divided bill for bill. Numbers fell upon other trusted friends. In many ways, he was an honest and clean man. He never drank. He never smoked. Cohen also made it a staunch rule never to use profanities in the presence of women. He surrounded himself with celebrities, and was often considered a genuine part of Hollywood. Rather than ignore or threaten the media, Cohen embraced them; always pausing for comments or photographs. His own autograph was treasured. There was little doubt danger surrounded all who were in his presence. A bomb demolished half his home during a large mafia war against Jack Dragna. Both opposing gangs and the police forces were after Meyer Cohen with a vengeance.

In the end; however, it was not for blood-chilling murders that he was brought to court. Like Al Capone, Cohen was jailed for tax evasion on several occasions. When he re-entered the world—supposedly reformed—he was often penniless; living off of the generosity of friends. Loyalty was priceless in his profession. A man under suspicion for betraying his friends was easily shot or tortured.

And yet, at the age of sixty-two, Meyer Cohen died in his sleep; not from bullet, nor murderous intent, but by complications to stomach cancer.

Biography. 2017. "Mickey Cohen." Biography. https://www.biography.com/crime-figure/mickey-cohen.

Crime Investigation. 2021. "Mickey Cohen." Crime Investigation. https://www.crimeandinvestigation.co.uk/crime-files/mickey-cohen.

Also by Elyse Lortz

Lawrence and Keane
Come Away
The Crimson Shaw
A Very Merry Monster

Poetry for the Wandering Mind
This Midnight Hour

CPSIA information can be obtained
at www.ICGtesting.com
Printed in the USA
LVHW080951240322
714297LV00016B/251